ALMOST HAPPY

ALMOST HAPPY

THE CHRONICLES OF TABBY

JAYLONNA STEVETTE

J. Merrill
PUBLISHING

J Merrill Publishing, Inc.
434 Hillpine Drive
Columbus, OH 43207
www.JMerrill.pub

Library of Congress Control Number: 2022918135
ISBN-13: 978-1-954414-58-7 (Paperback)
ISBN-13: 978-1-954414-57-0 (eBook)
ISBN-13: 978-1-954414-59-4 (Audio)

Book Title: Almost Happy
Author: Jaylonna Stevette
Cover Artwork: Safeerr Ahmed

CONTENTS

1

THE STORM

Usually, when a storm is coming, there's some warning. But, depending on the type of storm, there are always signs. With a thunderstorm, the sky gets dark first, then the wind, then the rain. Even a hurricane shows signs of its existence long before the destruction hits. So, it is with love and relationships. The signs are always there. It's a matter of us paying attention and running for cover. If you read the last book, well damn, you know there were signs.

So here I am in a storm that I contributed to by going on a crazy journey called love. Or so I thought it was love. But, man, I fell HARD. And what do I have in return? A fucked-up situation that I feel like I can't get myself out of. Two years ago, this time, I was getting my life back on track, getting back to happy. And now, I'm like, what the fuck. I know I'm talking in circles, but so much has happened that you have to give me a chance to take you there. Just know that there were signs along the way. Or were there? "Damn, Tabby, how did you fucking get here?" I thought.

I tried to rationalize in my mind what led me here. Was it a spiritual connection? Sometimes it felt like the Universe was in play, forcing us to continue to dance long after our favorite song had played. I was so caught up in the situation that I could no longer tell as the lines were blurred. Maybe I was just dickmatized. Hell, who knows. All I know is being with Jaquan was amazing until it wasn't anymore. And now, my heart has a void that needs to be filled, and sometimes I feel like he's still the only one that can fill it. Oh, this ain't no love story, and right now, I'm angry and need to heal. But how can I do it in the situation I'm in right here, right now?

"Oh Jaquan, you have me so fucked up, Sir," I yelled to no one in particular. That was more of my thing these days, yelling obscenities about my young flame, who used to be my twin. The one who encouraged me to risk it all, to take love's journey, only to deceive me, having me second guess who I am, my worth, and my being. "Oh, you got me REAL FUCKED UP, SIR! I HATE YOU!" I said yet again to no one. This shit had to stop, but I saw no real ending in sight. One thing I do know that works for me is that I am a Scorpio. That said, no matter what happens, I will get my revenge, for I am the phoenix rising from the ashes. And trust me, he has it coming.

My relationship with Jaquan left me feeling like I had had enough. I had wasted enough time and energy on people, so it seemed they did nothing but take, take, and take even more from me. I had introduced new people into my circle as a result of fucking with Jaquan and found out the hard way that I was getting played. This bastard tried his best to drain me physically, emotionally, and financially and he would have succeeded. My ass was stuck on stupid. I was exhausted yet again and back to square one, feeling unhappy. I said to myself, "Tabby, you don't fucking get it, do you? What is it gonna take for you to get your fucking life together? Yes, I talk to myself like that sometimes, dammit. I was angry at myself for several reasons:

1. I let him love the best part of me

2. He made me feel like a fucking fool

3. I didn't discover all his indiscretions until AFTER I handled the breakup peaceably for both of our sakes.

Who THE FUCK did he think he was fucking with? Oh, I was on a rampage, and I wanted revenge. I would make sure I would destroy his life like he rocked mine to the core. He had no idea what I had in my arsenal. Who should have been a bitter enemy has now become my biggest ally. Man, I swear, hell hath no fury like a woman scorned, and the side piece of that bitch ass nigga became my strange new bedfellow.

Let's not forget about James and Keisha. Do you think they would let me go away and live my happy? Hell no! I am constantly haunted by their presence in my home in one way or another. But that shit will unfold too. I find myself even with them in a fucked-up situation. James and Keisha have it all already. What more do they really need? I swear, if I turn on the television ONE MORE TIME and see their irritating faces, I'm gonna SCREAM! We've been divorced for two years now; it's clearly time for us to cut ties. But James and Keisha just won't let that shit happen. You would think the combination of the good Lord and the spiritual advice they have been getting from Pastor Doug would make them better people, but that isn't the case. What I don't get is how they have time to create misery in my life while airing out their dirty laundry for all the world to see. They have issues.

I thought about what had become of my life and how I got here. A part of me wanted to cry. Although two years had passed, it seemed like it was only yesterday when things were good. Hell, in the beginning, they were amazing. I snapped back to reality for a Moment and asked myself why I had put my mind through this torture. It was over, and Jaquan's actions made that loud and clear. I hated him for what he had put me through, but I still loved him because he loved me in a way that I had never experienced love before. For the first time in my life, I let a man actively and truly pursue me. Although there was a significant age difference, Jaquan gave me every part of him that he knew how. It was like he awakened something in my soul that had been sleeping for so long, a part of me longing to be loved, nurtured, and fed. Jaquan made it ok for me to let my guard down and be loved with no strings attached. And I fell in deep, like the heart of an ocean.

I reflected on love's journey. I recalled an evening I was preparing for my lover to come home. My home had become his home, and we had gotten great at playing house. With Jaquan's business being commission based, every day was different. Some days he would come home after having a fantastic day with gifts, products for the house, and electronic toys for himself. Then there were other days when he made no income. However, he was always optimistic and confident on those days that he could recover, and true to his word, he never failed. Jaquan was just lucky like that.

I thought back on the memory of better times. I had given Maria the day off and decided to pamper myself and cook for my man. I had the typical spa treatment, a premium pedicure, waxed brows, manicure, and dip gel overlay for my nails in my favorite shade of red. I also got the lash extensions because they brought out the brown in my eyes. My man's words, not mine. I then picked up some shells to smoke the weed he had left me for the day. For those who don't know that terminology, a "shell" is a tobacco cigar that is split and filled to make a marijuana "blunt." That blunt is then smoked, and the participants get really high if the weed is good. And Jaquan knew where to get the best weed, hands down. That was one of the perks of being with him; I never had to make that financial investment because he always had it. Oddly enough, I smoked more than before we moved in together.

I had just finished preparing shrimp alfredo, one of his favorite dishes and one that he loved for me to cook for him. I got in the shower and used the Chanel bath gel that Jaquan had given me as a gift "just because." My man loved the smell of Chanel on my body and wanted to ensure that he kept me in it. I lathered my body and thought about my lover. How good he was to me, and how amazing he made my body feel. Immediately got aroused. I took my hands and rubbed my arms; they felt so soft. I closed my eyes and thought about Jaquan. I wanted to please myself right then and there. My nipples became erect, and my juices were at the starting gate. I stopped myself; decided I wanted to wait to give all this pleasure to the man who had given me so much of the same. I stepped out of the shower, put on my lotion and perfume by Chanel, and thought about what my lover wanted to see me in.

I knew he loved breasts and ass equally. And fortunate for me, I had plenty of tits and enough ass for my body. I wanted to show him both of those assets when he got home that night. I decided on a black see-through net Cami and a black matching thong. I put on my diamond necklace to bring attention to my bustline and black Christian Louboutins, with the red bottoms accentuating my nails and feet. I wanted to make a statement to my man that was jaw-dropping. One that said, "Baby, you have everything you need right here." And true to form, I did not disappoint. As I admired my appearance in the mirror, I heard the front door open.

Jaquan quickly made his way to the bedroom of our condo and stopped when he saw me. He smiled and approached the mirror that I admired myself from. He said, "damn baby, you look so good," as he looked me up and down as I stood before my appearance. I looked at him through the mirror. I watched his eyes as he took in my appearance. He came from behind me and took in my aroma. "I love the way you smell," he said. Then he took more of me in. He touched my skin, talked about how soft I felt, told me how pretty I was, and applied soft kisses on my neck as he stroked my arms up and down. I began to melt into him. I tilted my neck to give him better access to it. That was one of my hot spots, and he knew it too. He applied more soft kisses and then applied pressure. It hurt so good, and I moaned.

My man applied more pressure to my neck and began to suck and nibble. I knew it would create a passion bruise later on, but I went with it and didn't mind because I was his. I moaned at his touch as he stroked my arms up and down while he licked and sucked on my neck. His mouth traveled to my ear, and his tongue sent chills down my spine. I moaned in pleasure at his touch. His hands traveled to my breasts, gently fondling my big black nipples. I gasped a little. Boo Boo Kitty was preparing for ecstasy, and those juices at the starting gate previously were waiting for the gunshot to take off.

I looked in the mirror at Jaquan. He looked up at me and smiled as he gently stroked my nipples. I moaned. I admired the look on my face as I moaned, and Jaquan did too. He could tell he was pleasing me, and his hands traveled south. He continued kissing my neck as he watched my reaction in the mirror. He was definitely hitting my spot. He bit down gently, and I moaned again as he looked at me intensely. I heard the gunshot sound, and my juices were off to the races. Jaquan rotated from my breasts to my thighs and then to my ass. He smacked it gently and looked down in admiration. "Damn, you got a fat ass," he said as he gently rubbed her and positioned himself behind me. I wiggled my ass a little for him. He chuckled and smacked her. Then gently massaged. I rubbed myself against him. I could feel the stiffness of his manhood. Jaquan was ready, and Boo Boo Kitty could take him whenever, wherever.

Jaquan unzipped his zipper and released his Johnson. I turned around to look at him. His penis was so amazing, like a sweet dark chocolate Hershey bar, that I wanted to devour it. I grabbed him and gently massaged him. He moaned his pleasure. I stroked him slowly as I watched his manhood extend more and more. His Johnson began to pulsate in my hands as I stroked. I looked at him. He moaned and said, "damn." He slid my thong to the side, and I took his chocolate and rubbed him into Boo Boo Kitty's wetness. We both listened to the sounds of our pleasure, of our wetness. I took the top of his shaft and rubbed him into my clit. She began to flicker. The sounds of wetness made a beautiful symphony that felt like pure heaven. Jaquan reached out for my twins. He placed them in his mouth and sucked gently. I gasped. I stroked his Johnson and rubbed him in tandem as he sucked my nipples. He took them in and out of his mouth. As he sucked, my body tingled from the pleasure of his mouth and his manhood. As I stroked and he sucked, Boo Boo Kitty gave her release.

Jaquan turned me to face the dresser. I looked at him in the mirror and smiled. I wanted him to enter me. I needed him to at that Moment. He did not disappoint as I arched my back. As he entered me, it felt like pure magic, and Jaquan moved slowly in and out of me. As he kept his cadence, we stared at each other. My mouth opened in pleasure, and his strokes intensified. I needed him to take me deeper. He grabbed both of my ass cheeks and entered me deeper, and his strokes intensified as if he had read my mind. I said, "Fuck me, Daddy," and he smacked my ass. He knew exactly what to do. His cadence increased as he went deeper and deeper inside me. I yelled louder, "Oh Daddy, fuck me, Baby," and he fucked me harder and faster. I grabbed hold of the dresser.

I tried to wiggle, but he grabbed me by the waist and pulled me deeper. He said, "Take this dick," "Oh, yes, Daddy," I said. He pounded deeper and harder. Faster and faster. Book Boo Kitty gave her release, and her creamy wetness covered his manhood. I yelled as she gave her release and Jaquan stroked faster and faster as his Johnson started to pulsate. Finally, he was ready to cum. I moved my hips in tandem with his strokes, and Jaquan gave a yell as he released his goodness into Boo Boo Kitty, and she took it all in.

We spent the rest of that night eating, making love, watching movies, and making love again. I thought about the memory, and I smiled. Those were good times, back when we were happy. I looked around at my present reality and felt a distinct pang in my heart. Life feels like it will never be the same. How can it be? I thought he was "the one," and he even said to himself that "this was it" for him. But now, all that's left of love's journey are the faded memories of what once was.

I looked around the room. It was my room, but it was the only space in this dwelling I could call mine. How did I get here? All my assets were frozen in a bitter post-divorce war with James and Keisha. It

appears there is an internal audit into account number 8, and until it
is complete, I have no access to any of my funds. So here I am with
nothing. Again. I guess I should be grateful for this room I live in free
of charge, but how can I, given the situation? I looked around again
and tried to focus on the things I did have. I heard distinct giggling
down the hall, a sound I had become all too familiar with these days.
It was Shaquita. She seemed to be over the moon these days, and I
couldn't understand it.

Meanwhile, I am in here bitter. But, again, I'm a Scorpio, so I have to
keep it cool. Plus, I don't even know what my next course of action is,
real talk, but I do know things can't go on like this much longer.
Shaquita giggled again, then Jaquan laughed. Jaquan? Yes, the man
that broke my heart is in the room right down the hall with his new
situation. She's an old situation, but we'll get into that later. My heart
sank as I imagined all kinds of things going on behind those closed
doors. Why the hell was I here, and what had I gotten myself into?
She seemed like an ally, but because of the condition of my heart, this
woman had to be my enemy too. Who accepts the invitation to move
in with her ex and his current situation? Tabby, that's who. I spent the
last six months breaking up with him, only to be sucked back into his
vortex by the Universe. It was like a cruel joke from the gods, but I
had nowhere else to go. My friends had become his circle, and my
children were off living their own lives. Vincent had moved to Las
Vegas with his high school love, and Vanessa had dropped out of
college and supposedly fallen in love. My assets were frozen, and I
had no money or place to go. Jaquan and Shaquita offered me a room
in her cozy section 8 apartment. Tabby, who was once that bitch was
now back in the hood; go figure. One thing was for sure, I knew I had
to get out of there, and I was determined no matter what it would
take. "Tabby, get your shit together," I said. Then I looked around my
room again. I decided at that moment that I would reclaim my
happiness no matter what it took or the situation.

This thing with Jaquan and Shaquita was temporary, and I needed to
see it as such. "Tabby, the first thing on your agenda is a new dick," I

said to myself. I firmly believed in getting a new dick to get over the old one. However, I have tried that as of late. Even dick was not making me happy these days. I didn't know what it was gonna take, but I had to get back to that place, back to happy. There was a knock on my door, and I summoned them to enter. It was Shaquita, of course, as Jaquan tried not to say much to me these days because we couldn't communicate without arguing.

Shaquita: Good morning, sunshine! I have to take Mickey to school, and I couldn't find your keys. Do you have them?

Tabby: Yea, they're on my table over there.

Shaquita: Ok, thanks, girl. So, listen, we weren't too loud last night, were we?

Did this bitch just ask me if they were too loud? The situation? Not even the girlfriend, but the fucking situation was asking ME if I heard them fucking...the situation was FUCKING what used to be MY MAN... See, this is the shit that makes me wanna snap. But I am a lady still; a broke one, but still a lady. I looked at her and blinked a few times.

Tabby: Well, I didn't hear anything, honestly. I already know how Jaquan can be, so I totally get it.

Shaquita: It doesn't bother you. Does it?

That bitch already knew the answer. I lied. She was satisfied with my response, grabbed the keys, and left the room. I immediately turned on my meditation music, rolled a blunt, and began the long journey ahead. It was no longer love's journey, but it was one I was willing to take to fight my way back.... To Happy.

2

BLISS

Bliss, as a noun, is defined as perfect happiness and great joy. Marriage, as an example, is often associated with this joyous feeling: People who are married and still in love are described as living in wedded bliss. Bliss is also an action word that means to reach a state of perfect happiness, typically to be oblivious to everything else. In non-marital relationships, bliss shows up at the beginning of relationships, lingers on in the middle, and fights like hell to hold on to the end. I would say that would be the perfect definition of how my relationship with Jaquan was, oblivious bliss. There were apparent signs I should have paid attention to, but I was so into him that nothing else seemed to matter. As you can remember, from Getting Back to Happy, Jaquan and I had just decided to take love's journey, and I hopped on the back of that motorcycle with that fine-ass young hottie, and we ended up in my newly acquired beach house in Atlanta.

The road trip itself was about 5 hours total. We made several stops along the way to pick up toiletry items and a few other things we thought we needed. Since this trip for the two of us was spontaneous, we left everything behind, including clothing; who does that? I wasn't worried because a shopping spree was in order to celebrate my newly acquired fame and fortune. The divorce had recently made me a millionaire, and since I recently won the marathon as a first-time runner, I was certain that offers of some sort would be pouring in. A few news outlets had already contacted me, and a local sports store even left a message with an offer of brand ambassadorship! Things were only looking up from here! And then there was Jaquan, my young hottie. Yea, I definitely would say that life was good. Jaquan and I enjoyed the scenery we took in on the way to the beach house, but he and I both could not wait to get there for a couple of reasons:

1. Although romantic, the five-hour ride was not the most ideal thing to do.

2. The obvious; was the sexual build-up that had been occurring since I got on the back of that motorcycle. Damn, he smelled so good! Mmm mmm mmm.

When we got to the beach house, I took in the view. I looked over at Jaquan, who also seemed to be impressed. When we were married, James used this place as his so-called get-away, so I never got to experience the perks of it; I had only seen pictures. The pictures, however, didn't capture the beauty of actually standing there in the Moment. The beach house was more like a small cottage in Tybee Island, about 30 minutes from Savanna, GA, along the coast. It was a 1000-square-foot bungalow with a wide-open deck that looked perfect for hanging with friends and family after a day lying in the sun on the beach. There were two floors with a living and dining space and a bedroom and bathroom on the first floor. Off the kitchen, a spiral staircase led to a second-floor sleeping loft with an adjoined bathroom with access to a small balcony. From the dining area, an entrance to the screened porch opened to another spacious deck at the back of the house. Again, I had to admit I was impressed.

Jaquan walked through the door and looked around. He looked at me and smiled.

Jaquan: Damn! Is this all you?

Tabby: (laughs) Yes, this is definitely all me! Although I haven't been here before.

Jaquan: For real? That's wild!

Jaquan pulls me in for an embrace and a kiss.

Jaquan: One thing I do know is that I definitely have to step my game up with a woman like you!

Tabby: And why is that?

Jaquan: Because look at you, everything about you says polish. I got my own and everything, but not like this.

Tabby: Jaquan, remember that we have a 15-year age difference; you're just getting started! I think you will do well for yourself, baby!

Jaquan smiles. He says, and that's why you shit, baby. A man loves a woman who can build him up. I ain't gonna lie. That shit is turning me on!

Jaquan drew me in closer and cupped my ass. I grabbed his face and kissed him. I looked him in the eyes, played with the hairs on his beard, grabbed his face, and kissed him again. Jaquan lifted me in the air, and I wrapped my legs around his waist. I giggled as he showered my neck with kisses. He played with me, and I became drunk from the touch of his full lips on my neck. Jaquan and I looked at each other, and I knew our thoughts were in synch. We were about to christen this beach house.

Jaquan sat me on the island in the kitchen. He positioned himself in between my legs. I smiled as he rubbed my thighs in a massage-like motion. It felt so good. His hands etched closer to my Boo Boo Kitty, and she became excited. I looked at him, and he stared back as he rubbed my thighs. His eyes were piercing. I rubbed his chest, and he moaned and pulled me closer. He leaned in for a kiss. His tongue tasted amazing as it danced with mine. Jaquan was a great kisser, and since it was one of my favorite past times, I didn't mind that we made out like that, with me on the island for what seemed like an eternity. My body was so hot. My hands reached down, and felt his manhood. It was rock-hard inside his designer jeans. I stroked him through the denim...until his stiff shaft made an imprint. Jaquan moaned, and the sounds of his moaning while I stroked his Johnson were a complete turn-on. My pussy was wet, and I wanted to feel the piece of steel inside me.

I laid across the island with great expectations. Jaquan stood over me. He grabbed my legs and hiked my body towards him. As he cupped my ass, Jaquan simultaneously removed my bottoms. Boo Boo Kitty's juices dripped from my vagina to my panties. He looked and smiled. Jaquan then opened my lower lady lips and gave her sweet soft kisses. My clit began to flicker. Jaquan kissed around it, and I begged him to taste her. He licked to the left, then right, then center. I exhaled a deep breath of pleasure. Jaquan licked me slowly. I moaned in ecstasy. I helped him help me get back to happy; I held both of my lips which allowed him free access to my kitty. Jaquan licked my clit. He put it in his mouth and sucked it. Kitty's pre-release started seeping out as he licked her into a frenzy. My clit flickered as he sucked like I was his. He took his mouth and licked, took his chin, and massaged. The hairs from his beard felt like heaven as he rubbed his chin into Boo Boo Kitty. Damn, this man had me on the edge. I screamed, "Oh, Daddy! Eat this pussy, baby!"

Jaquan said, "I'll never stop eatin' this pussy, baby. It tastes so good. Tell me it's my pussy

Tabby: Oh yes, it's your pussy, baby. I'm about to come!

In a matter of minutes, I came in an explosion, and Jaquan was ready and willing to receive my juices.

Jaquan took a step back. Looked around. He located a wooded mini stepper underneath the island. Jaquan placed the stepper in front of the island where he was standing and stepped on the first step. He looked at me and smiled. I wondered what he was up to. Jaquan grabbed my legs and spread them apart. He was in total control of my body. Jaquan entered me slowly at first, then deeply. I gasped. So did he. His dick felt incredible as he gave me long, deep, methodical strokes. Jaquan was in a position of power as he controlled my legs, moving them upward and wide to maximize his Johnson. I wanted to cry. It felt so good. Jaquan looked down at our bodies and the symphony we made together as he moved in and out of me. He said, "Damn, baby, you are creamin' all over this dick!" I said, "Oh yes, baby, don't stop giving me this dick, daddy!" Jaquan picked up the tempo. I felt his manhood rise and pulsate with every single stroke.

I moved my hips to match his intensity. Jaquan looked down at me. I looked up at him as I creamed. He said, "damn baby, your pussy feels so good on my dick.... I love this tight wet pussy." Jaquan pounded harder and faster. I screamed, "yes, Daddy, yes"! he said, "take this dick, baby," I moaned louder. Jaquan pounded and pounded until he came inside me. He collapsed on my chest. I stroked the top of his head. My lover had set out to do what he came to do; he had taken me to a place of bliss, a state of perfect happiness, typically to be oblivious of everything else.

Jaquan and I spent the rest of the day getting reacquainted with one another. Well, he and Boo Boo Kitty, that is. I can tell he really missed me. The truth is I missed him too. I don't know what it was, but he really did it for me, butterflies and all and shit. Right now, he was love, and I was willing to take that journey. Love. Did I love this man? Nah, it was too soon for that, wasn't it? I have to admit, what I felt in this short period was totally different than anything I felt with James in all the years that we had been married. Jaquan and James were different and came from two other worlds. James was a man of influence, well-connected, and wealthy. At the same time, Jaquan was a man from the streets that turned self-made businessman. To the average woman, James would be the most obvious choice. But given all the hell he put me through, I'd say I would take a man like Jaquan over him any day. Being with a man like James, I learned that money isn't everything. Although its allure makes a man like him more attractive, his narcissism is the worst price to pay for riches.

My thoughts were interrupted by a nibble on my ear that sent chills and fireworks throughout my body. Jaquan pulled me in closer to him and said,

Jaquan: Baby, your skin is so soft. You're so pretty. You're the shit. You know that?

I smiled. More like blushed. I guess I was the shit; I had new money, a new man, and a whole new perspective on life. But to hear him say that made me feel giddy in a schoolgirl kind of way. Being with James had gotten me accustomed to being depleted in the affirmation department. As a matter of fact, I can count on both hands the number of times James complimented me the whole time we were married, and unfortunately, I'm not exaggerating. So being with Jaquan was a definite breath of fresh air compared to the shell of happiness I called my marriage. Although it had its rewards financially, being married to James left me emotionally depleted.

Jaquan: Tabby, baby, did you hear me?

Tabby: I'm sorry, baby, what?

Jaquan: baby, never mind. I wanna tell you when I have your full attention.

Tabby: Well, you have it now.

Jaquan: I know, but it's ok. I look at you, and you're so beautiful. But I always seem to find you in your head, swimming in your thoughts. I want you to let me in there, in your thoughts. But not only in your thoughts, but Tabby, I want in here...

Jaquan pointed to my heart, and it skipped a few beats. He wanted in my heart, and a part of me wanted to let him in. But then there was the other part, the wounded Tabby, who was afraid to let go for a few reasons:

1. I had just ended a fucked-up marriage with James

2. Jaquan was 15 years younger than me, and

3. I was simply afraid

As a matter of fact, in my head, I was doing what I always did, re-evaluating the impulsive decisions that I made on a whim. What was I thinking about taking love's journey? Was Tara right? Was I making a mistake? I just hopped on the back of this man's motorcycle with no destination in mind promising a relationship! My life has NEVER been a romance novel! What the fuck was I doing? My heart started racing faster. I wondered if he could feel that. I began to panic. Ok, Tabby, breathe. Just act normal.

Jaquan: Tabby?

Tabby: Yes, babe? I did it again, didn't I?

Jaquan smiled and said, baby, it's ok. I know it's gonna take a little time. Relax, baby. I'm not goin' nowhere. We're just getting started.

Jaquan pulled me close and kissed me on the lips, nose, and forehead. It was passionate and yet endearing. Jaquan and I spent the rest of the evening watching movies, ordering take-out, planning our next move, and of course fucking. It was all surreal, and it felt like a dream. I had won my first marathon, taken love's journey, and gotten my man back. Everything was perfect. Almost too perfect, in fact.

Then the next day, Jaquan and I decided to get a rental car. Although the idea of being on the back of that man's bike for the next week was romantic, it wasn't necessarily ideal. We both wanted to do special things in the city, such as shopping and partying. Jaquan also mentioned going to the casino, but he also planned something special for us. I swear this man never ceased to amaze me! He was like my own little piece of heaven. Just for me. My phone rang, and I looked at the number. It was Liz from WGRU. I was a little surprised, but I answered the phone.

Tabby: Hello?

Liz: Good morning, Tabby. It's Liz McGee from WGRU! How are you this morning?

Tabby: I'm doing great. How are you?

Liz: I'm fantastic! Thanks for asking! Tabby, I don't know if you realize it, but what you accomplished is INCREDIBLE! Have you thought about what's next for you?

Tabby: Well, to be honest, I haven't had a chance to think about it. (I look over at Jaquan and smile) I've been a little preoccupied.

Liz: Tabby, I know all of this is happening so fast, but I have some fantastic news! WGRU would like to conduct an exclusive interview with you on the 5 o'clock news with our primary anchor Charles Brown! We want to know who the mystery lady behind the marathon medal is! You're a local hero, ya know! So, let's see here...how soon can you get to the studio!

Tabby: Oh, Liz, I'm sorry. I'm out of town and will be there for several days.

Liz: How unfortunate, Tabby! We have to strike while the iron is hot! No worries. Do you have some time early next week?

Tabby: How about I make myself available for your Liz

Liz: Perfect, Tabby! That's the spirit. So, listen, here are the deets. We need you at the studio at 3 pm for wardrobe and make-up. We also have another local hot story, so we'll interview you both at the same time; how's that?

Tabby: Sounds good to me, Liz.

Liz: Fantastic! I'll send you an email with all the details!

We ended our call, and I shared the news with Jaquan. He said,

Jaquan: That's what's up! I told you that you were the shit, baby! Pretty soon, you're gonna need a manager!

Tabby: (I giggled) baby, you so silly.

Jaquan: I'm serious, baby, you the shit, and you don't even know it. You're smart; you're pretty; you're a boss.

Tabby: Jaquan I am not a boss. I'm a woman who lost her job and best friend within weeks of each other. I happen to be lucky enough to get a huge divorce settlement, that's all.

Jaquan: Tabby, did you forget already about the call you just got? You won a whole marathon, the first time running. Who does that? And that's why you're the shit.

I smiled. Jaquan sure made me feel like I was everything when I felt like I was nothing. That's the kind of thing he did for me. Jaquan said,

Jaquan: Tabby, we should celebrate your celebrity status. Let me take you out tonight. I already had something special planned; now I'm gonna add another layer to that.

Tabby: Awe, baby! It's just an interview. But any time I spend with you, I'm down for that.

Jaquan: Well, let me finish putting the details together. I gotta run out, but I'll be back in a few hours.

Tabby: A few hours? What do you need to do, Jaquan?

Jaquan: Tabby. Baby. Trust me. I got this. I got a few connections myself.

Jaquan hugs me tight and kisses me on the forehead. We look into each other's eyes, and we both smile. He kisses me again. And again, and again, and again...until I laugh. Jaquan grabs the keys to the rental and heads out the door to God knows where. I sit alone in my thoughts of him and smile. I'm officially happy.

True to his word, Jaquan returned a few hours later with several bags in tow. This man went shopping for himself! He pulled out a brand-new pair of black imperial jeans that looked like the ones he already had on. He also bought himself a flashy red designer tee, a pair of Nike shoes, and a ball cap. Jaquan topped his outfit off with a pair of designer sunglasses. Was this what this man was doing? Shopping? I was really confused. Jaquan then pulled out a bag from Neiman Marcus.

Jaquan: Baby, I got something for you too. For our date.

Tabby: Oh really! (I got excited) Let me see!

Jaquan pulled out a red and black Michael Kors Camo-Print mini t-shirt dress. It looked like the perfect fit. I said,

Tabby: Oh, Thank you, baby! I love it

Jaquan: Yea, it's kind of casual, but where we're going is casual but special. But I see how you live, how you move. I know you like the finer shit in life. So, I know I gotta come hard or go home.

Tabby: Jaquan, do you think I'm impressed by all this money? I could lose it all today, and then what would I have?

Jaquan: Baby, the type of money you got from your divorce, you can buy jets and shit. C'mon, let's be real. Honestly, I don't understand what you see in a man like me. I'm a street nigga, like, really?

Tabby: And somehow, that doesn't seem to matter, now, does it? When I hopped on the back of that motorcycle, I decided that I wanted to be with you.

Jaquan smiled and breathed deeply. This time I drew him in for a hug. One that was reassuring and let him know I wasn't going anywhere. At that moment, I had an epiphany; this man was just as insecure as I was, but for different reasons. I was so busy thinking about my own that I didn't believe Jaquan would have some of his own. In my eyes, this man had it going on, not financially so much, but everything else. But at the same time, he was looking at me like I had it all together. I guess we were mirroring each other. I hugged him tighter. He breathed in my aroma. He looked at me and kissed me. I knew we would be ok. Jaquan said,

Jaquan: Baby, I need you to pack a bag. I know we just got to this beautiful place, but what I planned will have us run into tomorrow.

Tabby: Oh really? What's going on in that head of yours? What have you got planned?

Jaquan: Trust me, baby, you're gonna have a good time.

And just like that, I packed a bag, and Jaquan and I headed to Atlanta to have a good time.

We got to Atlanta around early dusk, and our first stop was the MLK Memorial. It was typically closed at dusk, but Jaquan pulled some strings to keep the memorial open for our own personal tour. I was very excited and yet impressed at this man's creativity! He really was thinking way out of the box to impress me. In my previous marriage with James, I was privy to all the finest restaurants and exotic trips. After a while, as I became accustomed to those things, James stopped putting in the effort to make our marriage spicy. Date nights fizzled and only existed during birthdays and holidays as our relationship declined. Where was the spice in that?

We first stopped at the crypt of Dr. And Mrs. King. I stood in awe and took in the scenery as it glowed in the dusk. Jaquan and I stood in silence. We thought about the history of Dr. King and our history; as African-American people. The struggles we went through, and Dr. King's contribution to moving our lives forward. We found out that Dr. King was not originally buried there. Dr. King was initially carried upon a farm wagon drawn by mules to Southview Cemetery, where he was initially laid to rest. In 1970, Dr. King's remains were removed from the Southview Cemetery to what is currently known as the t King Center campus, and in 2006 his crypt was also rebuilt to include the remains of Mrs. Coretta Scott King. We also learned that the vault was constructed of Georgia Marble, a staple and timeless acknowledgment of its southern roots and traditions. In addition to freedom hall, we visited Dr. King's home and the historic church where he served as co-pastor until he left to attend a theological seminary in 1948. It was all so beautiful and amazing. Now, this was a great date so far!

Our next stop was to get a bite to eat. We made a stop at Nana's Chicken and Waffles, which is a staple in Atlanta. When I sat down to order, upon looking at the menu, I had no idea that chicken and waffles could be served in so many different ways. For example, I saw strawberries, whipped cream, and red velvet waffles. I decided to live on the edge and get the red velvet waffles with the whipped cream. I know, I had just completed a marathon, so I needed to keep my body in shape for what was next. What was next anyway? I know I had the interview with Mr. Primetime Charles Brown, but beyond that, I had no clue where this newfound money or fame would take me. All I know is that I was in the presence of this amazing guy who happened to be showing me the time of my life. Yea, this definitely was bliss.

After dinner, Jaquan was not finished.

Jaquan: Ok, for the next part of our night together, I need your help with this, Tabby.

Tabby: My help? Ok...you know I'm a team player, so how can I help?

Jaquan: For the last part of our date, you have two options to choose from; but you won't know what the option is beforehand, and you won't know where we're going until we get there. Are you down?

Kind of like love's journey, I thought. I said,

Tabby: Since you keep it spontaneous, I'm down.

Jaquan: Ok, so choose...option A or Option B

Tabby: And what is option A again?

Jaquan: Tabby... What did I just say?

Tabby: I know, I know... I was just seeing if you would give away anything. Ok, Option A. So, what is it?

Jaquan: Like I said, you won't know until we get there. But know that no matter what option you choose, we were gonna end the night in the hotel room fucking our brains out.

I smiled and said,

Tabby: Well, I definitely like the sound of that. Lead the way, sir. I would say you could blindfold me, but since I don't know my way around the city anyway, it doesn't matter.

We both laughed, and Jaquan drove to our next destination. When we got there, I was pleasantly surprised. I looked up at the words on the building and understood: Magic City...the baddest strip club in Atlanta and a staple of entertainment. How could we visit Atlanta without partaking in Magic City? Immediately Boo Boo Kitty got a little wet. I looked at Jaquan. What was he up to? We sat in the rental and decided to smoke before we went in. As we puffed and passed, he said,

Jaquan: I hope you don't mind, but I got us something a little extra.

Tabby: Extra?

Jaquan: I thought that since we were out livin' it up, we could try something other than weed together.

Tabby: Jaquan, I don't think this is a good idea. I have never done cocaine, and I'm sure not about to start that shit.

Jaquan: Cocaine? Whoa, slow down, baby. Who said anything about powder? I would never even think of going down that road. You kidding me, right? You're showing your age, baby.

Tabby: Ok, ok, as long as it's not cocaine, I'm good.

Jaquan: Well, I was thinking more like a hit of X.

I smiled. I knew exactly what he meant, ecstasy. It reminded me of my night in LA with Samson and Pretty Red. I smiled again and agreed to go with the flow. We smoked the rest of the blunt, took a hit of ecstasy, and proceeded to enter the club.

From the outside of the building, there wasn't much pizazz. Just a white building and a sign proclaiming its name. "This is it?" I thought. Even the sign was nothing to look at. I wondered what the big deal was. The only thing significant about the place from the outside was the line of patrons waiting to get in. A very long line of patrons. What was on the other side of this building that had everyone willing to brave the elements on a daily basis to get in? Oh, I had heard stories about this place. From what I heard, some come just to get a glimpse of the celebrities that come through this place daily. I thought to myself, although I was sure that it would be, this so better be worth it. I was not accustomed to standing in long lines as of late. Jaquan grabbed me close to him in the line. Now that was making it worth it. I swear there is nothing like a man who loves public displays of affection—a complete turn-on. Being with him made the time go by in that line like it wasn't even an inconvenience. Or maybe it was the ecstasy; I really couldn't tell. But when we finally stepped into the building, I was enamored by the energy in the room.

The stories I heard about Magic City did not do justice to being in the experience of it all. I looked around and took it all in. Magic City was not only the spot for ordinary people, but politicians, athletes, and entertainers all go there to be seen, and some were in full effect tonight! I had never seen so many rappers and entertainers, many famous, which I need not mention. With Magic City being a staple in Atlanta for years, it significantly impacted the culture in Atlanta. The club owner went out of his way to create a fantastic nightly experience for its patrons. You walk in, and the hottest DJs are spinning the newest sounds. It's also known that strip clubs determine the music we hear every day on the radio. So while the hottest sounds play, the women strip while men throw money...there were strippers, gorgeous strippers, and cash everywhere! Sexy waitresses served hot wings, and plenty of bottles were popped all over the place. I swear, it felt like I was in a music video. There were private VIP areas where men smoked cigars laced with the chronic while the women put on the show of their lives. I took in the atmosphere and thought it was all surreal. I watched the women dance in different levels of undress as they seduced their customers. It was a lot to take in.

Jaquan looked around and smiled. I could tell he was impressed as well. We sat down at our reserved table and ordered drinks. A cute little light-skinned girl with tattoos covering her body showed up at our table. She wore a red lace thong bikini with a net overlay wrapped around her waist.

Bottle girl: A bottle of Dom courtesy of the house for your reserved seating.

Jaquan looked over at her and admired her. He then looked at me with an embarrassing smile. I smiled back and looked at her in approval. Looked at him. I gave him the ok to admire her beauty. She looked to be in her mid-twenties. Jaquan said,

Jaquan: Thank you, shorty. You know red is my favorite color.

Bottle girl: Is that right?

Jaquan: Yea, a cute lil' redbone in my favorite color? Thick in all the right places too? That's what's up.

Bottle girl (giggles), is there anything else I can get you? Perhaps some ones to make this night a little more eventful?

Jaquan: Now that's what I'm talking 'bout right there. Let's start with a stack.

Tabby: Go ahead and make it two.

Jaquan looks at me and smiles.

Jaquan: Oh shit, look at you.

Bottle girl: Two stacks, coming right up. Did you want to start a tab?

Jaquan: Oh, fa sure.

He handed her his credit card. Redbone walked away, and Jaquan looked over at me and smiled.

Jaquan: Baby??

Tabby: I smiled…. Yes, Jaquan

Jaquan: Redbone was fine, right?

Tabby: I must admit she is gorgeous.

Jaquan: But you know what? She ain't got nothing on you, babe. You like fine wine. You get sexier with age.

I smiled.

Tabby: Thank you, baby.

We picked up the glasses that redbone had previously filled with Dom. We toasted to the night ahead and what was about to go down.

As the DJ played the music, I felt the effects of the X, and the bottle Jaquan ordered. I swear there were songs I had never played before. The crowd was hyped, and the ladies twerked their asses to the beat of the music. I looked over at Jaquan, who was admiring the thicker dancers with tiny waists and huge derrieres. Dollar bills rained in the air from all over the club, and the ladies did tricks on the floor as they collected their reward. Jaquan said,

Jaquan: Babe, can you move like that?

Tabby: A little (I laughed). I used to dance in high school, so I'm sure I can pick up some of those moves.

Jaquan: Is that a fact?

Tabby: Oh, hell yea!

Jaquan: Good thing I got a room. You can give me a private show tonight

Tabby: All you got to do is say the word, and baby, I'll show you moves you ain't never seen before...

And that night, I did just that. When we got back to the hotel room, I set the atmosphere by dimming the lights in the hotel room and lighting candles. We were still high off the events from Magic City, the drugs, and the alcohol. I turned on my "fuck me" playlist that began with "Inside" by Jaquees and told Jaquan to sit in the middle of the floor. Jaquan did as instructed, and I began to dance seductively in circles around him. I took off my dress. Jaquan looked up and smiled. I walked around him seductively and leaned in for a kiss. Our tongues danced in cadence, and I could feel the sensations all over my body begin to awaken. I withdrew and began dancing again. This time I took off my bra. Jaquan licked his lips in approval and started massaging my legs and thighs as I swayed to the music. Finally, I took my panties off and got on my knees.

As Jaquan looked at my naked body in appreciation, I gyrated to the music. I swayed seductively to the left and the right and got on all fours. Then moved my ass in a twerk-like manner, and Jaquan slapped my cheeks as the music played. "Let me massage the pussy, let me massage the pussy" blasted through the speakers, and Jaquan took his hands and explored my body. He told me to turn over, and I obliged. Jaquan's hands reached up for my twins, massaged my nipples with his thumbs, and I moaned. "Damn, you got some big ass titties," he said, and I looked into his eyes as he continued to massage. That shit felt so good. Jaquan leaned in, and his mouth gave my girls the attention they deserved. He sucked my nipples lightly, and I moaned. He took the left one in his mouth, licked it, and I exhaled. He turned his attention to the right one and did the same. Boo Boo Kitty was getting moist, and I wanted him to taste her. I grinded my hips into him as he continued to suck on my twins. I could feel his manhood growing, and my clit flickered in anticipation of the pleasure he was about to give me. Jaquan began to grind with me, and I wanted him to put all 9 inches inside me. I was so turned on that Boo Boo Kitty's juices were overflowing.

Jaquan began kissing my body slowly. As he ventured lower, he showered kisses on my midsection, legs, and thighs. I moaned in pleasure. Jaquan brushed my lips lightly with his tongue and tasted my wetness. I exhaled again in a sigh of relief. He licked my Lovebox into a frenzy. Boo Boo Kitty purred. I said, "damn baby, lick this pussy." He looked up and said, "This pussy tastes good," then returned to his feast. Jaquan pulled my lips apart and licked my center. She rose to attention. He put my clit in his mouth and sucked it, took it back out, and licked it. He took his tongue and swirled my center like candy. My legs began to shake. I said, "oh, I'm coming," and Boo Boo Kitty's juices exploded everywhere.

Jaquan got up to unbuckle his pants. I reached up in a sex-crazed frenzy to help him. As he stood to release his designer jeans, I massaged his rock-hard penis from the inside. Jaquan's pants fell to the floor, and I massaged his massive cock. He moaned. I smiled as I looked at that beautiful chocolate. I took my mouth and licked it like a lollipop. Licked him from the bottom to the top and all along the edges. I took all of him in my mouth slowly, and he gasped. Took him in and out of my mouth. I licked the tip of his shaft. I tasted a little of his pre-release and massaged his twins as his shaft bounced in and out of my mouth. Jaquan said, "damn baby, take all this dick." I took it out of my mouth and said, "Yes, daddy," as I licked the tip and went up and down his long shaft.

Jaquan grabbed my face as I put his manhood back in my mouth. Jaquan moved his hips in tandem with my mouth. I sucked and slobbered. Jaquan moaned. I added more saliva and sucked as he pounded my face. I made blow sounds, and the wetness of my mouth intensified the sensation, and Jaquan moaned louder. I sucked and blew as he pounded. He moaned again. As his manhood explored my throat cavity, I began to choke. He pounded harder, and I gagged. He yelled, "FUCK! I'M ABOUT TO CUM! Jaquan released his goodness in my mouth, and I took in his soul.

I pulled Jaquan to the floor and got on top of him. I wanted this man inside me. I wanted to devour him. I looked deep into his eyes as I sat on his shaft. His dick felt so intense inside my Boo Boo Kitty. I looked down at him as I bounced up and down slowly. Jaquan's hands gripped my hips and stroked in tandem with my sway. Our eyes locked as the pleasure of every single stroke filled my vagina. I moaned and said, "damn baby, your dick is so amazing." He said, "Nah, baby, it's this pussy." He grabbed my twins and began to suck. I leaned forward and gave him better access. As he sucked, I rode, and our pleasures were intensified. As he sucked my nipples, Boo Boo Kitty began to flicker.

Tabby: Damn, Daddy, this feels so good

Jaquan: I love this pussy, baby. Give me those big ass titties.

Jaquan began to suck again.

Tabby: Oooh baby, don't stop. It feels so good.

I said as I continued to bounce up and down his shaft. I picked up speed, and the feeling intensified. Jaquan matched my cadence. Boo Boo Kitty flickered, and I changed speeds again. As Jaquan sucked, he matched my energy.

Jaquan: Gimme this pussy

Tabby: Yes, daddy, YES!

Jaquan moved faster, and I matched him. He grabbed me by the hips and lifted my body in the air. I had no control. Jaquan pounded faster and harder, harder and faster. I yelled, AHHHHHHHHHHHHHHHHHH.......... Then creamy wetness flowed from Boo Boo Kitty like a waterfall. Jaquan yelled, AHHHHHHHHHHHHHHHHHHHHHHHHH I'M CUMMMMMMMMMINNNNNNNNNNNNNNNGGGGG.......and

Jaquan released again, this time inside me. I collapsed next to my man on the bed. My man? Yes, I believe this man-child was my man. Jaquan reached over and cuddled me. I chuckled to myself at the thought of him being my man. It didn't matter, though, because I was happy. Yea, I had finally gotten back to happy. I smiled at that thought, and Jaquan and I fell asleep peacefully in each other's arms.

The following day, we headed back to the beach house, packed our things, and headed back towards my condo and our future reality. What was our reality? We were a couple, but what did that mean anyway? Would we date and move in? Was this all too soon? Should I even be thinking about any of this? I quieted my mind for a little bit. I decided to live in the Moment and enjoy this man-child of mine. He was fun, and my life could use a lot of that, especially with everything I had been through. I nibbled his neck and held him tight on the ride home. The rest of the ride back was pretty uneventful. We stopped for gas, took potty breaks, and he slapped my ass as I entered the gas station, typical stuff. For us, this felt like bliss. We were back together, and we were happy. I smiled about that thought all the way back home. It seemed as if our bliss was just a vacation when we pulled up to the condo to see my son Vincent and a young lady who looked vaguely familiar. "This is about to be interesting," I thought. Jaquan stopped the motorcycle and pulled his helmet off; I did the same. I looked up at Vincent and waived; he looked on in disapproval. I could tell. I kissed Jaquan, and we both got off the motorcycle and headed toward the front porch. I said,

Tabby: Hey, Son, how you been?

Vincent: Mother, I've been well. You remember Hope, don't you?

Tabby: Ahhh, Hope, how have you been?

Hope: I've been well, thanks for asking.

Vincent: Mother, I don't believe I've had the pleasure of meeting your friend. Actually, I don't know what's been going on lately with you. That's why I stopped by.

Tabby: Excuse me, where are my manners? Jaquan, this is my son Vincent. Vincent, Jaquan.

Jaquan: Nice to meet you

Vincent: Yea, likewise. Mother, can we have a word, please? Hope, you can wait in the car.

Hope smiles and walks away. Jaquan kisses me on the forehead, excuses himself, and walks into the house. Vincent glares at Jaquan until he disappears into the condo.

Tabby: So, Vincent, when did you start seeing Hope again? What happened to Rebecca?

Vincent: Mom, I started seeing Hope again before Ebony passed, remember? Where have you been, mother?

Tabby: Jaquan and I just came back from Atlanta

Vincent: That's not what I was asking. You seem so out of touch these days and unavailable, but now I see why. What's going on with you besides you riding around the country on a motorcycle with a man that looks like he's dang near half your age?

Tabby: Watch yourself, son. I know you're grown, but you are not THAT grown.

Vincent: All I'm saying is a lot has been going on that you don't know about, and I have been trying to reach you for months now.

Tabby: I had a lot going on, son with the divorce, the marathon.... Oh my god! I have to be at the studio for my interview in a couple of hours! I completely forgot.

Vincent: Congratulations on that, by the way. I called right after your interview; you didn't see my number?

Tabby: I can't even remember, son. A lot was going on that week. So, what else is going on, Vincent?

Vincent: It's Vanessa. She's failing out of college.

Tabby: Excuse me, what?

Vincent: Yea, she is half-assing her schoolwork and spending most of her time partying with her friends.

I shook my head in disbelief.

Tabby: Let me talk to her and see where her head is.

Vincent: She's not gonna listen, Mom. I've tried, believe me.

Tabby: Maybe she doesn't want to be there anymore. I don't think she really was ready to go in the first place. I said that, didn't I?

Vincent: Mother, what does that even matter right now? Vanessa wants to do what SHE wants to do.

Tabby: Well, I'm going to talk to her, but I'm going to do the listening. Let's see what she wants to do. If my baby girl wants to come back home, she is more than welcome. I have possession of the house, and if she wants independence, she can stay in the condo.

Vincent: I don't think that's wise, mother. She's not ready for that kind of independence.

Tabby: First things first. Let me reach out to her after my interview.

Vincent: Ok, Mom. Now, what about that "man" you got in the house? Has he moved in yet? (He rolls his eyes)

Tabby: Mind your business, son. I'm not in yours.

I look over at the car with Hope in the passenger seat. We both looked at each other in understanding and agreed to leave the subject of our love lives alone for now. Vincent hugged me, and I promised to call Vanessa and keep in touch with him more often. I smiled and walked through the door of my condo.

Jaquan walked out of the bedroom and asked,

Jaquan: So, I can imagine that was awkward. Your son don't like me. I can feel his energy.

Tabby: Baby, you are focused on the wrong thing. I'm a grown woman, remember?

Jaquan: Grown and sexy, for sure.

Tabby: Thank you, baby! Well, all of this grown and sexy has an interview in less than 2 hours, remember?

Jaquan: The interview, oh yea! That's gonna be dope. Get yo' sexy ass in there and get ready. I gotta make a run real quick and park the bike. I was gonna get my game and a few things and bring them back here. That way we can ride together to the studio.

This man was supportive already! I smiled and walked over to Jaquan. I planted a kiss on his mouth, and he smacked my ass. Then pulled me closer and cupped it tight.

Tabby: Don't start nothin' we can't finish. You gotta put the bike away, and I have to get ready.

Jaquan continued to massage my cheeks. He said,

Jaquan: We got time to do it ALL, baby.

Jaquan pulled me in for a kiss and a quickie. And just like that, Jaquan was right. We had mind-blowing sex that lasted five minutes, AND we both had enough time to do what we needed; he ran his errands, and I got amazingly fabulous for my celebrity debut. Jaquan picked me up in his Ford Expedition, and I could hear the trap music about a block away from my house. My condo had a strict noise policy, and I would have to address this with him later. But for now, I was in too good of spirits, and the city was gonna see me give an amazing interview with Jaquan waiting in the wings. Maybe one day, he will be right by my side. But for now, his support was appreciated and what I needed for now. Jaquan picked me up, and we headed to the studio.

When we got there, we were greeted by none other than Liz McGee herself. Her bubbly disposition always knew how to make a person feel welcome.

Liz: Tabby! Hello! Welcome to WGRU! How was the trip over? Did you find it ok?

Tabby: Why yes, Ms. McKee, they let us through the gate and gave us special parking

Liz: Perfect! You both can call me Liz! And may I say? I am so excited to have you in the studio! I would say we need to get you to hair and make-up, but you're FLAWLESS!

Tabby: Why thank you, Liz (I smiled)

Liz: You're quite welcome! Well, let me show you to the waiting area. You still have about 30 minutes until we go live. The other guests are in makeup now and are going on right after you. So, make yourself comfortable.

Liz walked us to a huge waiting area set up like a modern-day living room. Liz said, "help yourself to any of the refreshments! We have coffee, tea, and Chardonnay"! I said, "Don't mind if we do," Liz smiled and said she'd be back shortly. I looked around the waiting area. There was a huge sectional in the middle of the room, and a kitchen area with a huge marble island, oak cabinets, and a stainless-steel refrigerator. A bottle of chardonnay was already chilling on the island. I grabbed two glasses from the cabinet and poured the chardonnay for Jaquan and me. I handed him his glass and snuggled next to him. As I began to take a drink, he said,

Jaquan: Wait, it's bad luck to have a drink in the presence of company without making a toast.

Tabby: What should we toast to?

Jaquan: To a successful interview. And how can I forget? To one of the sexiest women alive.

Tabby: Jaquan! You're so fucking sweet!

I smiled, and we clinked glasses, shared a toast, and had an intimate kiss. In the distance, I heard a voice say, "I don't believe this; we haven't been divorced two months, and here Stella is getting her groove back." I heard another voice say, "The blood of Jesus! Lord, cover us all, um, um, um." I unlocked lips with Jaquan to look up and see an angry-faced James. Not only was I in his presence, but there stood Pastor Doug, a production crew, and my old nemesis Keisha.

Keisha... James Taylor's baby mama is what I like to affectionately call her. She will never garner my respect, as I have put up with her disrespect for about ten years. She would call my husband at all hours of the night under the pretense of distress of their son Christopher. And, of course, he would go running! In the middle of the night, no less, for years! As she called it, I was the dummy who didn't play my position. But I was his wife, so how was I SUPPOSED to play it? This bitch had it twisted. And now here she is, ENGAGED to my former husband. James and Keisha both had pure audacity coming in here, judging my relationship with Jaquan. Oh, they were judging, I could tell. All three were looking at us in shock, disgust, and horror. And now they've been blessed with a so-called reality show. The reality show...I had forgotten about that news story. That's why they're here, that fucking reality show. How the fuck did they land that anyway. I guess some people were just fortunate like that, and when you're connected like James and Pastor Doug, anything is possible, like the good book says. On the other hand, Keisha just happened to be in the right place at the right time. In essence, that bitch knew how to play her position.

Keisha came into the room, slayed to the gods. She rocked a simple black Dolce & Gabbana pencil skirt with a matching bustier blouse. Her outfit was complimented with a vintage Saint Laurent rhinestone short necklace and matching bracelet. She also rocked the classic Christian Louboutin black bird leather stilettos. But, of course, her outfit wouldn't be complete without her Paloma clutch, which was also Christian Louboutin. Her hair was laced with a long black sew-in with a part down the middle. Only quality hair I could imagine. And, of course, her face was flawlessly beat. Not to mention the 8-carat diamond dangling from that bitch's fingers.

I looked closely at the diamond. Oh, that was not a Tiffany's diamond. Harry Chad Enterprises was more like it. It was BEAUTIFUL! The stone cut of her ring was round and baguette. There was one center round diamond about three carats in diameter and small diamonds around the center diamond. The ring enhancer also had diamonds, approximately 2 carats to be exact. And when the light hit that diamond, it sparkled more, the color blue than clear. Jaquan looked Keisha up and down in a bit of admiration. I shrank a little, even though Liz had just told me I looked amazing. Humph. I could tell he was impressed by all the designers; most young boys were. Keisha looked at me and then back at her ring in admiration. She swept her ring finger through her hair as if her hair was in her way. She then looked Jaquan and I up and down like we were two insignificant bugs she wanted to crush. Keisha stepped next to James, looking into one of the cameras.

Keisha: Oh my god, James, are you so serious? What is she doing here? Baby, this is our show!

The cameras zoomed in on a pouty-faced Keisha.

Tabby: Oh my god, Keisha, are YOU so serious? Life does NOT revolve around you, although you think you're the center of the universe.

James: Don't you dare talk to my wife that way, especially coming in here with... that THUG.

Jaquan: Watch ya mouth, homey. You don't want these problems.

Tabby: Jaquan, baby, please

The cameraman zoomed in on my expression and then quickly moved to James to get his reaction.

James: Baby? Yea, that's exactly what he is, too, a baby!

Jaquan: Nigga you got one more time to disrespect me, and I'm gone show you how quick this baby will beat that ass

Pastor Doug steps in between James and Jaquan. The cameras continued to roll, and the production crew appeared pleased with the chaos they were captured on film.

Pastor Doug: Gentlemen! Calm down. There is a better way to resolve this. We are all intelligent Black men and must conduct ourselves as such. Do we want the world to see us acting stereotypically? We're better than that. This is NOT Love and Hip Hop!

Pastor Doug looks over at the camera and says, "The Bible says to treat those the way you want to be treated, amen? God called us to be examples. To be better." Then Pastor Doug commanded us all to retreat to our respective corners of the waiting room and allow him to mediate the situation; after all, the waiting area was big enough to accommodate us all. I walked over to the island to refresh my chardonnay. I could see Pastor Doug approach Jaquan for a conversation. One of the cameramen followed Pastor Doug. I shook my head in disgust. This was all turning into a circus. But what did I expect? James, Keisha, and Pastor Doug were here. This was no surprise to me. I looked over to see Keisha had also made her way to the island and began pouring a glass of wine. The cameraman also in tow. Keisha looked at me and said,

Keisha: It's just like you, Tabby, to try to ruin my television debut. You just can't leave us alone now, can you? You look nice, by the way; not something I would've chosen to be interviewed in, but...

Tabby: Keisha, really? You think that I am so pressed about your reality show that I would come here and cause a scene? Girl, if you don't sit down somewhere. Oh, and nice ring, by the way; I could've sworn your engagement ring came from Tiffany's.

Keisha: No, that was just a million-dollar shopping spree, honey. My engagement ring had to come from somewhere special, custom-made.

Keisha holds her hand up to me in admiration. The camera zooms in on her magnificent diamond. Keisha lifts her hand to eye level, admiring the diamond, and smiles. She then looked at me with a bit of venom in her smile and said...

Keisha: Tabby, I know you like to distract issues with backhanded compliments, but we both know you came today to complicate my storyline. You know how these television shows love sensation and drama? I mean, it all makes sense; we've been celebrities since our engagement made the news; hell, it went viral. Why wouldn't you take the time to flaunt your new young boo, and on camera, nonetheless? So go ahead, get your five minutes of fame; I would have made sure I looked better if I was in your shoes. But mine are red bottoms, yours?

Tabby: (chuckles) Keisha, you are really pushing it, dear. As far as sensation and drama goes, you don't need me for that. Look at the company you keep. The last thing I wanted to do was run into the 3 of you.

The cameraman zoomed in the judge the sincerity of my reaction.

Tabby: And furthermore, Keisha, if you MUST KNOW, me and my Boo, as you put it, were here before you by personal invitation. Did you forget that I JUST won the Nantucket Marathon? As a first-time runner, nonetheless. That's a pretty big deal, too. About to go viral even.

I looked at the camera and winked. Keisha turned a shade of red. I looked over, and Pastor Doug and Jaquan were laughing and engaged in conversation, another cameraman capturing it all. James was sitting across from them on the island, sulking, sipping what appeared to be scotch. Scotch? Wait, how did he get scotch?

Keisha: Are you serious, Tabby? Are you gonna ignore me? You're a childish bitch for this, and you know it.

Tabby: Wait, what?

Keisha: I'm not gonna repeat myself!

The production manager yells, "AND CUT." Liz McGee returns to the waiting area with her overly bubbly disposition.

Liz: Ok, Tabby, are you ready? You've got ten minutes, and you're up! Come with me!

I looked over at Jaquan, who blew me a kiss and waved, then continued to engage Pastor Doug in conversation. I was starting to feel like he was there to support them, not me. And I followed Liz down the corridor to prepare for my interview. I tried to refocus and erase the last 15 minutes of my life from my existence, which was hard. Coming face-to-face with James and Keisha shook me a little. Seeing Judgmental James and slayed to the gods Keisha was not on my agenda for today. As a matter of fact, I was hoping never to see them again. Ever. We no longer ran in the same circles. I had new money, but James had wealth. New money and wealth very rarely intertwine with one another. I shook off the events in the waiting room, gave a successful interview, and met Jaquan back in the waiting area afterward. I noticed one cameraman and an associate of the production team were still talking to Jaquan. He was so enamored in whatever they talked about that he didn't even see me enter the room.

Associate: You know, you have a certain charisma that is perfect for television

Jaquan: Pastor Doug said the same thing! Interesting.

Associate: Absolutely, Jaquan, you have the look, the swag. I'm telling you, the social media world would LOVE YOU! Here's my card. Let me know if you're interested in some future opportunities. Call me, let's talk.

Jaquan takes the card and says,

Jaquan: I may just do that. You never know; everything happens for a reason. Pastor Doug just said that too!

Tabby; (clears her throat) Hey, Babe.

Jaquan: Baby, how'd it go? That's probably a dumb question; you're one of the smartest people I know.

I smiled and said,

Tabby: I think it went quite well. But after everything else that happened, I'm honestly exhausted. Can we go home now?

Jaquan: Sure baby, let's go.

Jaquan and I got in the car and headed to my condo. For the first few minutes, there was an awkward silence. Jaquan then said,

Jaquan: To be honest, I don't see how you could ever have been married to that guy. He's arrogant and thinks too much of himself. He's an asshole who needs to be dealt with. He was lucky Pastor Doug had the brilliance of a level head.

Tabby: Brilliance of a level head? Pastor Doug? You act like you know these people personally. But, Jaquan, you know NOTHING about them.

Jaquan: What I do know is Pastor Doug seems to be an upstanding guy.

Tabby: And that is your first mistake there

Jaquan: Well, according to Pastor Doug, there may be some things I don't know about you.

According to Pastor Doug? Well, this shit surely sounded familiar.

Tabby: Oh, is that a fact? When did you and Pastor Doug have time to get so acquainted? Oh, I remember it must have been while you were there to support me for MY interview that he had time to tell you how amazing you were on camera. Go figure!

Jaquan: Tabby, what is your problem anyway? You're acting like a real bitch right now for no reason.

Tabby: A bitch? Oh, I got your bitch, sir.

Jaquan: I didn't call you a bitch; I said you were acting like one. What is the problem, Tabby?

Tabby: The problem is that instead of coming to the station to support me, you end up fraternizing with the enemy.

Jaquan: Fraternizing? I don't even know what that means, Tabby, but I assume you mean I was getting really chummy. You think that's a problem? How about the fact that we come back to your condo, and your son gives me dirty looks? Then we go to the studio, and I almost get into it with your ex-husband. On top of that, he and that bougie fiancé stared at me the whole time like I had a disease. Pastor Doug was the only person acting decent at that Moment, including you.

Tabby: Me?

Jaquan: Yea you! I saw you over there taunting Keisha and winking into the camera; you think I'm stupid? I don't miss nothing, Tabby, and what you did was childish and messy. Grow up, Tabby.

Tabby: Yea, you're real mature yourself over there smiling for the cameras. Kiss my ass, Jaquan.

Jaquan: Oh, there's that chick I was waiting to come out. You act all sweet and sophisticated, but there's a whole other side to you, and I saw it at the studio today and now here in the car.

Jaquan pulls up to my condo. There was another awkward silence. I said,

Tabby: Baby, let's just go in the house and forget about today, ok?

Jaquan: Easy for you to do. Nah, I'm good on that.

Tabby: Excuse me?

Jaquan: Tabby, you heard me. Everything that happened today was a bit extra for me. And messy. And I believe things don't happen for no reason. Maybe I was meant to see this side of you. I don't know if I'm ready to deal with this level of messiness. I'm a low-key person Tabby.

Tabby: Says the guy who JUST took the producer's card for acting opportunities, but ok, I get it.

Jaquan: And that's what I'm talking about. My television opportunities ain't got nothing to do with you and how messy this is Tabby. Could you please leave my vehicle so I can go home and think?

I was seething but didn't say a word. I got out of the vehicle and slammed the door as hard as I could. I was hoping the glass shattered. Jaquan pulled out of the driveway and put his music on full blast. The bass from his stereo system shook the condos nearby. I was even more pissed. And just like that, Jaquan and I were on a break, and his young ass accused me of being messy. I not only had my son Vincent to blame for that, but also James, Pastor Doug, and Keisha. So much for Bliss.

3

IT'S COMPLICATED

The word complicated is an adjective defined as consisting of many interconnecting parts, to be intricate. In the medical world, complications are secondary conditions that arise as a result of something primary, which is the source of the condition. In layman's terms, if you say that something is complicated, it means that it has so many parts to the situation or aspects of it that make it difficult to understand or sometimes even deal with. Complicated. I pondered on the definition of that thought as I thought about the current-day Tabby. Things were complicated, and Jaquan was the primary source of it all. There were a few factors involved:

1. Jaquan and I were no longer lovers, and he had a whole new situation

2. Even his situation in itself was complicated because they were lovers but not in love

3. I now lived with Jaquan and his situation

4. And then there was Angela, a permanent fixture in his life. I refer to her as his primary source of income, while Shaquita- affectionally refers to her as "His Pet."

Those things alone complicated things, but what could I even do, given the situation?

I picked up the phone to dial Vanessa. As soon as I began to dial, I saw Jaquan's number appear. I rolled my eyes and answered.

Tabby: Hello

Jaquan: How you doing, pretty?

Tabby: Jaquan, last I checked in, you weren't even speaking to me, remember?

Jaquan: (sucks his teeth) see that's your problem, always dwellin' on shit.

Tabby: Jaquan, how can I help you?

Jaquan: Well, I needed to make some money while you were sleeping. So, Shaquita and I are headed to the casino. I need to hit the blackjack table. You know my ID is expired, and I'm banned from the one in town, so I'm headed to Middleport. I needed her to drive.

I got up out the bed and looked out the back window. I noticed my car was gone, just as he said.

Tabby: Jaquan excuse me? That's over 2 hours away. Where's Mickey? How do you know I didn't have plans?

Jaquan: We dropped Mickey off at her grandmother's, and what kind of plans you got with that nigga from the other night?

So that was it. This nigga was jealous. He had a whole situation in the room up the hall, and he was pissed because I was entertaining? I said,

Tabby: What the fuck difference does it make the point is you took my car without my knowledge Jaquan; this shit has to stop.

Jaquan: It will quit playing, Tabby. The bottom line is that part of the agreement was for all of us to help each other until we could get back on our feet. Right now, you have the only car.

Tabby: That happens to be a Mercedes that you have no problem having access to. You would have a car if Angela hadn't set yours on fire, with you IN IT, and you STILL continue to deal with her. I can't!

Jaquan: First of all, you can't prove that she set the car on fire. Second, she was with me when the car caught on fire, so how was she gonna hurt herself? Think Tabby

Tabby: All I know is that your car caught on fire shortly after your business shut down. Maybe it was just karma.

Jaquan: There you go with that Karma shit. Maybe your karma is the situation you are in right now. I swear you too old to be going through this; you are almost 50.

Tabby: Perhaps this is my Karma Jaquan, but best believe I won't be in this situation too much longer. I'm making moves.

Jaquan: I bet you are. One thing you have always been is optimistic. I also see you have been on social media a lot more since that reality show was on the air showing your naked ass. What's that about? Again, you are too old for that. It's not a good look.

Tabby, how about you worry about getting a new vehicle so you can keep your ass out of mine.

Jaquan: I'm workin' on it, Tabby, baby steps; that's why I'm here.

I ended my conversation with Jaquan, which seemed pointless. What was I gonna do now? I was trapped in the house with no transportation. I had already scheduled my photos to be posted on social media and had the topic for my next blog. I was restless and needed to cleanse myself from the conversation I had with Jaquan. My phone dinged, and it was Raymond. The guy from the other night, I said out loud as I thought about Jaquan's audacity to be jealous. The crazy part is that I didn't sleep with him out of respect for my complicated situation, and I explained that to Raymond. After that, the most we did was cuddle and kiss a little. When we left the room and headed down the stairs, we came face to face with Jaquan. Jaquan, of course, was the first to speak, and it was a quick introduction. I couldn't gauge Jaquan's reaction at the moment, and to be honest, I had not entertained anyone in that townhouse since I moved in.

I knew afterwards, though, that he was pissed about the situation. A couple of hours later, I was summoned into the bedroom by Shaquita, and while we were engaging in conversation, Jaquan wouldn't even look at me. I tried to talk to him, but he wouldn't answer. Then finally, he interrupted our conversation to tell Shaquita that the next episode of "A Love Like Ours" had dropped. He knows I don't wanna know anything about that damn show James and Keisha is on. I knew that was my cue to leave the room and the conversation. I then went downstairs to clean the kitchen. I turned on my music and began to dance as I cleaned. As "On Chill" by Wale hit my speakers, I began to sway seductively to the music back and forth. I was in my sexy, and I knew it. I turned around. Jaquan was standing there staring. I looked over at the camera located in the kitchen. I knew Shaquita was watching.

I told you that this situation is complicated, but I decided to focus on my present-day restlessness and how Raymond was the perfect guy to alleviate that in the here and now. Jaquan and Shaquita wouldn't be back until the wee hours of the morning, so what did I have to lose? My kitty began to purr. So I texted Raymond back and asked him to come over. It just so happens that he was fortunate enough to get away.

Raymond could be classified as complicated, too, but I'll get into that in a bit here. I met Raymond on a horny night trolling an online dating site; I ain't gonna lie. I was restless, and Jaquan and Shaquita had just finished the latest episode of "A Love Like Ours." Either they liked watching Pastor Doug and the crew, or they did that shit to piss me off. They were down there giggling and shit, so I knew what was happening next. They would listen to music, Jaquan's choice of course, which would be some subliminal message into how he was feeling that night. Depending on the music, Jaquan would be into her, take a local ride with another chick, or take a ride 45 minutes away to Angela's. In all 3 cases, somehow, Shaquita was not pleased with the situation. And I didn't want to be around to witness how it was about to go down.

Jaquan turned on Jaquees, who was Shaquita's favorite artist. Yep. She was the one for the night. I swear, there was so much about this man that I had no clue about until now. But anywho, I was upstairs bored, and social media was my go-to these days. I was also rolling up my second blunt and thought it would be nice to get the hell out of here tonight. Hearing my ex fuck that not-so-attractive bitch in the other room was not my idea of having a good time. And she plays that shit up way too much. "Oooh, Jaquan, fuck me harder." That bitch weighs over 300 pounds; I mean, what can they really do?

While scrolling down my social media page, I got a ding on the dating app. It was Raymond. Raymond was exactly the distraction I needed to get the hell out of there. I hit the blunt slowly as Raymond and I engaged in conversation. I found out that he lived not too far from me, but he was babysitting for his sister. He said he wanted to see me and asked if I didn't mind coming to his sister's house to get to know him better. I agreed, and we exchanged numbers. Raymond called me; his voice was just as sexy as his photos. I also noticed he had a southern draw which was an actual turn-on. Raymond asked me what I was drinking, I told him I preferred light liquor, and he said that wouldn't be a problem. Raymond texted me the address, and I hopped in the shower and got myself together. I headed to meet Raymond with the expectation that it was about to go down.

I pulled up to Raymond's spot, and he greeted me at the door. He was a tall brown chocolate bar with bowed legs and a slender frame.

Raymond was slightly over six feet tall, with a mole above his lip. When he saw me, he smiled, and I noticed he had the most beautiful set of teeth. I was pleased with what I saw and could tell he was too. Raymond drew me in for a hug, and it felt warm, like a teddy bear. He smelled amazing too. Raymond invited me in, and as he poured our drinks, I looked around and took in my environment. It was a typical living room in a black home; nice furniture, exotic pictures, and a huge flat-screen television mounted on the walls. Music was playing through the soundbar connected to the television. I asked, "where are the kids?" and he handed me a drink and said,

Raymond: They just went to sleep right before I texted you; we're good.

He smiled, and I noticed he had the prettiest set of teeth. I smiled back. Raymond then pulled out his weed and began rolling up. I took a huge gulp of my drink and thought about Raymond. Yea, it was going down tonight. I was gonna drink this man like I took in that gulp. He looked up at me and smiled. Looked me up and down in admiration. He went back to rolling up, and we had light conversation. As we smoked the blunt, Raymond's complex situation began to be unfolded to me. I don't know if it was the weed or the alcohol that proved to be the truth serum, but Raymond began to spill all the tea on his situation.

Raymond had just broken up with his kid's mother. They had been together for about five years, he had a three-year-old with her, and she had an older son who was seven. The older child wasn't his, but he played daddy because he had been in his life for so long. Needless to say, they started growing apart and began having an open relationship. Raymond decided he wanted to be totally free from it, so he moved out of the house and back with his sister. He also confessed that the children upstairs were not his sister's but his own, the little girl and the boy. He said the mother was out of town again. Apparently, her new boo lived out of town. As I took in another drink, my senses began to tingle. I couldn't tell if it was my Spidey senses or

Boo Boo Kitty. I took a mental note of how I felt, and Raymond smiled at me again and told me to come closer. I thought about his southern draw and those beautiful teeth, and I came closer and sat on Raymond's lap.

The alcohol and weed had kicked in, and my body was on full alert. Raymond placed his hands around my neck and drew me in for a kiss. He wasn't a bad kisser, either. He stroked my neck as our tongues danced in and out of our mouths. I was starting to feel my body heat up. As we kissed, Raymond's hands traveled from my neck to my chest and brushed my nipples lightly. That shit was turning me on. My mouth watered as his tongue continued to dance in and out as he stroked my nipples lightly. He knew he was turning me on. As he kissed me, I rubbed his chest, and he moaned. His hands traveled from my breasts to my thighs, and I could feel Boo Boo Kitty becoming wet. Raymond edged closer to my love cave and stroked her wetness through my panties. She wanted him to stick his fingers there and called to him. He answered her with gentle strokes on her kitty as his tongue continued to make love to my mouth. My head was spinning in ecstasy, and I leaned back as he stroked my clit. While he kissed me, we heard the sound of my wetness as he stroked me, and Boo Boo kitty flickered. My lower lady stood straight at attention. Raymond laid my head on the couch and leaned over me. He reached down for my panties, pulled them down, and took them off. Raymond looked down at my kitty and licked his lips. I knew exactly what time it was. I opened my legs for him and exhaled as he administered that first lick.

Pure heaven is what it felt like. Raymond started with slow deep licks around my lips. My kitty was eager. Raymond didn't disappoint as his tongue flickered the tip of my clit. I was so turned on. Raymond licked me slowly, then fast, then flickered in and out. I moved my hips in cadence. I then took my hands and opened my lips, giving him full access to what he was tasting. Raymond licked her intensely. He focused like a sniper on my clit, administering lick after lick, then Raymond began to suck. I moaned and swayed my hips as my hands continued to hold my lips back. I rocked, and he licked. I swayed, and he sucked. I moved my hips in a circular motion, and Raymond flickered my clit. Boo Boo Kitty began to pulsate. I increased the tempo of my hips, and Raymond matched my intensity as his tongue moved in and out of me. Boo Boo Kitty exploded, and Raymond was there to catch all of her goodness.

Raymond stood before me. I massaged his manhood through his pants. I was impressed with what I felt and even more impressed when he dropped his bottoms. I wanted him and could not wait anymore. I massaged his cock and stroked his twins in tandem. He moaned his pleasure. I stood up and pushed him onto the couch. I straddled Raymond but did not enter him. I took his manhood and massaged it on Boo Boo Kitty. I could feel him pulsate, and my clit flickered against his cock, which sent an electric charge through our bodies. I massaged fast, then slow. Raymond rotated his hips as I massaged his cock against my lady love. He was trying to maneuver his manhood for entry, but I continued to tease him. He moaned, more like begged. I stroked and rubbed him against my clit, and he pulsated and went insane. I inserted the tip, grinded a little, took it out, and rubbed him on my clit again. He didn't know that he felt so good inside me that I wanted all of him, but I also wanted to savor this feeling. I looked at him as I massaged his Johnson. His eyes were intense, and I knew I was pleasing him. I finally decided to put him out of his misery; I sat right on his shaft. Raymond was the one that exhaled this time as our hips moved in tandem. I bounced slowly. I wanted to feel every inch of him inside me. As I bounced, he reciprocated with slow intense thrusts, and my kitty flickered each time he went inside me.

Raymond's shaft pulsated. I increased the tempo slightly. Raymond matched me with his thrusts. I grinded into him. As he thrust, my juices lined his shaft. He said, "damn, your pussy's so wet." I moaned as I rocked back and forth. I leaned in for a kiss, and our tongues danced as he continued to thrust inside me. Raymond took on hand and massaged my nipples. Boo Boo Kitty began to flicker in a frenzy from the sensation of the three; His pulsating Johnson, the wetness of his tongue, and the intense pleasure his thumb gave my nipple. I increased the tempo some more and grinded hard into him. His shaft rubbed up against my clit as he administered flickers to my nipple. I put it in his mouth as I bounced up and down. Finally, I couldn't take it anymore and said, "oh god, I'm cumming!" he said, "Baby, let's cum together. Let me cum inside you." I looked Raymond in the eyes as he stroked me. Raymond lifted my hips and began to stroke my pussy at lightning speed. I was on top, but he was in control. Raymond stroked, and I yelped and yodeled! Finally, he yelled, and Raymond came inside me.

As I thought back on that memory, I smiled. I was glad that Jaquan and Shaquita were gone. I could get my groove on in private. Partially, anyway. Shaquita and these damn cameras. Luckily the person she's trying to watch closely is right there with her. Shaquita is never concerned about me unless Jaquan is in the vicinity. Insecure bitch. I focused on the task at hand: Raymond, who absolutely didn't disappoint. After our rendezvous, I walked Raymond to the door, laid down for a good night's rest, and slept like a baby. I woke up late the following day to the sound of Jaquees playing downstairs in the living room.

I looked up at the nightstand and noticed my keys placed neatly there. I heard music playing from the shower. There was a knock on my door; it was Shaquita. I told her to come in.

Shaquita: Good morning, Tabby. Did you sleep well? Probably like a baby, I can imagine. (She smiled)

Tabby: As a matter of fact, I did! But I'm sure you knew that.

Shaquita: (laughs) well, I did see that Raymond showed up at the door, and he didn't leave until early this morning. I'm sorry; you know how I get when those notifications go off. But you go, girl! Way to get some last night!

Tabby: Girl, you need to stop with the cameras. Jaquan was with you last night! But yes, Raymond and I did get our freak on! So, the fact that Jaquan took my keys without asking made it all worth it.

Shaquita: I feel you, girl! But don't let Jaquan see him again; you know how he got the last time. I don't get it. The two of you are not together anymore. So why does he act like that?

Tabby: And that's why I gotta get the hell out of here! The time is coming, and very soon, I am leaving! So, Jaquan better get his shit together! I swear it's like having another kid to raise!

Shaquita: Well, you obviously don't understand Jaquan like you thought you did. Once he trusts you, he has a hold on you that never goes away. I've been dealing with him for seven years, and Angela 4. All I can tell you is welcome to the club!

She laughs. I looked at her like she had some sort of sickness. This woman was more than willing to deal with a man who openly had multiples. And from what I was beginning to see, he didn't give a damn about anyone or anything in his life but himself. After all, I had already been through; there was no fucking way I was gonna stay entangled in this bullshit. My thoughts were interrupted by Shaquita as she began to speak again.

Shaquita: Girl, you know I'm joking. Stop being so dramatic! Last night was good for us, so we won't need to use the car anymore!

Tabby: Oh really, that's good news!

Shaquita: Yea! Jaquan won $25,000 at the casino last night! We stayed at a hotel, and then I got a rental car this morning for the week. Jaquan and I are gonna go car shopping today and later on in the week. Once we find a car, he's gonna put it in my name, and we'll be set! That way, you don't have to worry about me using the car for my own personal stuff.

Tabby: Well, that is great news, Shaquita! Congratulations! What's next, a job?

Shaquita: A job? Oh god, no, I'll lose my section 8.

Tabby: Oh yea, I forgot about that. Well, good job anyway!

The shower turns off in the faint distance. Shaquita excitedly excused herself from my room to get ready. As she left the room, I could see Jaquan's skinny frame headed down the hall to their bedroom. The sounds of Shaquita's favorite artist filled the bathroom, and 30 minutes later, she was dressed. Shaquita had a floral dress that landed mid-thigh. She wore no lotion, so her arms, legs, and feet were ashy. Shaquita had a pair of dirty gray flip-flops on her crusty feet. It was a sight to see. I thought, "He went from a dime to a penny." That's what he wanted. Shaquita went into her bedroom and came out quickly. She then went downstairs and then came back up. She said,

Shaquita: Did Jaquan tell you he was leaving? Where did he go?

Tabby: I have no idea where Jaquan went. You know he ain't speaking to me much these days, so why would he tell me?

Shaquita: Maybe he went to Lil Jason's house

Shaquita calls Jaquan. He sends her to voicemail. She sits her fat ass on my bed. She checks her messenger. She notices he's active, then goes inactive. She then goes to Facebook, pulls up her fake page, and begins to spy. Not on him, but on Angela.

Tabby: Shaquita, what the fuck are you doing, girl?

Shaquita: I need to find out what the fuck he's doing, Tabby. I just got a rental in MY NAME, and he better not be with Angela!

Shaquita gets up and storms out of the room. She slams the door to her bedroom, and I can hear weeping from her door. Poor girl. I get it; loving Jaquan is hard and a sickness, which made me question why I was still here. The tender and understanding part could relate to how she was feeling. I got out of bed and softly knocked on her door. Shaquita told me to enter, and I came in and gave her a consoling hug. This woman had been with this man on and off longer than I had even known him. He had taken her to hell and back again. But that was Jaquan, either pure heaven or extreme hell. There were no in-betweens. Shaquita wiped her eyes and began to cough. She then sprinted to the bathroom and started vomiting. I went in to rub her back. There was no hair to hold back as Shaquita's hair was as long as a second is short. And that was in a pigtail on top of her head. Lovesick. I shook my head. I wanted to stay and console her, but I knew things would worsen. Thanksgiving was just around the corner, and right now, these were not blessings I was counting. When Shaquita was finished being sick, I would try to make arrangements for the evening because I was certain Jaquan was not coming home anytime soon.

I went back to my room and texted Raymond. He responded immediately. He said he was down for some company tonight and that his sister went out of town yesterday and would be gone all week. I thought this could be good, and we agreed to meet later. Hours had passed, and still no Jaquan. I felt bad for Shaquita as I got myself together to see Raymond, but I was not gonna let her issues with Jaquan affect what I had going on. I didn't care if I was occupying a room or not. When this mess was done with James and Keisha, I would cash them out to get them out of my life. I meant that. I refused to be entangled in this bullshit year after year. Being in this complicated situation showed me another side of Jaquan I had never seen before. I looked at myself in the mirror and nodded in approval. I told Shaquita I was headed out. She was sitting on the couch, numb in her thoughts and tears. I told her goodbye and decided I couldn't worry about her or Jaquan. Boo Boo Kitty and I had a dick appointment with Raymond.

When I got to Raymond's house, he opened the door quietly.

Raymond: We have to be quiet. The kids are upstairs asleep. Don't worry, though; I'll show you where I live. I have a whole space to myself.

Raymond showed me downstairs to the basement. We hadn't made it that far the first time, but like he said, Raymond had the whole space to himself. The basement was more like a mini apartment because it was finished. There was a bedroom, bathroom, kitchen, and entertainment area. It was very nice. I sat on the sofa, and Raymond poured me a drink and turned on some soft music. Raymond said he needed to check on the kids and left me the weed to roll up while he went upstairs. I did as instructed, and he returned and said the kids were still stirring. I thought it was so sweet that he would keep the kids while his sister was out of town. That was quite a responsibility on his hands. Raymond spent the first hour checking on the kids until they were tucked away and asleep. Now it was our turn to play. We laughed and chilled as the music played and just enjoyed each other. That felt good. In that small Moment, I felt happy again. Happy...I was almost there once. I thought I had it with Jaquan. The painful memories of happy started flooding in. Instead of getting emotional, I took a shot of tequila to numb the pain. This was not the time nor the place for old issues to come to the surface.

My emotions were interrupted by a knock on the door. Raymond and I looked at each other puzzled. I asked,

Tabby: Are you expecting company? Are you trying to get me into a secret threesome I don't know about?

Raymond: (laughs) baby, I wish I would have thought of a threesome, but no. I'm not expecting anybody. I'll be right back.

Raymond left the basement to answer the door, and I sipped on my drink. A few minutes passed, and he was still upstairs. I decided to be proactive and roll another blunt. After smoking that blunt, 10 minutes later, Raymond STILL hadn't resurfaced, and I was getting not only a little suspicious but a little irritated. What the fuck was going on, and why was I down here by myself? Finally, Raymond returned with his fingers to his lips. I said audibly,

Tabby: Excuse me? Shhh... What for?

Raymond: (whispers) I got a situation upstairs, please.

Tabby: Raymond, you have a situation down here. What the fuck is going on? And please don't leave anything out.

Raymond: My kids' grandmother is upstairs. She came by.

Tabby: Your kids' grandmother? Why the fuck would she be coming by?

Raymond puts his head down. He says,

Raymond: She came by to check on the kids

Tabby: I thought you had your sister's kids this week. You have yours too?

Raymond: Honestly, I have just my kids. My kids' mother is away this week, so I have them.

Tabby: Well, why didn't you say that, Raymond? Did you ask her to come by?

Raymond: No.

Tabby: So why would she come here out of the blue to check on them? Raymond, there is something you are not telling me, and if you don't start talking, I'm gonna yell at the top of my lungs, I swear!

Raymond: Apparently, her son called grandma while he was upstairs, supposed to be sleeping.

Tabby: But why? I still don't get it.

Raymond: Hold that thought; I'll be right back.

Raymond tiptoes back upstairs and stays ANOTHER 10 minutes. Now, I am steaming. As Raymond comes back down the stairs, I gather my things and say,

Tabby: You know, your baby Momma's Momma has been a real buzz kill for me, I don't know what you got going on, but I gotta go.

Raymond: Tabby, wait.

Tabby: Fuck this

Raymond: Ok, let me explain. So, me and my baby's Mom live together, but we are not together. I stay in the basement, and she stays upstairs. We both live our own lives, and she is out of town right now with a nigga.

Tabby: If you arc so separate, why do I have to be quiet in the basement?

Raymond: I know it's a lot, but I can't explain it all right now. If you want to leave, that's fine. I get it. But her mother is still upstairs.

Tabby: What the fuck does that have to do with me? She ain't my baby Momma!

Raymond: Tabby, PLEASE! Just listen to me. Shhh… I can't let you go out that front door with her upstairs.

I whispered and yelled,

Tabby: Nigga what! Are you FUCKING KIDDING ME! Raymond, I'm grown with grown children. OH, HELL NO!

I looked at Raymond in disbelief. He looked at me with a merciful plea in his eyes.

Grandma: Raymond, what's going on down there? You got the TV on?

Raymond: No, ma, you hear the music, don't you? I'm coming back up.

Grandma: Ok, Raymond, we need to finish this conversation about this text I got from Jay-Jay.

Grandma closed the basement door. I shook my head, obviously no longer buzzed or horny.

Tabby: So, what the fuck now, Raymond, am I supposed to wait this shit out?

Raymond: No, I wouldn't let you do that, Tabby. But I do have a way to get you out of here.

Tabby: Nigga, I ain't climbing through no windows. Let's get that straight right now.

Raymond: No, no, don't worry, I got you. There's a door to the outside when you're coming into the basement, right up the stairs. Just tiptoe.

I rolled my eyes and followed Raymond. What other option did I have? We tiptoed up the stairs, and he slowly creaked the door to the outside open. I made sure I had everything, made my exit, and sprinted to my car. I turned on the engine, pulled further up the street, and parked the car. Thought for a Moment. What the fuck. I felt like I was in high school all over again. I was disgusted. Not just with what happened with Raymond. But with life in general. My housing situation was fucked up, my new potential dick had a whole situation going on, and I was sitting at the end of his street in a parked car. I had to get my life together. I took a deep breath in and out. I still had my overnight bag I packed to spend with Raymond. I didn't want to go home yet because I didn't know what chaos I was walking into with Jaquan and Shaquita. I checked my cash app and looked at my balance. Not bad, I thought and decided to treat myself to a night at the Homewood suites.

When I got to the hotel, lady luck was on my side. I booked the room for two nights with my past booking points while in management. I was feeling optimistic already. I also picked up a bottle of wine from their mini store to keep me company that night, just like the old times of traveling. One bottle of red Moscato was on the menu. I got to the room and stepped into the shower. I let the hot water consume my face first, then stream down my body. I felt refreshed. I got silent and tried to think about what was next. My life had gotten way too crazy all at once. Jaquan and I ended things when James and Keisha decided to freeze my assets. Talk about bad timing. I had to change that somehow and definitely had to make some real money in the interim. The marathon win had died down, and those opportunities had already passed. I washed over my body and thought some more. I tried to focus on the light at the end of a gloomy tunnel. Keisha and James were on top of things; why were they fucking with me anyway. AND from what Shaquita says, she throws little shade my way on the show, that bitch! Although it had gained me quite a following on social media. Hmmm. I might be able to turn that situation around and capitalize on it...

I jumped out of the shower and dried off. I put on one of the hotel robes and wrapped the towel around my sew-in. I felt a little bit of my power come back. I decided to leave my attorney Yvette Stevens a text. The next day we would strategize and discuss my case with James and how to make my new idea lucrative. I turned on the television and poured a glass of wine. I decided that I would try to no longer be a victim of the things that were happening to me or that I allowed to happen. I drank half the glass of wine and fell into a deep, peaceful sleep. The next morning, I ordered breakfast and had it delivered to my room. I smiled at the thought of having my own space again. It seemed like forever. When I thought about it for real, I had never actually had my own space for long:

1. I raised kids as a single Mom, so I was never alone.

2. I married, so again, not by myself.

3. I was separated but had so many lovers I never got to process being alone.

4. I divorced James, met Jaquan, and we, in essence, shacked up. He was the rebound that I tried to pretend it wasn't, so I again cohabitated.

That deepness was interrupted by the ring of my cell phone. It was Yvette, just the person that I wanted to talk to! I answered the phone with eagerness.

Tabby: Hello.

Yvette: Good Morning, Tabby. How are things going?

Tabby: Complete chaos, and I pray you have some good news for me.

Yvette: Well, Tabby, I wish I could say I have all good news, but I don't. No worries. However, the situation with James and Keisha is just a temporary setback.

Tabby: Ok, you said there was bad news, Yvette. Whatever it is, give it to me, please.

Yvette: Your pending divorce appeal is an interesting one. Typically, in divorce decrees, the decision is final. However, in this county, a quirky precedent set over seven hundred years ago allows a spouse to appeal or revisit the conditions outlined in the divorce due to specific stipulations. James believes he has found a loophole. James found out that the judge assigned to your case had a daughter going through a nasty divorce at the same time. James' attorney is arguing that it was impossible for the judge to be fair and impartial. As a result, the terms of the divorce are in review by an interim judge. Until then, all accounts the two of you had in question will remain frozen.

Tabby: How long is this review going to take, Yvette? Level with me.

Yvette: Tabby, honestly, it can take just as long as it did to get a divorce hearing. About nine months. Let me look at Judge Carlson's schedule. Hmm... actually, it looks more like ten months. The silver lining in all of this is if the judge has a schedule change between now and then, we may be able to push the date up a couple of months. But you have to be ready at a Moment's notice, Tabby. Can you do that?

Tabby: You have to be fucking kidding me! Ten months of frozen assets? It's already been two months! That son of a bitch! All of my money from the marathon promos, my leisure money, EVERYTHING was in those accounts. All I had was access to my savings.

Yvette: And I'm confident James was very well aware of that. The good news is that any income you earn is free game. My advice would be to create another account at another bank and create an income for yourself until this is resolved. You may have to go back to work for a while, Tabby.

Back to work. Back to work? I had forgotten that working was an option. I had gone from divorced and rich to having my high-powered attorney tell me I may have to get a job. What?

Tabby: Ok, Yvette, I do have to bring in income. I agree, and I have an idea of how to do that, and I will need some advice on how to do that. James and Keisha are capitalizing off my misery, and I've had enough. It's time for me to fight back.

Yvette: I agree. And I'm here to support you. There is also more good news on the proceedings. You don't have to worry about the decree overturning Tabby, no matter who the judge is. This quirky legislation is simply a stall tactic. Once we go before the judge, there will be no problem getting what's rightfully yours. Now, as far as this new business idea is concerned, what did you have in mind?

I shared my idea with Yvette. She was very intrigued. She gave me some pointers from a legal perspective and then encouraged me to get started immediately. I spent the rest of the day formulating my plan of action for my new stream of income. I figured I needed to do something if I couldn't access my money. I knew I couldn't stay in my current situation much longer. Honestly, I didn't even want to think about the place I lived in. I surely didn't call it home. I slowly took a deep breath in and out and decided to enjoy the getaway I had created for myself for the next two days. Hell, I'd deal with the troubles of my roommates later.

At the end of my eutopia, it was check-out time. I felt an uneasiness in my stomach. I didn't know if it was me not wanting to return to Shaquita's or if there was a storm brewing. I wondered what I was walking into; I could never tell with them. Shaquita would go from being radio silent, crying, to arguing and putting him out of her room. Then she would surprise me days later by being cuddled up with him watching him eat cheeseburgers that she prepared for him.

Classic freakshow. The bottom line was that whatever I was going home to would not be a good situation.

I pulled up to the house and noticed there was no car, no rental, no new car, nothing. That was not a good sign. The door was unlocked, so I let myself in. Shaquita was sitting on the broken-down sofa, smoking a cigarette. "All you need" by Jaquees played in the background as the tears streamed from her eyes. I felt bad for her. I asked,

Tabby: Are you ok?

Shaquita: (pauses). Yea, I'll be ok.

Tabby: Where's Mickey?

Shaquita: She's upstairs playing. (she sobs a little) I can't believe he did this. It's so unfair.

Tabby: Has he been back yet?

Shaquita: No! Two days and not a word. What did I do to him to deserve this?

Shaquita starts to cry. I stood there Momentarily, trying to decide if I should sit next to her and console her. The song stopped and repeated. I walked over to the sofa, sat down, and hugged her. She broke down a little bit more.

Shaquita: We were supposed to get a car and some furniture. Thanksgiving is coming up, and I wanted it to be really special. I swear Jaquan fucks up everything.

Tabby: Yea, I can't argue with you there. But you have to pull yourself out of this girl. What can you do but wait? But while you're waiting for his return, you have a whole daughter upstairs that needs to be taken care of. You can't keep her in that room in front of the flat screen or tablet. How is that effective? Get out and spend time with Mickey. Do something.

Shaquita: Yea, you're right. Maybe I can call my friend and take her out for a few hours.

Tabby: Now that's the right idea! It will do you both well.

I gave her one last squeeze and retreated to my bedroom. It was my place of solace. I looked around at my vision boards as I heard Shaquita come up the steps. She headed to the bathroom and got in the shower. About 30 minutes later, she called for Mickey to get ready, and she and Mickey left with her friend. While she was gone, I decided to begin the new venture Yvette and I had discussed. I showered, put on something sexy, and picked up my phone. I went to FB and looked at my profile. Five thousand friends and 17,649 followers. Yea, the fact that James and Keisha had this reality show would be beneficial for me as well, I thought. I tapped on "what's on your mind." I pinned my cash app to the comment section and hit Facebook LIVE. As soon as I hit start, over 100 viewers tuned in. Nervously, I opened my mouth and began to speak. I began to tell my truth, and the people listened. 30 minutes later, when I exited the Live, I knew that my idea was genius. My view had been shared almost 100 times, and a platform for me had begun. I also checked my cash app, in which donations had continued to pour in. I was well on the way to sustaining myself for however long this ordeal with James and Keisha would draw out, but it also served another purpose. I was not gonna allow that trio to walk all over me on national television. It's time I fought fire with fire.

Several hours later, Shaquita and Mickey returned both in good spirits. They went to the park and got a bite to eat. Mickey retreated to her room and back to what she loved best, YouTube. Shaquita went to her room and turned on the latest episode of "A Love Like Ours," her guilty pleasure that irritated my soul. The fact that they watched that show every week, KNOWING that those folks know me and hate me personally, was the biggest shade of all. I could hear Keisha on the television in her bitchy voice, "Pastor Doug, you are a true spiritual genius." I rolled my eyes and turned on my TV. Of course, the advertisement for THAT show was the first to pop up. And I have to admit it did seem intriguing. I thought, "I wonder what kind of shit this bitch has been talking about me on National television." I clicked the remote and selected episode one.

I started talking to myself...Tabby, what are you doing? And to turn to the first episode? Girl? Really? I must admit curiosity is getting the best of me. This shit ain't right, and you know it. Well, what do we do about it? How is watching this bullshit helping? I'll tell you how, not that I have MY new venture, I can use this show as research AND ammunition, don't play with me. Ok, ok...Well, it sounds like you have this all under control. I'll ride with it. And just like that, I stomached the first three episodes of "A Love Like Ours" and the antics of the beloved trio.

As I watched, I could see why the show was so popular. Pastor Doug had an apparent charisma and wisdom that the world was dying to fall in love with. Not to mention how James and Keisha made their love story seem like a fairy tale, a very lavish one at that. And then there was the hidden shade towards me—the supposed bitter ex-wife. I swear it made me furious. However, I couldn't just get on my platform and vent. I had to be methodical. If anything, watching their show gave me ammunition and ideas on adding polish to my own. I took the remote and turned the television off. I said a quick prayer of gratitude and thanksgiving and drifted off to sleep.

The following day, it was business as usual, and still no Jaquan. As a matter of fact, Jaquan stayed away until day 6, just in time to turn in the rental the next day. Then, he appeared with bags of clothing, boxes of shoes, no money, and Angela in tow. I knew that the shit was about to hit the fan....

4

RED FLAGS FOR RED ROSES

Red flags, what are they? A red flag is *a literal warning of some kind of danger*, like a tornado siren in the night, used to warn locals that the twister is coming. In corporate America training environments, the red edits in systems are indicators of hard stops to look at the information causing the edit. You then have to correct it to move forward. Red flags can also be a figurative warning, like the red flag R Kelly's angry outburst on television sent to America as a whole about his temperament. Either way, the flags are there, and they tell you that the shit ain't right. Well, you know there were red flags on love's journey, and I chose not to see or ignore what was in plain sight. Jaquan seemed to have that effect on everyone around him. Turning red flags into red roses. How did I get so swept away, you may ask? Damned if I know. What I do know is that I didn't see the following things coming, and that year was a hell of a ride:

1. Jaquan's whole life was a facade, from his job to his so-called lifestyle

2. The red flags of his and Vanessa's hate-hate relationship

3. And then there was Angela

All those red flags, and then some, should have been enough for me to walk away and set that man's whole life on fire. But I believe karma is a real thing. And if I knew then what I know now, I would have blocked Jaquan from my Facebook when he stormed off from my condo, blasting his fucking music.

When Jaquan pulled off from my condo, I went fuming in the house and slammed my door. He was an inconsiderate asshole. I pulled out my phone and dialed his number. He didn't answer. I called again. No answer again. I got pissed. I repeatedly called until he eventually started sending my calls straight to voicemail. That son of a bitch! I paced the floor. He had some audacity. I poured a shot of tequila and sat down on the couch alone in my thoughts. My phone dinged. It was a text from Vanessa.

> Vanessa: Mom

> Tabby: Yes, Vanessa

> Vanessa: Do you have a minute? I need to talk to you.

My phone rings.

Tabby: Vanessa, why didn't you call me in the first place, girl? That is so irritating.

Vanessa: Anyway, Mom. How you been?

Tabby: Just living, child. So, what's going on in Arizona?

Vanessa: Mom, don't act like you don't already know; I'm sure Vincent called you.

Tabby: No, he didn't call. He made a personal visit with Hope, nonetheless.

Vanessa: He came by the house? Really? Mom, it's not that serious.

Tabby: Well, Vanessa, tell me, what is it, love? From what I understand, you're failing out of college. What do you plan to do about it?

Vanessa: I really don't know, Mom. Maybe I'll stay one more semester and see if I can get my grades up.

Tabby: Vanessa, you have to get a 3.5 to stay for another quarter and re-take what you failed. Can you do that?

Vanessa: MOM! I don't know. This feels like pressure, Mom. I'm coming home for the weekend, and then I'll decide. Can you pay for my ticket, please?

Tabby: Yes, child. Come home.

I hung the phone up and shook my head. I got on my phone and sent Vanessa some money for her airline ticket. And just like that, Vanessa was coming home for the weekend, and I had no time to worry about Jaquan. I got the condo together in anticipation of seeing Vanessa in the next 24 hours.

Vanessa came home like the emotional storm I sensed she was. From the moment she came through the door, she dropped everything in the living room and ran straight to the bathroom to relieve herself with the door open. I looked over at her, laughed, and wondered if this was truly the child I had raised. Vanessa then came out of the bathroom, making demands of Maria for a light snack and to take her things to her room like an entitled little brat. I rolled my eyes.

Vanessa: What, Mom? I'm exhausted. I hope you don't mind, but I bumped myself up to business class on the flight. You know I hate to be uncomfortable.

Tabby: Business class? How nice. I'm so glad you were comfortable... Vanessa! Have you lost that beautiful mind of yours? What's wrong with you? Maria, can you make Vanessa something light to eat? Vanessa can get her own things.

Vanessa: Ok, Mom. Can I get a minute, though? I literally just walked in the door. That was a long flight. I'm exhausted.

Tabby: Ok, Vanessa. So what are your plans for the next few days?

Vanessa: I don't know, Mom. We could hang out tonight and watch movies. Then, I can go with my friends tomorrow.

Vanessa gets off the couch and walks over to the mirror. She admires herself for a minute, grabs her phone, and takes a selfie. Then takes another. And another. She then grabs her bags and heads to her room, and the music plays. I let Vanessa be the young adult she was meant to be and poured myself a glass of wine. I thought about Jaquan. Still pissed that he had blocked me. I swear he was acting so immature. It was like having another kid around, and I sure didn't sign up for that. I decided to leave Jaquan right where he was. If it was over, then I would let it be so. Besides, I had to figure out what was happening with my baby girl. Vanessa has always been a quiet storm, keeping everything bottled in. Her acting out as of late was her way of letting her emotions out. But according to Vincent, she was out of control. Maybe a little time at home would help with that. I decided I would get to the bottom of this and help her as much as possible.

A few hours later, after a nap, Vanessa emerged, and we sat and watched movies the rest of the night and well into the morning. It was kind of fun. We watched a comedy and a drama and then binged on a new series. It was good for both of us. I think the quality time helped us forget about our very present realities; her failing out of school and me failing with my love child. However, a part of me couldn't help but wonder what he was doing. I tried to keep my mind focused on our time, but thoughts of Jaquan kept creeping in. I couldn't stand that man, but I was crazy about him at the same time. As I rolled my eyes with my thoughts about Jaquan, I noticed that Vanessa was deep into her phone.

Vanessa: Mom, I know it's late, but Sugar is coming by, and her brother Antonio is in town. They're gonna stop by to say hi.

Tabby: At this hour?

Vanessa: Mom, they just came from going out. I won't be outside long, I promise. Did I mention how fine Antonio is? Emm emm emm

Tabby: Girl, that's the last thing you need to be worrying about. But you're grown so...

Vanessa: Mom, I already know.

Tabby: Your famous last words Vanessa, always have been.

Vanessa: MOM!

Tabby: Ok, Vanessa, I won't say anything else.

Vanessa smiles and gets off the couch to get herself ready. A few minutes later, she was in the driveway talking to Sugar and what appeared to be her brother and another guy. I closed the blinds with my nosy ass and smiled to myself as I remembered the days when I was in my twenties. I decided to chill and not put too much pressure on Vanessa. After all, I went through my twenties and came out ok. I poured myself a drink and headed to my bedroom. When I closed my door, I heard the distinct sound of bass music from the window outside. My heart began to beat faster. Was it Jaquan? The music got louder, then, all of a sudden, it was gone. Nah, that couldn't have been him. If it was Jaquan, he would have pulled in and come to see me. It was just wishful thinking, I guess. I took a few sips of my drink, got in bed, and went off into a deep sleep.

The following day I woke up to the smell of breakfast in the kitchen. Maria had cooked breakfast for what appeared to be Vanessa's guests; Sugar and Antonio. I looked around the kitchen in confusion when Vanessa smiled and said,

Vanessa: Morning, Mom! I hope you don't mind, but Sugar and Antonio stayed over last night in the spare room. It was really late when we finished kickin' it. I didn't want them to drink and drive.

Tabby: Well, that's understandable. Did they starve to death as well? From the looks of all this food, you had Maria cooking like they'd never had a meal.

I looked around at the homemade waffles, bacon, hashbrowns, sausage, fresh orange juice, and what appeared to be an omelet bar. Maria smiled as she served Sugar her omelet, but I could tell she was slightly irritated.

Vanessa: Mom, that is so rude!

Tabby: No, what's rude is having Maria in here first thing in the morning cooking for guests that she didn't intend to. Maria is not a slave.

Vanessa: But that is what she gets paid for, Mom. Maria, can you add some seasoning salt to the potatoes? We're Black, ya know.

Tabby: Black? Baby, you sound like an entitled little white girl. Stop it right now, Vanessa. Did you forget where WE came from?

Vanessa: Mom, no, I don't remember where we came from. I was a toddler when you married James, so if I act like an entitled little white girl, it's because you made me that way.

I gave Vanessa a look that said, "don't push me," and then I said,

Tabby: Sugar, Antonio, unfortunately, you're gonna have to take this meal to go. And since Vanessa is being rude, you can take her with you. I would ask Maria to pack things up, but since she works for me and not Vanessa, the three of you able-bodied people can kindly pack up the food, take what you want and please go. Maria has a long day ahead of her already planned.

Vanessa looked at me and glared. I glared back. We glared at each other for about twenty seconds, and Vanessa rolled her eyes and went back to tending to her guests. The three of them hurriedly packed up all the food and left. Vanessa knew what time it was. I apologized to Maria for Vanessa's rudeness and gave her half the day off. After my conversation with Vanessa, I knew I had to blow off some steam. I decided to go to the gym and relax in the pool. The truth was, I loved the water. Although I never learned to swim, I always wanted to be around it, at the gym, the beach, and then with James on cruises staring at the ocean. It was something about it that was relaxing and gave me a sense of peace and quiet. Perhaps splashing around would help me clear my mind about my situations as of late; Vanessa and Jaquan. Both right now seemed to be stressing me out. Perhaps I would spend two hours today and then hit the sauna.

I would make a day of it and schedule a massage. I called my favorite spa, made an appointment, and headed for the shower. My phone dinged. It was my messenger. I looked to see it, and it was Jaquan. I left him unread to say his peace. I decided to give that man-child a dose of the medicine he was giving me. I silenced his messages, turned on Cardi B's "Be Careful with Me," and sang the lyrics as I took my clothes off and danced in the mirror as I admired my naked body. I got in the shower, packed my day bag, and headed to the spa in my Mercedes C300. I took the smaller Mercedes since I was riding solo.

My spa day was everything I imagined; cool, calm, and relaxing. It was everything I needed. I got back to the big house. As usual, it was as peaceful as Maria had left it; spotless, with classical music playing through the surround sound. I looked around at the décor and smiled. Since James left, I was able to remove the staunch from this massive place and turn it into my showroom. Now classical music is something I picked up from James. He insisted on it every Sunday and on holidays after he watched old karate movies all day. I swear that man was weird. But the classical music was soothing and something I implemented when Ebony passed. I used it with meditation, and soon I began listening when I needed to think. I turned my phone back on, and the messages started to pour in from Vanessa and Jaquan.

The first few messages from Vanessa were her asking me where I was and why I wasn't responding. Then she tracked down my whereabouts by contacting Maria, so since she realized I was at the spa and didn't want to be bothered, she decided to message me about her plans. Vanessa is dropping out of school and found a job at Burger World as the Assistant Manager today. Good for her. Oh, and she's also gonna get an apartment with Antonio. The hell she is. She doesn't know this kid! I was gonna put a stop to this shit immediately. Classical music continued to play in the background. But this time, it seemed so loud. I told Alexa to pause the music, and I picked up the phone and called Vanessa.

Vanessa: Hey, Mom, did you get my messages? I got a job! That's great, right?

Tabby: Yes, Vanessa, I'm excited to hear that. And if you are coming back here, you definitely need to support yourself. But getting an apartment? And then moving in with a man you don't really know? Nah, Vanessa, that's not happening, love.

Vanessa: Mom! I'm coming home and being responsible. I got a job.

Tabby: But what's the rush, Vanessa? I don't get it. They need to be solid if you're going to make rush decisions.

Vanessa: I know how to live on my own, Mom. I went to college for two years.

Tabby: Do you think that experience has prepared you for your own place? C'mon Vanessa.

Vanessa: Yeah, because some of my friends had apartments off campus. I already know what it's like.

Tabby: You know you seem to have an answer for everything, Vanessa. I need you to stop and think. Listen, take a few days and stay at the condo. Think about this. Let Antonio get the apartment, and you can visit as often as you like. If you stay home for a few months, you can save money and move out in a good position. And if the two of you are still dating by then, I guess you're grown have at it. But all I ask is that you stay home for 90 days. Can you do that?

Vanessa: Yes, Mom, I guess.

Tabby: Well, don't sound so excited. It's called compromise, my love.

Vanessa: I know, Mom. Well, I'm gonna spend the rest of the day with Antonio, and then I'll head to the condo.

I told her to have fun. I figured 90 days from now that Vanessa would move on from Antonio and have money to do whatever she pleased. I knew Vanessa, and she changed her mind quickly about everything. And just like that, problem solved. I now had to deal with the 36 unread messages from Jaquan.

The first message started with an apology. It went on and on about how his mother raised him as a small child better than that, and if he crossed any lines, he was deeply sorry. Awe. How nice. Then when I didn't respond, he accused me of cheating with unknown company. What the fuck? The bass I heard the other night was his, interesting. Then he began to try to insult me by saying I was too old to be out here sleeping with young guys. I rolled my eyes. He then showed me screenshots of my social media posts where several guys gave hearts to my status. Then the last string of messages was him apologizing again and begging me to talk to him. I sighed. This was truly exhausting. I turned the classical music back on and decided to deal with Jaquan later. I loved him, but this was a bit much right now. I poured a glass of wine and decided to call him later that night.

I spent the rest of the evening with my wine and music and catching up with old friends. Tara had damn near taken over the bar she was managing. The owner had gotten sick as of late, so she was making a lot of critical decisions. Business had picked up for them, and she implemented a few special night events like karaoke and Wine Down Wednesdays.

Tara: You should come. Especially on karaoke night. I wanna see you hit that stage!

Tabby: Girl, you are NOT getting me up there! But I definitely will come out to support you.

Tara: Yea, you can even bring your young thang. I wanna meet him; I need to make sure he's worthy of you, Tabby. You been through a lot. The last thing you need is someone who's not on your level. I mean it, girl.

Tabby: Relax, Tara, I got this.

Tara: Your famous last words Tabby.

We agreed to disagree and got off the phone with a promise that I would bring Jaquan up to the bar to meet her. My next call was to Samantha, who was a few hours away.

Tabby: Good morning, foxy!

Samantha: Hey, sexy mama! I'm glad you called! I thought you had gotten kidnapped! Girl, what's been going on?

Tabby: Well, for starters, I wasn't kidnapped, Foxy! Jaquan and I went to the beach house in Savannah.

Samantha: Oooh, Sexy Mami, how romantic!

Tabby: Yea, it was...until we got back. As soon as we got to the house, Vincent was there, and then we got to the studio and had a run-in with none other than who? James and Keisha!!!

Samantha: Mami, you've got to be kidding me!

Tabby: Yes, Foxy! And Vanessa's back, and Jaquan and I are mad at each other.

Samantha: Whoa, sexy Mami! Slow down! Start from the beginning!

I told my second best-bestie everything. She listened without judgment. She assured me that everything was gonna be ok and that she was there if I needed her, even if only a text away. We talked for about an hour, and I felt much better. I knew in my heart that I had this. God wouldn't give me more than I could handle, right?

A few hours later, Vanessa emerged to get some of her things to take to the condo. As she was in her room packing, I heard the distinct sound of bass music—Jaquees, "Inside You," to be exact. I knew who that was, and my heart skipped a beat. Jaquan. As the Tahoe got closer and closer to the house, I wondered what kind of sick test this was. I just said God would not give me more than I could handle, and then my two issues come smacking me in the face at the same time? I took a deep breath in and out and prepared to try to put out two fires at once. Vanessa came down the stairs with a large bag.

Vanessa: So, Mom, who is that in the driveway? Blasting the music, nonetheless. If this were the condo or me and my friends, you would have a fit!

Tabby: Not now, Vanessa.

Vanessa: Ahh...the fuckboy that Vincent was telling me about (she laughs)

Tabby: Fuckboy? Excuse me? So now, you and Vincent are having conversations about me?

Vanessa: I mean, when Vincent said it, I didn't believe it, but here he is in living color. Here he comes too. How old is he, Mom? GEESH!

Tabby: Vanessa, be on your best behavior

Vanessa: Ok, Mom. But I'm not calling him dad.

We both laughed as Jaquan knocked on the door. I let him in and introduced him to Vanessa. She was cordial enough but gave me a look sideways. I wondered what she was thinking. Sure, Jaquan was not like the men she was accustomed to seeing me with, James in particular. But that's what I liked about him; he was self-made. Jaquan didn't come from money but was able to build a successful business. I admired and respected that. After a few pleasantries, Vanessa dismissed herself and told me she would see me in a few days. She closed the door, and Jaquan and I looked at each other. He broke the silence by saying,

Jaquan: I see your other child doesn't like me either. (He chuckles) one big happy family.

Tabby: Oh, so we gonna start the conversation off like this? Oh, I can tell how this night is gonna go.

Jaquan: Don't worry about it, Tabby. I ain't come over here for all that. Why ain't you answer my messages? I know you saw them.

Tabby: As you can see, Vanessa is here. I had a lot going on, like you sending my calls to voicemail.

Jaquan: I was pissed, Tabby! I came to support you, and you treated me like I was your ex and that boogie bitch he's marrying.

I smiled at Jaquan's keen observation of Keisha. That bitch thought she was better than everybody in the room. I couldn't stand that bitch, and the fact that our worlds had intertwined once again was pissing me off. The fact that we were in the same city was too close for comfort for me. A small voice in my head thought about selling the house and the condo and getting the hell out of there.

Jaquan: Tabby, are you fucking listening to me? You can't be serious, baby. I mean, where the fuck did you go.

Tabby: I'm sorry, you know how I get. One thought led to another.

Jaquan: Then BOOM! You leave the fucking conversation, Tabby! FOCUS! Please, for once.

Tabby: Ok, Jaquan, you have my attention.

Jaquan: What you saw was me being cordial, Tabby. With your son at the studio. I was hella uncomfortable at both places. So, I tried to fit in as best I could by making conversation. I was there to support you, to keep the peace. And you turned on me. I felt betrayed. And we both got heated, and I left. And then when I came over to talk to you the other night, you were all over some guy in the driveway, and I said fuck it!

Tabby: Turn on you? All of who, Jaquan?

Jaquan: Oh, so you gonna play dumb now?

Tabby: Jaquan, I'm too grown for games.

Jaquan: Yea, considering you're older than me, you should be.

Tabby: Considering you're younger than me, you should grow up and be a bit more mature. Stop making assumptions.

Jaquan: So that wasn't you the other night. I know what I saw.

Tabby: Do you really? What you saw was Vanessa apparently hugging up with Antonio.

I rolled my eyes. He looked me in the face with deep intensity. Like he was trying to read me. I looked back. I wasn't afraid. I had nothing to hide, and he knew it. Jaquan nodded. He took his shoes off and took them to my bedroom. He then went to his truck, got a backpack, and brought it back into the house. I watched as he unpacked a few of the contents. His gaming system, what looked like a change of clothes, and some toiletries. This man had an overnight bag. And just like that, I guess we were done arguing, being on a break, or whatever we were doing. Problem solved? Not by a long shot. Jaquan changed the conversation as he hooked his gaming system to my flat-screen television. I decided to go with it and enjoy the night. I went to freshen up in the shower, and when I returned, I noticed Jaquan had started rolling a blunt. I also noticed there were fresh flowers on the table and the lights were dimmed, and candles were lit. I looked over at Jaquan and smiled. I walked over to him, and he pulled me onto his lap and drew me in for a kiss, and said,

Jaquan: You crazy as hell, but I'm crazy about you.

I said,

Tabby: You drive me crazy, but I'm still crazy about you

We both laughed, and he finished rolling the blunt, and I poured myself a shot of tequila. Jaquan was a Hennessy drinker, so he had his own bottle. I took a shot and watched him play the game as we smoked the blunt. In between the game, we would take a shot or two or three. An hour later, I was very mellow and happy he was there. The truth was I was missing him, and so was Boo Boo Kitty. Jaquan must have sensed what I felt because he turned off the game, and the music began to play from the speakers. This time though, there was nothing classical about it. Surprisingly, he had old-school favorites on his playlist, such as Mary J. Blige. I was impressed at his ability to try to adapt to who I was. Older, different than the type of woman he was used to being with, apparently. I appreciated that.

Jaquan pulled me onto his lap and drew me in for another kiss. I melted into him as our tongues danced with one another. My juices began to flow with just a simple kiss. I thought about my Boo Boo kitty and how much of a slut she was. Jaquan grabbed my face with both hands and continued to kiss me passionately. That man kissed me like he was in love with me or missed me. I kissed him back and gave him the same energy. Our tongues continued to dance as our bodies heated up. I moaned as we came up for air. We kissed again, and Jaquan's hands traveled my body as his tongue gave my mouth pleasure. Jaquan touched my breasts lightly through my shirt. My nipples became erect. He circled them with his hands while he licked my ear. My senses were on overload. I let my hands travel his chest and his stomach. I played with the hair on his chest. Jaquan moaned at my touch. I let my hands travel to his manhood. Rubbed his Johnson through his trousers, felt him rise. Jaquan moaned again as his Johnson pulsated at the sensation of my touch. I wanted him inside me, but I wanted to taste his chocolate even more. I got off Jaquan's lap and stood before him. He looked at me intensely. I took my clothing off piece by piece as he watched. "Dance for You" by

Beyonce played on the airwaves, and I allowed my naked body to sway from side to side, and he watched in pleasure. I dropped to my knees in front of him. I took off his boxers as I massaged his thighs. I looked at his manhood, who stood at attention. It was a beautiful piece of chocolate. I grabbed his shaft and gently massaged him. Jaquan moaned his pleasure. As I massaged, I gently cupped his twins, massaged them too. As Jaquan's dick stood at attention, I took my mouth and licked from the bottom to the top in long teasing licks. Jaquan looked at me. He begged me with his eyes to take him in my mouth. I refused. I licked and stroked as his pre-release began to reveal itself. I knew then that he was ready. I massaged his balls and took him in my mouth slowly. Jaquan exhaled. I licked and sucked and stroked his Johnson. Jaquan moved his hips to match the sensation I was giving. My mouth went deeper onto his shaft. I pretended she was a pussy, and made my mouth wet. I spat on his dick and massaged his shaft. Put it back in my mouth and sucked. I stroked his balls as my mouth covered his manhood. He tasted so good in my mouth. I took it out of my mouth and looked at it. It was perfect. I smiled and put it back in my mouth. I licked and sucked and took it out again and stroked him. His shaft was still wet from my mouth. I looked into his eyes as "At Your Best, The Remix" by Aliyah played through the speakers. He stared back at me intensely, and the lyrics told the story of what was meant to be understood. Jaquan bent down and lifted my body on top of him, and I prepared to ride that amazing pony of his.

I eased down on his shaft. Although it had only been a few days, it seemed like months. I slid deep onto him, and it felt like home. Jaquan moved his hips slowly, and I moved in tandem. My clit began to awaken, and I gave him a deep kiss. As our tongues danced, so did our lower counterparts. Jaquan's hands moved from my hips to my nipples. He fingered my girls, and my clit began to flicker. I said, "damn, this feels so good." He said, "It's this good pussy." I increased the speed of my hips as his mouth traveled to my breasts. He licked them softly as I bounced up and down on his sweet chocolate. That shit felt amazing. He said, "Damn baby, your pussy is so wet right now. This shit feels SOO good." I moaned my pleasure. I leaned into his chest, and Jaquan grabbed me by the hips and took control. He guided me inside him. Grinded our bodies deep inside one another. I moaned louder, and he dug deeper. Boo Boo Kitty pulsated, and I moaned louder. He said, "yea, there it is, baby. Cum for me, baby." "Ooh, yes, baby," I yelled. I'M CUMMMMING! Jaquan moved his hips faster and grinded inside me. He said, "That's my baby...now cum again" .... Jaquan continued to stroke deep inside me, and I lost control. I bounced up and down on his amazingness. I came again, and again and again....then Jaquan released love's journey deep inside me. I dropped down on his chest and lay playing with his hair and the lining of his tattoos for a while. Jaquan returned the favor by continually showering my forehead with kisses. I felt loved, I felt safe, and I felt protected.

Over the next 30 days, things went swimmingly in my life. Vanessa had taken my advice and grudgingly stayed at home and worked. However, she spent most of the weekends at the condo with Antonio. I didn't mind, though, because it gave me and Jaquan time to be alone together. His apparent work schedule kept him busy from the afternoon until late evening. That meant our time was mostly a late-night schedule. And with Vanessa being a late-nighter, it also left for awkward moments during the week. I would catch Vanessa giving Jaquan the side eye. Then he would mention later how he noticed her giving him the side eye. And there was me in the middle. Vanessa would have conversations with me on the side about Jaquan's lifestyle and his job. She swore he was a big weed dealer in the city.

Vanessa: I swear, Mom think about it. He's young. His messenger is constantly popping up, AND look at his work hours.

Tabby: Vanessa, why are you in this man's business?

Vanessa: AND he always has weed, Mom! You haven't seen Ray Ray since you met him. PLUS, Sugar told me she used to buy weed from him. Mom.... Jaquan is a drug dealer; face it!

Tabby: First of all, Jaquan smokes way too much weed to sell it, dear. Second, how are you keeping track of his hours managing a restaurant?

Vincent: I'm just sayin'. Mom, think about it.

Tabby: Speaking of jobs, what exactly do Antonio and Sugar do anyway?

End of discussion. She knew that I knew that man had no job or aspirations. So how were they gonna get an apartment together? Oh, it was ok for her to be in my business, but I better not dare pry into her affairs. So the weekend getaways were everything that Jaquan and I needed.

Jaquan was spontaneous, and I loved that about him. But it wasn't just on weekends. Jaquan would get up at 2 am and decide he wanted to take a drive. We would ride around and listen to music; somehow, that drive would take us out of town. Sometimes we would hit the casino, Jaquan was a master at blackjack, and he would win big. We'd leave the casino with 50K and stay the night in one of the most expensive hotels there. We'd then hit a shopping spree, where he'd buy shoes, belts, and jewelry. Of course, I always got something special. And then there were other times when our drives would lead to parks for a quiet lunch where it was just the two of us. That was fun. Sometimes we ended up at an amusement park where he would force me to get on the highest roller coasters. I would scream and hold him the whole time. Jaquan added an element of adventure to my life, and the more we spent time together, the more I enjoyed being with him. As I wondered what he had in store for me this weekend, my thoughts were interrupted by the vibration of my phone. It was Vanessa.

Vanessa: Hey, Mom, whatcha doin'?

Tabby: Not much, figuring out my life and outfit for later. Me and Jaquan have a date.

Vanessa: Gross, Mom. But anyway, I called because I have some great news! I got an apartment!

Tabby: You got a WHAT!

Vanessa: Mom, don't freak out. I've been saving my money and Antonio and I saw a really nice place. Plus, I can put him on the lease when he gets this job at the gas station.

Tabby: Vanessa, what are you doing, child? Absolutely not. Do you really think you can handle the financial responsibilities of an apartment? You were just over here demanding Maria to pack your lunch. Where is this fabulous apartment, anyway?

Vanessa: Linden Arms Townhomes

Tabby: Linden Arms? In the hood Vanessa?

Vanessa: They're nice on the inside, Mom.

Tabby: Vanessa, that's a big HELL NO! Stay here and keep saving.

Vanessa: Mom, I signed the lease two days ago...

Tabby: YOU DID WHAT?

Vanessa: Mom! It's ok. It's gonna be ok. Antonio's dad is gonna come and help move my bed and other things, and you can meet him.

I rolled my eyes and took a deep sigh into the phone. This girl was determined to go down a path of hard-headedness that would not end well; I could see that. Vanessa, however, would not listen to reason.

Tabby: You know what, Vanessa, if you're grown enough to sign an apartment lease, then I need to let you be grown. I'm here if you need me, but I'll tell you now I refuse to help you help a grown-ass man. We've been through way too much for that.

Vanessa: I know, Mom. I already know. I got this, trust me.

We ended the call. I paced back and forth in anger, confusion, and fear. That girl was a handful and very sneaky too. I thought she was content stacking her money, but all the while, she was planning her exit. I had to come to grips with this situation. It was already happening. I decided I needed to support my daughter by making sure she wouldn't fail at this. But I also decided to keep close tabs on her relationship as well. I didn't like Antonio. He appeared to have no goals or ambitions. If he had his way, he would stay locked in my condo, playing video games. I had to make sure that leech was not intending to live off my daughter. My phone rang again, and this time it was Vincent. I rolled my eyes because, as of late, he acted like my father instead of my son.

Vincent: Good afternoon mother

Tabby: Afternoon Son

Vincent: I just had an interesting conversation with Vanessa. So, she's moving out, huh?

Tabby: Apparently, she is, and since she signed the lease days ago, she's locked into it.

Vincent: How could you let this happen, Mom? Vanessa moved back home, and things are worse than when she was here. And have you met that Antonio kid? Straight trash. Why would he want her to move to Linden Arms? Vanessa knows NOTHING about that lifestyle. You gotta step in and do something.

Tabby: And what am I supposed to do, Vincent?

Vincent: Get your attorneys and get her out of this!

Tabby: Why? So, she can resent me and run off somewhere with this guy? I don't like Antonio either, but Vanessa is adamant about going head-first into this crazy relationship.

At that moment, Jaquan entered the house. He started a conversation with Maria, which could be heard in the background.

Vincent: And who is that, Mother?

Tabby: Maria.

Vincent: And who? Never mind, I get it. But, once again, you are way too preoccupied to be concerned about making sure Vanessa doesn't get her life together.

Tabby: Really, son? The reality is that Vanessa is an adult. She is grown enough to make her own decisions, no matter how poor they appear. You can't make an adult do anything they don't want to do. So, Son, I need you to back up and handle your affairs in the place you live.

Vincent: Mother, I don't agree. But the two of you are adults, and I will fall back this time out of respect for you. But as a man and the apparent head of our legacy, if I need to step in, I will.

Vincent and I got off the phone and agreed to have a cease-fire. I wondered where he got that male egocentric attitude as of late. Reminded me of James. Perhaps being raised in that household had done more damage to my children than I had thought. I sighed, and Jaquan came over and kissed me on the forehead. I looked up at him and smiled. I said,

Tabby: Baby! What are you doing here so early?

Jaquan: I shut operations down early today. Got all the money I needed quickly, so I wanted to spend time with my baby. What's wrong?

I told him what happened. He listened silently and told me he agreed with Vincent but could also see my point.

Jaquan: All I'm saying is I wished my mother would have fought for me in life. I don't have what you have with your kids. My mom gave all that love to my siblings; she said fuck me. Don't leave her out there. At least let her stay in the condo.

Tabby: Can we not talk about this?

Jaquan: You don't wanna talk about it because I disagree. Baby, I ain't come here to argue with you; you'll figure it out. I came to take you for a ride. Let's hit the casino. I already booked a room at the Estoria so we can go right up to our room after we play!

It would take my mind off things. I smiled at him again and said, "ok, let me pack my bag!" Jaquan's invitation was a whole mood changer, and I packed my back and handed him the keys to the Mercedes truck. I figured we might as well ride in style. I thought about his Tahoe. It was older, but nice too. Jaquan had all the bells and whistles on it, and he loved it. I just needed him to upgrade a little. Perhaps this 50k wouldn't be spent on jewelry, furs, motorcycles, etc. I needed to add some polish to my man.

The ride to the casino was pretty chill. We smoked and listened to music as he drove with one hand on my thigh and the other on the steering wheel. I loved it when he drove. Jaquan was a great driver who anticipated the moves of every other driver, and I felt safe with him. It was crazy, this man was 15 years younger than me, and I felt safer with him than in any relationship I had ever been in. I smiled as I took in all the scenery, the sunny skies, the beautiful trees, and my gorgeous man. I looked over at him. He was focused on the road and the lyrics on the lyrics that played through the speaker. Mary J Blige was singing "I Wanna Be with You." I thought to myself, "yes, I wanna be with you, babe." So I leaned back, hit the blunt, and enjoyed the rest of the ride to the casino.

When we got there, we had a quickie, and then I got in the shower. The events from earlier in the day came flooding back into my mind. I wondered what I did as a parent that made Vanessa go way left. Then I thought about Vincent and how he blamed me for all of this —accused me of not being focused. On what? The truth is I had raised them and provided a good life for them. Now the rest was up to them. I scrubbed my body and tried to shake off the thoughts that tried to keep flooding my mind. I reminded myself I was here with Jaquan, and I promised to have a good time. When I got out of the shower, I noticed Jaquan was preoccupied with his phone. I asked if he was ok. He barely looked up and nodded. Then he said,

Jaquan: I ordered some food so we can eat before we go. I know you are hungry. I'll be back. I got to get some air.

Tabby: Ok, babe.

I kissed him, and he left. About 30 minutes later, the food arrived, and no Jaquan. I called him. The phone went to voicemail. Saw that he was offline on social media. What the fuck was going on? Another 30 minutes passed, and I lost my appetite. Jaquan still wasn't responding, and a part of me was getting concerned. I decided I needed to find him and figure out what was happening. I grabbed the extra key and my jacket and headed out the door of the hotel. My first stop was to the front desk to see if maybe they knew where my man could be. And just like that, mystery solved. Jaquan had headed straight for the casino.

As I walked into the casino, I took in the scenery. Beautiful slot machines stood taller than humans and were themed-based, like the money gods or superheroes. The players sat glued to their stations feeding the machines coins from their little cups. There were two slot machine sections: One for smokers and a non-smoking section. I headed for the smoker section because I knew Jaquan used the slot machines as a warm-up. I looked around, and no Jaquan. I headed back inside, passed all the crap tables, and headed straight to his game of choice; the blackjack tables. I walked past several tables until I spotted him heavily concentrated on a game. The dealer was a cute dark-skinned younger woman with 30-inch bundles, big ass dimples when she smiled, and breasts that spilled out of her uniform. I noticed her table was full of men. Most of them were focused on her, but Jaquan was there to get that money. He seemed to be winning. And every time he did, she bent a little lower, giving him access to her tits, one of his favorite things to look at. I watched their interaction. Then I saw him watching me. He smiled and waved me over. I walked over to Jaquan, and he pulled me into him. The dealer looked over with a half-smile. "You win again," she said and slid his chips with no extras, imagine that. Jaquan chuckled, grabbed his earnings, and we left the table. Jaquan wasn't finished. However, he walked around the rest of the blackjack tables, surveying them; watching the dealers. He spotted a table he wanted to post up at. Jaquan handed me $500 to spend at the slot machines. He also handed me $2,000 for emergency money. He said, "under no condition do you give me this money, Tabby. This is for something specific I need to account for." I had a sneaky suspicion that this trip to the casino had nothing to do with spending time with me. The impromptu afternoon drive, the quickie in the room, distracted by his phone. Not only that but the focus on his face and the anticipation of returning to the tables. It made me wonder if this man had an addiction to winning big. At the time, I didn't want to press the issue, so I agreed and took my free money to the slot machines to take my chance at winning.

And winning BIG did I do! I won $5000, to be exact, on one slot machine; The Goddess, Mighty Aphrodite. It was one of those animated machines where her beautiful image blinked and smiled. As I was walking up, a couple was walking away. Just as they walked away, a free coin dropped from the machine. I took it as a sign and sat down. I was glad I did because, as I stated, I won big! So much so that I didn't realize a couple of hours had passed, and I noticed Jaquan had been blowing my phone up for the last 15 minutes. I recall him telling me not to give him money that he wanted to be saved, and I thought about ignoring his calls. Then I thought better of the situation, looked up at mighty Aphrodite, and cashed in my ticket with my earnings. I then went on a quest to find Jaquan. As I headed towards the blackjack tables, I bumped right into him.

Jaquan: Where the fuck have you been, Tabby? I've been blowing your phone up. Where's that money at?

Tabby: I got it right here, babe. I was on the slot machines, guess what!

Jaquan: Tabby, the money, where is it? I need it.

I try to lighten the mood and giggle.

Tabby: Now, baby, you told me not to give you this money under no circumstances. What happened over there? Did you lose all that money?

Jaquan: Most of it, not all. I've been invited to the player's room, and the buy-in to the table is $5000. Gimme the money so I can use it to buy in.

Tabby: But Jaquan, you said not to. Plus, if you take this money, you realize that you're breaking your own rule.

Jaquan: I don't give a fuck about that, Tabby. Give me the money.

Tabby: Jaquan, no.

Jaquan: If you don't give me that fucking money! How are you gonna keep what's mine? GIVE IT HERE.

Jaquan leaps at me and grabs my bag. I snatch it back, and the two of us struggle and begin yelling. As we both struggle for the bag, I look up to see everyone staring at us. We look like a crazy couple in the casino. I wonder what story our actions told; boyfriend addicted to gambling fights his girlfriend in the casino for cash to continue fueling his addictions. I gave up the struggle and let him have the bag. He took his money from the bag and threw it back at me. I had never felt so disrespected in my life. I tried to play it off and headed in the opposite direction to the slot machines in hopes of reuniting with mighty Aphrodite, and I was in luck. But this time, our interaction was not so lucky. I lost $500, the amount that Jaquan had given me. At that moment, I stopped. I knew to quit while I still had a chance. I was still up a few thousand, so I took my earnings and returned to the room. Several hours later, a drunk and very broke Jaquan entered. He looked at me with an attitude and said,

Jaquan: Don't judge me. I ain't worried; I'll make that money back tomorrow easy.

Tabby: I'm sure you will. (I scoffed)

Jaquan: So why the fuck are you so worried about how I spend MY MONEY? You sure don't have a problem with me when I spend it on you. This money's easy come, easy go, baby.

Tabby: You got one more time to be disrespectful to me, Jaquan. And to be honest, I don't give a fuck what you do with YOUR money, as you keep reminding me. I don't know what kind of women you are accustomed to dealing with, but I have always had my own. I don't need you, Sir.

Jaquan: Yea, courtesy of that ex-husband of yours. I'm self-made in these streets. Like I said, easy come, easy go.

Tabby: Self-made in these streets? So because my money isn't ill-gotten, it means nothing?

Jaquan: Ill-gotten? What are you implying, Tabby?

Tabby: Oh, you know EXACTLY what I'm implying, Jaquan. C'MON, what builder keeps the hours you do? You sleep until early afternoon and don't get home until after 11. Those are definitely hours kept by the ill-gotten, Sir.

Jaquan: Sir? Oh, you my momma now? So what is it that I do, Tabby? Since you're so intelligent. You have NO IDEA what I do.

Tabby: You're right, Jaquan, but I know you ain't no home builder! I was born during the day, but surely not yesterday. So, what is it, weed, cocaine, pills, what?

Jaquan: You are so smart that you're dumb, Tabby. I smoke too much weed to sell weed. You already know I used to sell drugs, but that was years ago. That's not what I do, Tabby.

Tabby: Well, what is it that you really do, Jaquan, because clearly, you have been lying to me for months. And is that what had you preoccupied with your phone today? Your work?

Jaquan: No, that's not it at all. Tabby, there's a lot I need to tell you about my job, about what's been going on.

He pauses. I look at him and wait for him to finish.

Jaquan: A few days ago, my first ex reached out to me. White girl, ghetto, from the west side.

I thought to myself, yuck. Nothing good ever came from the west side of town.

Jaquan: Anyway, we were together for like six years, but I was in my mid-twenties when we broke up. Her family was racist as fuck, and she even fought my momma. That was my last straw; I had to leave her crazy ass alone. But anyway, she contacted me to let me know we had a son.

Tabby: Excuse me? A son? How do you know he's yours, Jaquan?

Jaquan: Well, last month, when we were arguing, I had a blood test done. He's mine, Tabby. And now she has been hitting me up for money and shit.

Tabby: So, you've known for over a month that you had a son? Un-fucking believable!

Jaquan: I know, I know, Tabby. But I didn't know how to tell you. Plus, you had all this shit going on with your daughter, so it never seemed to be the right time to bring it up. So I came up here to make some extra money to start paying this bitch so she won't take me to court, and I wanted to tell you about it.

I sighed deeply. It was a lot to take in. This sounded familiar to me. My high school friend Rico kept a whole kid from me, and I had to stumble upon it. I tried not to compare the two, but I had to admit I was a bit triggered. And all this right on the heels of Vanessa going behind my back and signing a lease. It appeared both Jaquan and Vanessa were moving in secret this whole time. The two people closest to me were stressing me the hell out. I thought I had this shit handled, but it was spiraling out of control. I rubbed my temples. How the fuck was I supposed to respond to this?

Jaquan: Tabby, say something.

Tabby: And what the fuck am I supposed to say, Jaquan?

Jaquan: Something, anything.

Tabby: So how does this new son of yours factor into things? And why didn't you feel like you could tell me? Especially after you found out?

Jaquan: We were just getting good again, Tabby. I really wanted to, and like I said, I wanted to tell you. The energy of everything was off from the moment I walked into the house today. Then we came up here, and I started losing; that never happens. Then we started arguing, and now here we are. A whole fucked up day that didn't go how I planned.

I was still silent. I didn't know what to say. Jaquan had a young child, which I knew his lifestyle was in no way, shape, or form prepared to handle. I also thought about the fact that I still didn't know how he made his money or how he afforded this lifestyle that he was living. We got sidetracked because he dropped the atomic bomb about his son. Red flags all over the fucking place. Jaquan got my attention and said,

Jaquan: I can understand if you think all this is a lot; I get it. It's a lot for me too. I even understand if you wanna walk away from me after all this because I lied. But I promise I'll never keep nothin' from you again.

Tabby: And your "job," Jaquan?

Jaquan: I promise you I am not a drug dealer. I never lied about that. What I do is kinda hard to explain, but I promise you I will take you with me very soon and you will know exactly what I do. I don't want no secrets, Tabby. And as far as my son goes, I will handle that. I'm gonna be honest with you she's crazy. I'll make sure my dealings with her are strictly about that kid. All she wants is money anyway.

Tabby: I am not in a place in my life where I want to deal with a crazy baby mama, Jaquan.

Jaquan: You won't, I promise. I'm just asking that you give me a chance to show you.

Jaquan comes over and lays his head on my stomach. He tells me he needs me and makes all kinds of promises. I decided to let him have this one to keep the peace in our relationship. He would, however, have to walk a fine line for a while until I saw that he was reformed. We both went to sleep that night for the first time in a long time without making love. Where was love's journey about to take me now? I was afraid even to ask.

The ceasefire between Jaquan and I had lasted a few months, and he was true to his word; he made money, fed his baby mama, and kept her drama far away from me. He even started bringing his son around in an attempt to form a relationship with him. I had to admit I was a bit impressed by it all. I also noticed that Jaquan had begun furnishing things in the house. Parts of my home began to look more like his taste than mine. I also noticed that he pretty much moved in with me; this man had a whole walk-in closet to himself. I didn't care, though; I was crazy about him. At the same time, Vanessa appeared to be handling things in her new apartment. I wasn't sure if Antonio was working, but she seemed to have made enough to keep herself afloat. She also didn't come around as much, only every now and again to get good leftovers from Maria's cooking and toiletry items that Jaquan happened to keep this place stocked with. It irritated him because he felt like she didn't purchase it. So, she shouldn't take it with her. Of course, Vanessa didn't care and helped herself as she pleased. Her only defense was to ask me about his job, which I still didn't know the answer to. Imagine that. Well, imagine my surprise when Jaquan decided to free himself out of the blue.

Jaquan: Baby, things have been going really well with us, and I promised to be honest about everything.

Tabby: Holy shit, is there another child

Jaquan: Hell no (chuckles). No more surprises like that, babe. I know you have been wondering for a while about my job and I promised to tell you everything. And I appreciate that you gave me the time and space I needed. I love that about you. You're the shit, and you know it.

Tabby: Well, thank you, baby.

Jaquan: What I do is one of those things that I can't explain in detail; I have to show you. It's gonna be long and tedious, and it's gonna take a couple of days. What are you doing tomorrow?

Tabby: Well, I'll be hanging out with you and finding out what you do. Are we taking the Benz?

Jaquan: Absolutely not. No fucking way for what I do. We need to get up early to get started. Our first stop is Daytona to pick up Angela.

Tabby: Angela? Who's Angela?

Jaquan: Angela is a very intricate part of my whole operation. I'll tell you all about it tomorrow. But for now, let's chill. I found a bomb-ass movie we can watch. It's based on a true story....

I took in our conversation about tomorrow, his operation, and Angela. My intuition began to be on alert. Something about her name and the way he said it. There wasn't anything endearing, but something was off. I had to wait until tomorrow to catch this bitch's vibe. Was she a bitch? Oh, the Scorpio in me could feel it. Something about her didn't sit right already. I put my thoughts to the side for the rest of the night. Jaquan and I caught a vibe of our own. We ordered takeout, watched a movie, and blazed the Zsa-Zsa. We also played a little that night. He gave me amazing head, and I rode that pony until its leg could take no more. Finally, we both laid down for a deep sleep in preparation for the days ahead.

The following day, we got up early. Jaquan seemed a little nervous but also focused. He showered first and prepared the truck for the trip ahead while I showered. I had packed some light snacks for the day, although I had no clue what was in store. As soon as I got dressed, Jaquan and I hit the road and headed to pick up Angela. Daytonia was a small city that served as the gateway to bigger cities in our state. The city itself took 45 minutes to drive through. Daytonia highlighted three prominent shopping places; Walmart, Home Depot, and Lowes. There were no malls, small shopping strips, or anything exciting to see in the town, just those three places, a few small bars, and plenty of gas stations. Not to mention the plethora of low-income apartments, which I noticed that we happened to be headed to. Jaquan pulled into one of the complexes and put the car in park.

Jaquan: I'll be back. Lock the doors because I don't trust nobody out here, Tabby. I'm going upstairs to get Angela. I would have you come, but she has roaches.

Jaquan leaves the truck and leaves me alone with my thoughts. Roaches? What kind of people was this man dealing with? I didn't want to stay in that truck longer than I had to. I silently prayed to myself as I waited for my man to come back to the car. Five minutes later, Jaquan arrived with a tall, dark-skinned, funny-built woman. Angela. Angela was not much to look at. She had a cheap sew-in and fake lashes where you could see the residue of the glue from around her eyes. Angela's appearance was basic. She wore black leggings, a t-shirt, and a pair of off-brand shoes. Interesting. As they came closer to the truck, Jaquan instructed her to get in the back behind him, and she obeyed. I wondered if the woman was slow. Jaquan made the introductions, and her "hello" was very lackluster. Yea, my Spidey senses were definitely on to something. Jaquan said,

Jaquan: Angie, we gotta hit these stores first. Then we moved to Allentown and Jacob's Grove. If we're lucky, we'll have all we need. Did you talk to your sister?

Angela: Yea, you can drop me off there when we are done.

Jaquan: What about the kids?

Angela: They daddies got 'em.

I looked over at Angela. She looked at me and then down at her phone. This chick was pure weirdness. I decided to keep my conversation between my man and me. As we talked, Angela sat there in silence. We got to Home Depot and parked the truck. Angela got out of the back, grabbed a large tote, and headed into the store. Jaquan said,

Jaquan: In about five minutes, I gotta go in the store and check on her.

Tabby: Jaquan, what is she doing

Jaquan: What do you think she's doing, Tabby? She's stealing.

Tabby: WHAT!

Jaquan: Calm down; we have been doing this for a few years. Right now, loss prevention is not in the building.

Tabby: How the hell is she gonna get out of Home Depot with stolen goods? What's she stealing? Drills?

Jaquan: (laughs) relax, Tabby, we got this all under control. Angela is the key to my whole operation. There's a lot of money to be made from what we do. Like I said, we have been doing this for years. Tabby, I wanted to be honest and show you what I did. Don't judge me, ok, until you see it all.

Tabby: I won't judge, I promise.

But I was secretly judging. My man was a booster. I think. Well, he wasn't boosting Angela. Out of Home Depot. What the fuck. There is no way this is how this man was bringing in so much money every day. I couldn't believe it. Five minutes later, true to his word Jaquan went to check on Angela. Three minutes later, both of them came back to the truck. Angela dumped all of her stealings on the floor in the back. My nosy ass looked to see what it was. A few tools, mainly drill bits and other weird-looking parts. To me, it looked like a bunch of trash. I was puzzled.

Our next stop was Lowes. Angela performed the same action and got the same results. More parts and drill bits and such. Our next stop was Walmart. When we got to Walmart, the two of them went in together. He had to watch Angela's back in there. Ten minutes later, they both returned with plenty of Walmart plunder. We spent the rest of the day hitting nearby cities, and the two performed the same actions; in and out of the local Home Depots, Lowe's, and Walmarts until the truck was completely full of items. This made for a very long day. It made me wonder how many days of the week he spent doing this. The whole thing could be dangerous. We then drove back to town later that evening, and Jaquan dropped Angela off at her sister's and took the goods to my house. He separated the goods into bags of value and prepared for the second part of his operation. Jaquan told me we had to get up early again. He also told me not to worry; we would not be headed out of town again.

The very next morning, we got up early again. Jaquan told me to dress in something casual because we would be riding around all day. While I was in the shower, Jaquan went to get gas and to pick up Angela. I got dressed in a pair of Chanel leggings and a matching Cami. I put on my gym shoes and made sure my hair was flawless, and my make-up was natural and minimal. I looked casually cute if I thought so myself. I looked in the mirror and smiled. As I admired myself, I noticed that Jaquan was back and had entered the room. He smiled at me and approached me from behind. Jaquan grabbed me close for an embrace. He kissed my neck. Goosebumps began to form on my shoulders and arms. He said,

Jaquan: Damn, you got a fat ass.

As he smacked it. He kissed my neck again. Jaquan's hands then traveled from my ass to my breasts. He began massaging.

Tabby: Baby, what are you doing? We gotta leave

Jaquan: Nah, we got a few minutes, c'mon.

Tabby: What about Angela?

Jaquan: She's in the car. She'll be ok. (He whispers) C'mon, baby. Gimme that pussy.

Jaquan continues to massage my breasts. Boo Boo kitty was already moist, and he knew it. His hands traveled south to my love box. Jaquan played in my wetness. I looked at him in the mirror. My kitty throbbed at his touch. I lowered my leggings, and Jaquan released his manhood from his jeans. I leaned against the wall, and Jaquan entered me from behind as we looked at our reflections in the mirror. It felt so good. Jaquan stroked me from behind. I moaned in passion as my breath steamed the mirror. It was all so hot. I arched my back as Jaquan continued to stroke. I said,

Tabby: Fuck me, daddy, oooh, yes.

Jaquan: Take this dick, baby.

Tabby: Oh yes, daddy, give it to me.

Jaquan's strokes intensified. Boo Boo Kitty flickered. As he pounded, I moved my hips in tandem. Jaquan pounded harder and faster. I growled and said, "fuck me harder, baby! Yes!" he pounded harder, and I backed my ass up to match his intensity. He yelled,

Jaquan: Damn! You're pussy's wet as fuck! Cum all over daddy's dick.

As he thrust inside me, my pussy began to sing, and Boo Boo Kitty exploded all over her daddy's dick. Jaquan continued to dig deeper inside me. He said, "cum again," and I obliged. Jaquan yelled FUUUCKKKK, and in an instant, he came. That was one hell of a quickie. We quickly freshened up and smiled as we headed to the car. Jaquan instructed Angela to get in the back seat behind him. As she exited the passenger side of the car, I could have sworn that she scowled at me. I looked her up and down and gave her an uppity smile as if to say, "Bitch, stay in your place and sit in the back." I know she felt my energy. Angela did as instructed and got in the back seat of the Tahoe behind Jaquan. I could tell she had an instant attitude. Jaquan turned on the music and rolled a blunt. He put the car in reverse, and as we drove off from my beautiful neighborhood, Jaquan drove in the usual fashion; one hand on the steering wheel and the other on my thigh. Angela was sitting in the back, going through the bags of plunder, looking sour-faced as we drove to our first destination.

When we arrived at our first destination, I was a little surprised. It was in the heart of downtown but not in the gentrified area. There were a few abandoned storefronts, a non-used factory, and a building that we rode around in the parking lot of.... The homeless shelter. I wondered to myself what the hell we were doing here. Jaquan found a spot and parked. He lit up a cigarette and turned his music down. Jaquan instructed Angela to get out, and she did so and began to approach several men leaving the shelter. Jaquan said,

Jaquan: So, this is day two. I know you got a whole lot of shit running through your mind, Tabby.

Tabby: Well, I'm not gonna lie. I am very curious as to what is happening. Like why we're here at the homeless shelter?

Jaquan: Yea, the homeless work for me. You'll see. All your questions will be answered today. How well they perform will depend on how long it takes to accomplish our mission. You saw what Angela did. She's my booster and recruiter. The homeless are my returners.

Tabby: Returners? I've never heard that term before

Jaquan: Trust me, you'll see

At that moment, Angela returned to the car with three homeless men. Jaquan asked,

Jaquan: Do y'all have IDs?

They all said yes. He told them to get in the back of the truck and instructed Angela to sit in the extended seating at the very back with the goods. Angela did as she was instructed. Our first stop was a local Home Depot about 30 minutes away in the suburbs. Angela grabbed three bags of the goods and handed one to each man. Jaquan gave them the instructions to take the items to the return counter and show them their IDs. Once the items were returned, they would receive an in-store gift card. They were to return to the car with the gift card and the receipt. Their pay would be 5% of the amount of the gift cards. The men agreed, and they exited the car along with Angela.

Tabby: Ok, so why does Angela go in the store?

Jaquan: I send her in there to scope out security and to make sure the men return to the car with the gift cards.

Tabby: Oh, ok.

Jaquan: So now we sit and wait.

Jaquan lit a cigarette and rolled the window down. I didn't smoke, but it also didn't bother me that he did, but I appreciated the respect. He handed me the sack of weed and told me to roll up. I smiled and rolled a fat one. We listened to the music and smoked the blunt while he waited on the returners to bring the gift cards back. It was a whole vibe. Around fifteen minutes later, the men returned to the car with Angela behind them, and they handed the gift cards to Jaquan. Jaquan looked at the receipts, smiled, and gave them to me to look at. Each receipt was a little over $3000. The homeless men got in the car and smiled as well. Angela saw me looking at the receipts, rolled her eyes, and got in the back seat. What the fuck was her problem. Jaquan told the men they had a few more stops to make, and they seemed pleased to be making money. We stopped to get them something to eat and headed to our next stop, Lowe's.

The activity at Lowe's was the same. The returners went in, got gift cards, and handed them to Jaquan. Jaquan gave them to me to keep, and Angela had an apparent attitude that didn't go unnoticed. I chuckled on the inside at her irritation. When we got to Walmart, I decided to address what my senses were picking up. After Angel and the returners left the car, I turned my attention to Jaquan. He said,

Jaquan: Now, this part takes the longest. It's about 30 minutes per store. We have to space them out in the Walmart line so it won't look suspicious.

Tabby: Good, so now we have a chance to really talk.

Jaquan: Ok. So what are you thinking about all this so far? Like I said, I came up hard, Tabby. Being homeless made me have to survive in any way that I knew how.

Tabby: I'm not judging at all, babe. To be honest, I'm taking it all in. But I do have one burning question: What is the deal with Angela? She obviously has had an attitude all day, and I sense that it's my presence; what's up with that?

Jaquan: To be honest, that's just Angela. In her mind, every woman I have dealt with is temporary, so she honestly doesn't really talk to them because of that. It's been a long time since I had a real relationship, and since me and her have been working together, nobody has been around as long as you have.

Tabby: So, are you sleeping with her, Jaquan?

Jaquan: Man, HELL NO! Tabby, we live together; you are my woman; what kind of question is that?

Tabby: No woman has an attitude like she does unless she has feelings. So again, I ask, what is up with Angela?

Jaquan: Look at her, Tabby; she's fat, sloppy, and ghetto. And she doesn't spend time with her kids. What kind of woman is that? Angela is nothing more to me than a booster. Do you know how I met her? She tried to steal from me.

Tabby: Excuse me? And you trust her? Oh, I got to hear this story.

Jaquan: I met Angela at a club a couple of years ago. We got a room that night, and we fucked. The next morning some money came up missing from my jeans. Now me and her were the only ones in the room. She even had the audacity to look around the room and help me find it. While we were looking for the money, she didn't know that I called my cousin Tracie up to the hotel room. Tracie was ready to beat her ass! She confessed and begged me not to hurt her. Well, I came up with a plan. Before I met Angela, I was in the stores, trying to show this chick Shaquita, who I stayed with, how to steal. She was always nervous and shit. So, I figured she was good at it since she stole from me. She gave me the money back, but I let her keep it. Then I made her work for me. At first, for free, then after a few months, I started breaking her off just enough to pay her bills. And that's what it's been for the last three years. That's it, Tabby. Now there should be no reason for that girl to have any feelings. She got a whole nigga or two.

I sat in silence and took that conversation in. Jaquan and I passed the blunt and listened to music as we waited for the four of them to get back to the car. We hit a few more stores the rest of the day, then Jaquan made a few phone calls. Within minutes his phone dinged, and he headed back to the stores and told the men to stay in the car with Angela, and he asked me to go into the store with him. Angela looked irritated, and he gave her a sharp look as if to say, "don't start." Jaquan and I went into the store, and he grabbed a shopping cart. I pushed the cart down the aisles as Jaquan looked through his phone. He showed me his phone and said,

Jaquan: You see this. These are pictures of the items from my buyers. After we get the gift cards, I pick up the items and pay for them with the gift cards. Once I'm done shopping, they meet me here, pick up the goods and pay me. Now I also have buyers lined up for the Walmart cards. They meet me here also, and it's a 60/40 cash transaction.

Tabby: Interesting.

After about 20 minutes of shopping, we paid for the items and headed out of the store. His buyer pulled up in a Chevy F150 and got out to meet Jaquan. I recognized him. He was Jerry Stewart, one of the biggest home flippers in the city! imagine that. Jerry handled a few projects for Pastor Doug when he was adding additions to his home and the sister church up the road. Jerry walked up to the shopping cart and loaded the items. He looked over at me in recognition and confusion. I smiled. We said nothing, and he handled his business with Jaquan. Jaquan and I walked to the truck and got in. Several minutes later, a small car pulled up, and a woman got out and approached the truck. She handed Jaquan the cash, and he gave her the Walmart gift cards. Jaquan rolled the window up, said, "all in a day's work," and laughed. Jaquan then handed each man their cut of the day's work and asked them if they needed a ride back. Two men asked to be dropped off at the shelter, and one decided to spend part of his earnings in a hotel. Hey, I wasn't mad at him for wanting a better place to sleep. We dropped the men at the shelter and took the 45-minute drive to Daytonia to drop off Angela. Jaquan pulled out the day's earnings when we got to the apartment. He handed Angela a couple hundred dollars and looked at me, and said,

Jaquan: Baby, get you something nice. Here's a couple of thousand.

Angela: OH, HELL NO! WHAT THE FUCK! I SWEAR TO GOD!

Jaquan: You swear to God, what bitch? If you don't get out of my fucking car with your money and get the fuck out of my face! You know what it is!

Angela looked over at me, slightly embarrassed. She got out of the car and slammed the door.

Tabby: Now, Jaquan, you can't tell me that girl ain't got a problem with me or feelings for you?

Jaquan: Man, fuck her feelings.

Jaquan turned the music up, lit the blunt, and we headed back to the house. We spent the evening in the usual fashion; eating what Maria had prepared, watching movies, and making love. At the end of the night, I lay in Jaquan's arms, taking in all the last few days' activities. I finally knew how Jaquan's operation went down. Was I pleased? No. But he was my man, and who was I to judge how he made his money? All I know is that even after all that, I was still crazy about him. But there was the thing about Angela. And who was Shaquita? He never mentioned living with someone. As much as I wanted to relax in his honesty, all the red flags seemed to be swirling in my head. But what was I to do? For now, I would relax on love's journey yet again.

5

THE LONG KISS GOODBYE

Saying goodbye is never an easy thing. Some prefer to say, "see ya later," in hopes of never having to say goodbye. Why? Because goodbye represents an ending. When you have good people and things in your life, you never want to see them go. When Ebony left this world, I wasn't prepared. We had talked about living here to at least 70. So, her passing was a shock to everyone who loved her. When you lose a loved one, you always think about everything you wanted to say to them that you never got to express, praying that they know from the other side how much you loved them. There's often a bit of regret and sorrow. In relationships, goodbye is never easy; now, in the day and age of social media, it's intensified. When marriages break apart, lives are changed forever. Like I said before, goodbye is never easy, and letting go of Jaquan was harder than I imagined. They say all good things must come to an end, and Karma was calling for the transition from love to a lesson. As the seasons changed with Jaquan, so did our relationship. I wish I had better prepared myself....

Once Jaquan had revealed the nature of his job to me, things seemed to be going well. It was like a wave of peace had hit both of us, and we could finally be free. The nature of our relationship continued; we were fun and free. Jaquan made sure we had food for Thanksgiving, and I did most of the cooking; imagine that! Jaquan's son Tiquan had even come over, along with Vanessa, Antonio, and his two-year-old son. We had a nice peaceful dinner, and Jaquan, Antonio, and the boys bonded over video games while Vanessa and I took pictures, updated our social media profiles, and watched movies. I was happy; hell, we all seemed to be. It was our first official holiday together and a huge success! It looked like nothing but up from here.

During Christmas, it was even better. Jaquan had mentioned that he had not had a good Christmas before he was a kid before his Mom kicked him out. It made me sad on the inside. Christmas was always one of those holidays that I loved. The hustle and bustle of shopping and all the beautiful decorations. Well, I surprised him one day while he was out and decorated the whole house. When he got to the house, it was filled with Christmas music, and Maria had even baked some sugar cookies before she left. The whole season was filled with amazement as we hung stockings for everyone, hid gifts around the house, and Jaquan even slowed down in business and talked about using his talents to do something legitimate. I was also in the gift-giving mood for the kids. I had sold the condo and put it in trust for Vincent and Vanessa until they reached 25. That was a couple of years off for Vincent, but Vanessa had a few years which was perfect. Vincent could handle the responsibility. On the other hand, Vanessa would have a few years to get to a level of maturity to handle that kind of money. Either way, both kids were more than happy to get the gift I gave them.

Jaquan was very generous with his gifts as well. He gave Maria the week off with pay and a complete spa treatment at one of the local franchises. She was more than happy to return after the new year. For me, he got a lot of the usual gifts; my stocking was stuffed with Bath and Body Works and nice-smelling perfumes. And, of course, an ounce of weed for me to smoke at leisure. He also got me a 72-inch fireplace to add to the living room. But the small box with the classic black Christian Louboutins made the holiday for me. He got me a couple of outfits, some boots, and a few other items. And he captured my response to everything on video. It was truly magical.

For New Year's Eve, Jaquan wanted to invite his best friend Maurice and his new girlfriend. Maurice was Jaquan's age, so I wondered what kind of night we would have. I worried a little about the age difference, but I would be hospitable. Jaquan also decided to move the rest of his things out of his roommate's place and into mine. It only made sense anyway; he was here every night. Maurice helped him get situated, and I got a chance to meet him before the evening started. He was friendly and very well-mannered. He had a good job and his own place and talked a lot about his new girlfriend. I was glad Jaquan had such a good influence in his life, and New Year's Eve was nice and chill. Nadia was a beautiful brown-skinned woman in her 30s who had hood polish. She looked around my home and smiled. I poured the drinks, and the weed got passed around. We talked about everything from our relationships to raising children, and she told me she wanted her and Maurice to have what Jaquan and I had. We had relationship goals; imagine that. I smiled. We brought in the new year with a kiss and a promise from Jaquan,

Jaquan: This is it. I ain't goin' nowhere, and neither are you. You stuck with me. Can you handle that?

Tabby: Baby, I think I got this.

We celebrated the new year with the promise that we would be on love's journey for the long haul. We were committed to whatever the ride would bring.

As Valentine's Day came around, love was in the air for us. Several days before the holiday, I was minding my business. Maria had already left for the evening, so I pulled up Facebook because I was bored. I happened to notice a post from Jaquan. He had been posting a lot more lately, but this post I saw had over 1,000 likes, hearts, etc. Jaquan had posted a video about all of the early Valentine's gifts he had gotten for his woman. In the video, the camera zoomed in on the back seat of my car. It was filled with stuffed animals, baskets of fragrances, and lingerie. He then moved to the trunk and opened it. I noticed a big box from Louis Vuitton and more stuffed animals. The camera person zoomed in on Jaquan, and he said,

Jaquan: It ain't even Valentine's Day. Yes, and I'm thirsty to give my baby her gifts. I hope she don't see this!

I smiled at the video. I had seen it. The comments from the ladies ranged from, "oh, that's so sweet," to "relationship goals." There it was again. I smiled. One woman even shared the video saying, "For this reason alone, that man is getting his dick sucked tonight." I hollered with laughter at that. The whole thing was an amazing gesture. On Valentine's Day, Jaquan didn't disappoint. When I came home that evening, my entire kitchen island was decorated from end to end with Valentine's Day stuffed animals, chocolate, jewelry, and Louis Vuitton. I smiled. Mama had a brand bag. Not only that, there were hundred-dollar bills tucked away in the corners of the gifts. This man had outdone himself. As the hundreds added up from one end of the island to the next, it was about $5000 by the time I was finished counting. I was in love with this man, and he always kept it interesting. That night he moved some of my gifts to the side and took me right to that same island. We ended the night with love's long kiss, more promises of forever, and our souls were tied to one another. How we made love and how he told me how much he loved me when we made love was an amazingness that I had never experienced. I was drawn in more by each and every forehead kiss.

And that was the beginning of the long kiss goodbye.

As winter was in full swing, things were still a bit cozy. Jaquan had slowed down in his business because his truck broke down. Instead of fixing his truck when he did business, he used my car. I refused to allow him access to the Mercedes because he seemed too comfortable in my car. Most of his money was spent on household items and his spending habits. I had added paying Maria weekly to his contribution to the house, and he seemed a bit resentful about that. The red flags were appearing again. Since Jaquan was paying Maria, he felt like he could redecorate, and I would come home from running errands to find a rearranged house or items that he bought into the home from his business. After a while, I didn't even recognize my home because Jaquan had taken over.

What was I doing these days? Absolutely nothing. I spent my days at home, bustling around like a desperate housewife waiting for Jaquan to come home. I spent time mainly on the back of my deck smoking weed. Sometimes I would switch places and move to my porch. I had one of those big country swings, and I loved spending time there. Since the weather was mild this winter, it was perfect. So, there I was, high on the swing in the middle of winter. Imagine my surprise one day when I received an unexpected visitor. A black escalade with tented windows slowly crept up my driveway. I knew exactly who it was, Pastor Doug.

Pastor Doug waited for his armor bearer to get out of the front passenger seat and open the door for him. Pastor Doug stepped out of the vehicle, and as his black alligator shoes hit the gravel of my driveway, I could have sworn I heard theme music playing. There wasn't; he was just that sharp. Pastor Doug had tan Gucci slacks and a matching sweater, which fit him like a glove. I had to admit; the man had an aura. Don't get it twisted; his presence was not angelic. I reminded myself that I was not one of his congregants, and I also knew that where Pastor Doug was, foolishness followed. Pastor Doug walked up and said,

Pastor Doug: Well, Praise the Lord, Sister Tabby. How are you?

Tabby: I'm good, Pastor Doug. How are you?

Pastor Doug: Well, this is the day that the Lord has made. I will rejoice and be GLAD in it! Oh, glory!

Tabby: Pastor Doug, I don't mean to be short, but this comes as a surprise that you are here. I had a busy day ahead of me. Is there something I can help you with?

Pastor Doug: From the looks of things, you seem to have all the time in the world Tabby. But I won't take up much of your time; there are a few boxes that James left behind after the divorce. He asked me to do him a favor and stop by to get them.

Tabby: Well, it would have been nice if he called first.

Pastor Doug: Would you have really answered, Tabby? That's neither here nor there. Will it be ok if we get these things?

I agreed and allowed Pastor Doug and the two handlers into the home to get James' things. Pastor Doug did nothing but look around and ask questions about the new décor. He also asked questions about my new boyfriend.

Pastor Doug: What was that young man's name again, Jayvon?

Tabby: It's Jaquan, Pastor Doug.

Pastor Doug: Jaquan, yes! How's that going, by the way?

Tabby: Not that it's any of your business, but we're doing well.

Pastor Doug: I can imagine Tabby. You fought desperately to get out of your marriage to James. With everything, he had going on then too. You never really wanted to be married; to be honest, shacking seems to be more your speed. Lord have Mercy! Em em.

Tabby: You know, Pastor Doug, I refuse to get into what happened with James and I with you. You have no idea what really happened between us.

Pastor Doug: Oh, I already know what happened; the sex toys, the drugs. The same stuff it seems you're into now. And now you've added a man half your age to the mix. God is not mocked. Whatever a man sows that, he shall also reap, Tabby.

Tabby: Doug, did you come to lecture me or get the rest of James' items?

Pastor Doug: It's Pastor Doug. I am a man of God.

Tabby: But you are not MY pastor. And a man of God? Ok, I think we're done here.

I had Maria see Pastor Doug and his men out of the house with the rest of James' stuff. "Good Riddance," I thought. I was glad to be seeing the last of Pastor Doug. Several hours later, I received a call from an unknown number. It was James.

James: Tabby...

Tabby: Hello, James?

James: Yes, it's me. Thank you for giving my things to Pastor Doug. There were old family photos in some of those boxes. Pictures from my childhood, so I appreciate you giving those back.

Tabby: No problem, James, those were your items. I would never keep them from you.

James: Again, I appreciate that. But I want to ask you something, Tabby, and don't lie to me. Did you move that man into our house?

Tabby: Our house? James, I believe this is my house.

James: No, it's OUR HOUSE, Tabby.

Tabby: James, if you remember correctly, I got that house in the divorce. So it's my house, James, and I can have whoever I want here when I want them here.

James: Well, considering I still pay the mortgage on that house and the deed is still in my name, I believe I have a say as to who is there, including your children.

Tabby: Nigga don't you EVER bring my kids into any discussion! My kids can move in, have families and raise them in this bitch if I say so.

James: Calm down, Tabby.

Tabby: You crossed lines, James, and you know it.

James: You're right, and I'm sorry about bringing Vincent and Vanessa into this. All I'm saying is it's wrong to have this man living in a place where I still have to pay bills.

Tabby: Your finances are the consequences of the divorce, James, plain and simple.

James: Consequences of the divorce, huh? A divorce I never wanted in the first place. A divorce I tried to stop by giving you the world in the Tiffany's store, Tabby, remember? I never wanted this.

Tabby: Oh, so you propose to Keisha in that same store months later? A day late and a dollar short, James.

James: Dammit, Tabby! Who are you anymore?

Tabby: A woman who has moved on with her life. And clearly, you have, too. James, we have no more business left. Keisha is your business now. So, I suggest you focus on that and not worry about my new man and me, and YES, I said MY MAN!

I hung up the phone. I decided to continue my day and not let my conversation with him or Pastor Doug bother me. Pastor Doug. That man ran straight over there and told all my business to James. He was supposed to be a man of God. I shook my head, rolled a blunt, and smoked to put myself in a better frame of mind. Jaquan would be home soon, and things were starting to get strained between us. I prepared for our usual evening; homemade cheeseburgers and French fries, smoking weed, and watching him play the game. If I was lucky, we would squeeze in a movie and a quickie before we went to bed.

As we moved into spring, my relationship with Jaquan started diminishing slowly at first. The winter had faded away, and so did the honeymoon phase of our relationship. Jaquan had started spending the weekends going out. At first, it was just on a Friday; then, the Friday extended to all weekend. Our quality time seemed non-existent. Sure, he was living here, but it seemed like there was no more romance or spontaneity outside of everyday life. Had he lost that loving feeling? With our sex life, you couldn't tell. Jaquan still made sure to handle himself in the bedroom, but I needed more. As I tried to communicate my needs, I realized it was like talking to a teenager. Every conversation ended up with us focusing on his needs. I swear it became exhausting. Jaquan also seemed to lose motivation to get his truck fixed. So every day, my c class was the luxury taxi for the homeless. I began to become disgusted, not even wanting to drive it anymore.

And then there was Angela. Angela's presence became more and more visible. And I hardly noticed at first. In the beginning, she would sit in the car and wait for Jaquan to come out when he popped in from time to time during the day. Then, he invited her in to sit down. I would make conversation, and she was cordial, even nice at times, I thought. But for the most part, she said nothing. I then noticed that when he went out on weekends, so did she. When he went to the casino to gamble, she was there. I began to question the nature of their relationship and why she was accompanying him to the casino. He would say to me,

Jaquan: I know how you get when I gamble, Tabby, so I stopped asking you after we got into that fight. I take Angela because I don't like riding by myself, that's all.

All of the flags I noticed before were starting to irritate me. Sure, Monday through Thursday, he seemed to be on his best behavior, but when the weekend came, he always had plans to go out. Not only to the club but also to the after-hours bars. The after-hour bars in our town were small hole-in-the-wall establishments hidden in plain sight. They usually had food, illegal liquor, and strippers. When I confronted Jaquan about the happenings there, of course, he denied it, but I wasn't stupid. So, over the next few months, I decided to sit back and observe his behavior. At the same time, I asked for more time with him. He stepped it up a bit, but only when I mentioned it, and his weekends were still his weekends. I started putting Jaquan's responsibilities back on him, like fixing his truck. He complained and still made no attempts at getting it repaired. I took note of that too.

On one of his attempts to step it up, he decided to take me shopping, and we'd go on a ride together. He told me to get ready, and he'd pick me up. I got all dolled up in my dress to come out to the car to see Angela sitting in the back seat with an apparent attitude. He said he had to drop her off before we hit the mall, and he pulled out a wad of cash and handed me $1000. He kissed me and said, "that's your play money, baby, for a rainy day. So, where you wanna go today, Gucci, Louis? I smiled as Jaquan pulled over to stop in the store to get some cigars to roll up. We would shop, smoke, ride, and have a good time. As soon as Jaquan pulled over and got out of the car, Angela got on her phone and called someone. "I SWEAR TA GOD, I'M ABOUT TO KILL MYSELF," she said and got out of the car crying. We dropped Angela off and had an amazing date. Later on, I mentioned what I witnessed with Angela. Jaquan told me she was a cutter who battled depression. My heart went out for her, but his did not. He said, "I don't know what that bitch is trippin' on, but she weird." So, I left it alone because he apparently knew Angela better than I did.

I also noticed changes in his attitude towards me and social media. He hated the fact that I spent my leisure time posting. This man would follow my posts and get upset if he felt like I was oversharing. The same man that went all out to proclaim his love for me no longer wanted ME to engage; imagine that. He would comment about different men liking my posts and go to their pages to see if I liked theirs. Very insecure. I often found that when someone is insecure about your actions with the opposite sex, they are guilty of their own indiscretions.   And Jaquan was no different. Like I said, I was beginning to collect data, which was not good for Jaquan. Reason being, once I hit him with the indisputable facts, we were going to be done. The truth is, I've had enough of the merry-go-round of love's journey. It all just made me wonder.

So during the weeks that turned into months of me collecting data, I came across a post on his social media page. I was used to women putting hearts under his pictures, but it was something about one woman in particular. She was dark-skinned, more on the solid side, with incredibly huge breasts. I knew immediately she was his type, so I went to her page. I looked at her photos. Each and every one revealed a little more of her cleavage. I looked down at the likes; it said "JAQUAN WOODLAND and 169 others"! What the fuck! Each and every photo he liked. No wonder he was obsessed with who liked me because he was out here LOVING her! Oh, it was time for Jaquan and I to have a heart-to-heart. My phone rang; it was Jaquan,

Jaquan: Tabby, I know you had plans tonight, but I need a favor. Angela's birthday is this weekend, and she wanted to go out. Can we use the car?

Tabby: Hell no! is that bitch your woman? Jaquan, bring me my car.

Jaquan: I don't understand why you trippin'. It's her birthday.

Tabby: Then her broke ass needs to make other plans. Like I said, bring me my fucking car!

Jaquan: I ain't bringing you shit.

Tabby: Oh, I bet the fuck you do, Jaquan. How about I make a few phone calls? Did you forget who I know?

Jaquan: Bitch are you threatening me?

Tabby: Oh, I'm a bitch now? Jaquan, how about you bring me my fucking car before the authorities get involved? You definitely don't want that.

He hung up the phone. He knew what time it was. Jaquan would be bringing me my car. The truth is, I didn't have any concrete plans, but I decided to make some quickly. I got dressed and decided I would go to the bar and see Tara when he got there. Jaquan pulled up in my vehicle with Angela on the passenger side, dressed up, at least that's what she called it. She looked ghetto fabulous. I was pissed. They both got out of the car. I stopped Jaquan and grabbed my keys. I told him that he and Angela would need to find somewhere else to go and even offered to drop them off. Jaquan refused, so I waited for them to leave in an Uber. I headed to the bar to talk to Tara and vent.

Several hours later, I returned home from my drunken vent session with Tara to see Jaquan sitting on the couch playing a game; and Angela seated at the bar looking at her phone. I looked at him and said,

Tabby: Really, Jaquan? I asked you to leave and take that BITCH with you! So why are you still here?

Angela: Bitch? Who you callin' a bitch? I SWEAR TO GOD!

Tabby: You SWEAR TO GOD what BITCH! Jaquan, if you don't get her out of my house!

Jaquan: I'm dropping her off now, Tabby. Damn! Calm down! I see you been drinking!

Tabby: And I see you been causing me to drink.

Jaquan grabbed the keys to my Mercedes and headed out the door with Angela behind him. About an hour later, Jaquan returned and laid the keys on the counter. I called from the living room, and he entered. I told him we needed to have a serious talk. He sat down and said,

Jaquan: I already know what you want to talk about, Tabby. Me. My actions, my attitude.

Tabby: Yea, at first, I struggled to understand, Jaquan. But I already know what it is. Jaquan, deep down, you're not ready to be in a relationship, and I know it.

Jaquan: I just don't know, Tabby.

Tabby: Well, let me help you. You have spent more time in the clubs and with Angela in the last few months than with me.

Jaquan: Is this about Angela? I swear y'all women are never satisfied

Tabby: Y'all women? Well, how about Jah'ne doin' me Jones on Facebook? Who is she? You sure loved a lot of her photos.

Jaquan: What?

Tabby: Please don't play dumb, and don't play me like I'm dumb. Jaquan, there is a 15-year age difference between us. I get it. I told you that already. I believe you love me, but we also want different things, and you need to be single.

Jaquan nodded his head in agreement. We set a deadline for him to get his truck fixed and to have an exit date. I knew I felt a peace about deciding to break up with him, but I also felt sorrow. That night Jaquan slept on the couch wrapped in his favorite purple and black leopard print blanket. I always thought it looked a little girlish, but hey, to each their own. The next morning Jaquan asked me to call a towing service to have his car taken to his mechanic. I knew this was the beginning of the end, the long kiss goodbye.

Over the next few weeks in the house, things between Jaquan and me became chilly. Jaquan barely spoke to me while still using my car to get things done. His transmission and engine had gone out in his truck, so it took longer to fix than he anticipated. Honestly, I felt he was using it to stay in my home as a stall tactic. Jaquan walked around with a constant attitude, getting smart with me when he heard me making phone calls. What I thought was a peaceful break-up was quickly turning hostile. Jaquan stopped paying Maria and began stockpiling the household items he had bought into the house. I became even more hostile and began removing his clothing and other belongings from my closets. I put everything he owned in the hall to the left. I felt like the lyrics to Beyonce and even made my own personal video. That evening, he came home with news that his truck was fixed and saw his things against the wall. Jaquan took a deep breath in and made arrangements to get his truck. He returned with Angela and began moving some of his things out. It was happening; love's journey was coming to an end. Jaquan didn't come home that night, and he removed the rest of his things the following day. The big house that became my home, our home, seemed empty and lonely as hell. Jaquan had taken everything he came with, even down to the toothpaste and toilet paper. This big beautiful place felt barren, and as the day turned into night, the lyrics to "if you think you're lonely now" had never seemed more accurate in my heart.

Over the next few weeks, I hid myself in hermit mode. I only came out for food and water, literally. I missed Jaquan and hadn't realized how his presence affected me over the past year. Every time I heard bass coming out of a stereo system, it made me think of him. Driving past the park and the casino gave memories that stung me. I just didn't want to engage; I was still lovesick. I knew I had to overcome it, but it was hard. I didn't know where he was or what he was doing, and the fact that he had moved on with his life so easily without me left a pang in my heart that was too much to deal with. I tried to snap out of it, and with the aid of my girlfriends, I began to make an attempt. Tara had called me out of the blue and invited me to a movie premiere in our town. A local filmmaker had rented out the biggest theater to debut his third feature film, "Holy Roller Hustlers," which was supposed to be a comedy. I agreed at the last minute and got myself together. I was not going to put the pieces of my life back together, sitting and sulking every day. Finally, I met Tara at the theater in my red carpet best.

As we stepped into the theater, I noticed a couple of familiar faces; James, Keisha, and Pastor Doug with cameramen in tow. I should have known. This was one of the biggest events in the city, so why WOULDN'T they be there? Keisha, of course, was dressed to impress from head to toe. She wore a short beaded Chanel dress with a matching clutch, and her make-up was flawless. I was also in Chanel; I had a black and gold Chanel pencil skirt with a matching bustier. I wore the new Louboutins that Jaquan had bought me for Christmas, and I looked pretty darn good for a woman who had just had love's break-up. Keisha looked me up and down in secret admiration, and I smiled. As she walked over with her film crew, I rolled my eyes. She said,

Keisha: Why Tabby, is that you? Fancy seeing you in this circle, considering the company you've been keeping these days.

Tabby: Keisha, how are you? Not that the company I keep is any of your business, but I find it interesting that we seem to travel in the same circles.

Keisha: Oh no, Tabby, don't be mistaken, you and me. Anyway, I wanted to address something with you that I should have done a long time ago. Several months ago, you had a conversation with James...

Tabby: You know what, Keisha, let's not do this here. If you wanna know about my conversation with James, then perhaps you should discuss it with him. I don't have the time or energy to entertain you or this camera crew.

Keisha: You know, Tabby, you're right. James and I are good friends with the producer, and this is his big night; we don't want to ruin it. You look lovely, by the way.

Tabby: Well, thank you.

Keisha: Classic red bottom. Excellent choice. My favorite go-to pump. It gives one that sleek, elegant, classy look, even when they are not.

The cameraman zoomed in on Keisha's response. She gave a wicked grin. I walked away. I wasn't going to let Keisha make my life even worse. I joined Tara over on the red carpet, where the cast members were taking pictures. I looked over at the red carpet, and one man caught my eye. He was about 5'11", a deep brown skin with the biggest smile I had seen in a long time. I was struck immediately. He wore a pair of sunglasses, and I watched him pose for the camera celebrity style. I looked at the poster and realized he was the film's star. I smiled again and kept watching him. I wondered if he could feel me watching through those shades of his. Then I thought, "Nah," as plenty of beautiful women were eager to get that man's attention. He looked about 36 or 37, but I couldn't tell. I thought about what I had just been through trying to be Stella. I knew I was not ready to go back down that road. The young actor pulled off his glasses and looked in my direction. He winked at me; I smiled and gave him a look as if he could get it. Maybe that was Boo Boo Kitty, not me because that bitch sprang into action immediately. You see, Boo Boo Kitty's philosophy is the best way to get over one man is to get on top of another. So, she never misses an opportunity and apparently always gets what she wants. As I began to walk away, he yelled, "Yo, pencil skirt!" I turned around, and he said, "C'mere, take a picture with me." Just like that, I was on red carpet photos.

The actor drew me in like we were lovers in our pics, and I felt a little special. I looked over at the crowd, mostly in awe, except for the young groupies hoping to spend the night with him. I also noticed the sour-faced trio looking over at me and whispering to one another. Keisha looked me up and down and whispered to James. I smiled and put on a show for them. Pastor Doug shook his head in disgust, and I gave more of a performance by taking photos of him nibbling my ear to insinuate that we had a relationship. I didn't know this man from Adam. Well, I quickly got to know him when he took the time to introduce himself to me in one of the photo ops. This young actor moved his hand to the small of my back and whispered in my ear,

Ahmed: My name is Ahmed, who you shorty

Tabby: (laughs) I'm Tabby

Ahmed: Ok, Tee Baby! I see you looking good. I hope you enjoy the film. So, what you doin' after?

Tabby: Well, I came with my girl, so I plan to leave with her too

Ahmed: Ok then. Won't y'all come to the after-party as my guests? We have a private section, bottles, fun shit, you know, letting off some of this celebrity steam, baby!

I laughed and agreed on behalf of me and my girl. This man was serious because not only did he invite us to the after party, but we enjoyed the film from special seats along with him and the principal cast members. We snuggled and ate popcorn while we watched the film. He said,

Ahmed: This is our official first date, you know.

Tabby: Oh really?

Ahmed: Yea. Damn, you so fine, girl. You from here?

Tabby: Yep, born and raised.

Ahmed: I'm from Atlanta; I moved here a year ago with my sons. Just trying something new. I did a few movies in Detroit, so this is like a home base for me.

Tabby: So, you're an ACTOR actor! Like, for real. Ok! That's pretty dope!

Ahmed gave me that award-winning smile. I melted a little. He was so fucking cute. He said,

Ahmed: Yea, I do this for real, Tee!

He kissed me, and I smiled. Then, we turned our attention back to the movie. He was actually pretty good, I thought. He had a charisma that shined through on the big screen. I thought about the Moment I was in; and decided to live in it. I enjoyed Ahmed for the rest of the film, and then we went to the after-party together. Ahmed and I exchanged numbers, but I didn't think anything would come of it, especially since we didn't have sex that night. He was an actor, and I was sure he could fuck anyone he wanted to. He was a lot younger than me, 11 years to be exact, so I'm sure he was on that young boy fuck shit. Yea, he had kids, but Jaquan also had a son. I rationalized in my mind all the reasons to stay away from him IF he called. But again, he was an actor, so I had minimal expectations. So when Ahmed did text me, I was surprised yet intrigued. After a few days of texting back and forth, Ahmed offered to come to my place and cook me dinner. I looked around this lonely place. It felt so empty and silent with Jaquan gone. And here was this man offering to come and cook for me. I decided to bring life back into this place and have a little fun! So, I had Ahmed come over, and it got hotter in the bedroom than it did in the kitchen.

Ahmed entered my home with a bag of groceries and that fucking smile of his. He was so fucking cute, I swear! I led him to the kitchen to work his magic. I grabbed the bottle of tequila and poured it as I watched him unload the bag of groceries. Chicken wings, flour, some sort of sauce, potatoes, and pancake batter. He said,

Ahmed: Tee baby! You're in for a treat, girl! I'm about to make you some chicken and waffles, Atlanta style! My Momma's recipe!

Tabby: Say what! Uh oh, I better watch out!

Ahmed: Yea, yea! Roll up while I cook.

Tabby: I can't wait to see this. Are you really that good in the kitchen?

Ahmed: Yea, Tee, for real, I LOVE to cook. My Momma showed me. She was the best cook. I remember when I was about nine, and it was Mother's Day. I made my Mom a steak, mashed potatoes, and steamed broccoli, and she said it was THE BEST.

Tabby: You were cooking that at 9?

Ahmed: Yea, you don't believe me. I'm 'bout to call my mom right now.

Ahmed grabs the phone and Facetimes his mother. She validates his story, and we all have a good conversation. I could feel his love for his Mom oozing out of the phone. It was refreshing seeing that, especially since Jaquan's relationship with his was so estranged. I relaxed and let this man cook for me and feed me. And then it was time for him to fuck me.

Ahmed and I took our evening to the bedroom to finish what we had started. I knew he had children at home, and eventually, he would have to get home to them. Ahmed pushed me onto the bed playfully. He leaned in slowly for a kiss. It was slow at first, but then quickly became passionate. I grabbed his face. We kissed for a while. His tongue sent shivers all through my body. I took off Ahmed's shirt as we kissed. We came up for air, and he took off mine. Ahmed kissed my body, first my neck, then my chest, and made his way to my twins. I moaned as he sucked them lightly. My pussy got wet. His tongue danced around my nipples, bushed them lightly, then blew. My lovebox began to tingle as her juices seeped through my shorts. I let him play between my bosoms. Ahmed pushed me back playfully and, in one swoop, scooped my shorts off my body. Ahmed looked down at Boo Boo Kitty and smiled. He licked his lips as he dived into her wetness. I moaned. Ahmed licked my kitty like a sharpshooter. He licked and sucked my center, and she got wetter and wetter. Ahmed took his fingers and spread my lips apart. He had full access to my button, and he took full advantage. Ahmed sucked my clit, and she stood at attention. He licked, and she flickered. He sucked, and she shivered. Boo Boo Kitty exploded, and Ahmed slurped up all her juices.

Ahmed got up and came in for a kiss. We kissed lightly, and I flipped him over on the bed playfully and went in for his manhood. I stroked him slowly as I looked up at him. He said, "damn girl," and I smiled wickedly. I took him in my mouth, and he gasped. I licked his Johnson slowly. As I licked his tip, I stroked his twins with my free hand. I looked up at him. He moaned as his eyes rolled up in his head. I took his shaft deeper in my mouth with slow deep intense strokes. Ahmed began to say "FUCK" as I noticed his toes began to curl. He was ready for the ride I was about to take him on.

I took my mouth off Ahmed's rock-hard dick. I gave him an intense look as my body eased on top of his. He wanted inside of me, and I grabbed his shaft. I pretended to allow him to enter me, took his manhood, and rubbed it against my clit. His manhood jumped, and my kitty flickered as we both felt the sensations of pleasure in every interaction. I rubbed his manhood slowly against my clit; pushed him in a little, took it out again, and rubbed him against her. Ahmed looked at me as if he were begging to feel my insides. I took him out of his misery and slowly sat down on him. I grinded my hips slowly and deeply, and Ahmed matched my cadence. Ahmed put my girls in his mouth as I moved up and down his shaft. The sensation of his mouth and his dick made my juices build up around his dick. Ahmed felt my wetness with every single stroke. He said, "Damn, your pussy is so wet, Tee. This shit feels so good." And it did. The shit felt amazing, if I did say so myself. Our bodies speed up the tempo. Ahmed grabbed my hips and grinded me inside him. He took control. As he moved my hips at lightning speed, his Johnson hit my clit as my hips matched his movements. I yelped, moaned, and came hard! Ahmed came quickly after that. We both collapsed on the bed and laughed. He asked me where the bathroom was so he could get himself together. I knew he had to get back to the boys, so I pointed him in that direction. Ahmed cleaned himself up, got dressed, and leaned in for a kiss. I thought I was saying farewell until the next time, but shit with Ahmed took an unusually freaky turn!

As Ahmed was getting dressed, he said to me,

Ahmed: I noticed that I been in this big ass bedroom and ain't seen the whole thing. There's the bathroom and this over here. What's that?

Tabby: Oh, that's my walk-in closet, well, two of them—one for my clothes and the other for my shoes and accessories.

Ahmed walks in the direction of my closets and looks around.

Ahmed: How can one woman have that many purses and shoes? And other things I see. Tabby, you're a naughty girl.

I walk into my walk-in closet naked to see that Ahmed has discovered my little arsenal; Johnson and Esteban. New versions, of course; I had worn the old ones out throughout the years. Ahmed looks at my naked body and smiles, holds Johnson in his hands, and says,

Ahmed: What you know about these, Tabby?

Tabby: Oh, I know plenty.

Ahmed: I bet you don't... have you ever squirted with one of these?

Tabby: Of course I have. Wanna watch?

I gave Ahmed a wicked grin, and he smiled back. Ahmed handed me Johnson, and I laid down on the floor of the walk-in closet. I grabbed my massage oil and poured it on Boo Boo Kitty. I felt the heat from the massage oil, which brought my clit to full attention. I turned on Johnson at mid-speed and looked up at Ahmed as I rubbed Johnson in my Kitty. I took Johnson and brushed him lightly against me as I moved my hips. Ahmed licked his lips and dropped his shorts. His manhood stood at attention as I stroked myself with Johnson. Ahmed began to stroke himself slowly as we looked at one another. I took Johnson and allowed him to pulsate on my clit. Sharp sensations went in and out of me as I rubbed my clit, and Ahmed stroked his dick. I opened my legs wide, so he could see all my insides and beckoned him to come to me with my eyes. He looked and stroked as Johnson pulsated on Boo Boo Kitty.

The sensation in my body got intense. I dug Johnson deeper inside me. I rubbed him on my clit and changed speeds. Kitty's walls overflowed like a waterfall as Ahmed watched in amazement. Ahmed dropped to the floor and entered me. I kept Johnson on my clit and stroked as he stroked my insides. We both felt the vibration of Johnson and my wetness as I squirted again and again with him stroking inside me. Ahmed stroked as I squirted and stroked more intensely as I squirted again. Ahmed stroked deeper and deeper as the vibration of Johnson moved from my clit to his dick. Finally, I placed Johnson directly on my clit, as Ahmed announced he was ready to cum. As he let out his release, Kitty released her upward waterfalls directly on his shaft. He came, and I squirted; it was all so intense.

Ahmed once again collapsed on me, and we laughed. We lay there for a few minutes in each other's arms in the walk-in closet. He then put his clothes back on and had to get home for real this time. I grabbed my robe and saw Ahmed at the door. I shut the door and took a deep breath in and out. This time it was a sigh of satisfaction. I showered and laid down for a deep sleep. That man had truly put it down! When I woke up, I smiled as he called me for a quick conversation. Ahmed was headed to Detroit to audition for a new series that was coming on STARZ. It was a big deal, and only his agent and his Momma knew, and now me. I felt a little special and smiled. I wished Ahmed the best of luck and continued my day. I knew he'd be back in a few days, and he promised that he wanted to spend it with me. I knew that Ahmed would be the perfect distraction from the hell I had just gone through. At that moment, my phone dinged. It was a text message from Jaquan. A video showing me how much money he made at the casino. Like, I gave a fuck. I rolled my eyes and decided to continue with the rest of my day.

True to his word, Ahmed returned home a few days later, and we spent his first day back talking about the audition. He mentioned a few A-list celebrities with guaranteed leading roles, and then there were people like him who had hopes of landing a seasonal role but would even be considered extras. He was very excited. While he was saying he should know in the next few days, he got a call from his manager. They offered him the role of one of the brothers of the main character. Ahmed got off the phone, jumped up and down, picked me up, and spun me around! This was a huge break for him. After all of that, he called his mother. She wished him well, and he got off the phone and turned his attention to me.

Ahmed: I will have to head out in a few weeks to begin the preliminary promo and get started on production. The downside is that I'll be gone for about eight weeks.

Tabby: Well damn! That's a long time, but I'm sure it will be well worth it.

Ahmed: Damn right, Tee! A role in a series on a major network? That's fucking huge! But don't worry, Tee baby, I'll be right back. You won't even miss me, girl. We can do the long-distance thing.

Tabby: The long-distance thing, huh?

Ahmed: Keep it nice and hot with your friend in the walk-in closet. We can get that video chat POPPIN! Plus, you can come up on the weekends when you are not busy.

Tabby: You got it all worked out. I see.

Ahmed: Yea, Tee! That's the kind of man I am.

Ahamed reached in and kissed me. I so enjoyed his light-heartedness. So I stayed in the moment, and Ahmed and I spent the next few weeks just doing that, being in the Moment.

Once Ahmed headed out for Detroit, I found myself restless. I needed something to do, but I didn't know what. Little did I know that my life would be turned upside down over the next eight weeks while Ahmed was away. It was like a cruel joke from God or the universe. I meet a great guy who is an amazing distraction before the shit hits the fan. What happened next had my life in a whirlwind, one that, once it got started that I couldn't stop it. Once again, I was almost happy! I should have known, though, because of the planetary alignments; Mercury was in retrograde. The last time that shit happened, Ebony died, and I divorced James. My life also spiraled a little after that, and I met love's journey. Fuck that, I thought to myself. The old saying goes, "The Lord giveth, and the Lord taketh away."

While Ahmed settled in Detroit, we began communicating primarily via text. I understood he was busy but seeing his Instagram with a hot new young castmate made me cringe. "It is what it is," I thought as I received a private message on my messenger from someone I was not connected to. Shaquita Turner. I looked at the picture. Just a face shot, interesting. I opened the message, and it was lengthy and stated:

Shaquita: I know you don't know me, but my name is Shaquita. I know you and Jaquan were dating, and I felt I needed to reach out to you. I have known Jaquan for years; we are good friends, nothing else, and I allowed him to stay here after the two of you broke up. Since he moved back in, he is not been the same; Jaquan drinks a lot more and listens to old-school music. He also has been focused on getting as much money as possible and has been in the casinos non-stop, taking his pet Angela with him. Also, the two of them almost got arrested on a return gone wrong, and when they caught her, she used my name to avoid going to jail. The police called me because Jaquan's truck is in my name, and when they pulled off from that Lowes, they captured the license plate. Jaquan doesn't care; he promises to return tomorrow to the store. Can you please talk some sense into him? He'll listen to you.

I looked down at the message in shock and disbelief. What the fuck was I supposed to do anyway? Jaquan was a grown-ass man, and if he wanted to self-destruct, that was on him! And besides, I hadn't spoken to Jaquan since the break-up, so I had no idea where his head was. I decided to ignore her message. Another came through with her number asking me to call her. This bitch sure was persistent. I picked up the phone and called.

Shaquita: Hi Tabby, I'm Shaquita. I know my message was a lot to take in, and I hope you can help.

Tabby: First of all, Shaquita, I don't mean to be rude, but Jaquan is a grown man. I can't control what he does.

Shaquita: We all know Jaquan has a mind of his own, but when he was with you, he was a completely different person; better. We have been friends for a long time, and I have seen women come and go, but you were different in his eyes. Do you know that when Valentine's day came around, I bumped into him while he was shopping for you? Jaquan had the look of a man in love.

I sighed. Why was she stirring up emotions I didn't want to deal with? I didn't want to feel anything for that man right now.

Shaquita: Tabby, please.

Tabby: Ok, I'll call and check on him. But I'm not making any promises to you.

I ended my conversation with Shaquita and hung up the phone. I remembered that Jaquan had recently texted me. I picked up the phone and called him.

Jaquan: Hey, stranger.

Tabby: Hey Jaquan, how you been?

Jaquan: You know me chillin', makin' money, that's it, that's all.

Tabby: I wouldn't expect anything less from you. I see you hit big at the casino; good for you!

Jaquan: Yea, you know how I do it. So, what you been up to, Tabby? You got a new man yet?

Tabby: I can't even believe you asked me that already

Jaquan: Well, I know how you are, a cougar and all. I know somebody has been in that bed. Don't deny it.

Tabby: Well, have you been spying on me again, Jaquan?

Jaquan: Yea, I already knew. I remember how fast we got together.

Tabby: Wow, Jaquan, it's like that? Who pissed in your cereal this morning?

Jaquan: Is that a reference to me being a child, Tabby? See, that's why we ain't together now.

Tabby: But you can call me a cougar, ok. You know what Jaquan talking to you is pointless.

Jaquan: Then why the fuck did you call Tabby? Look, girl, I gotta finish my business today and break off Angela some cash, who has been breathing down my fucking neck this whole conversation.

Angela: Nigga, I SWEAR TO GOD! A BITCH ain't PRESSED ABOUT WHAT THE FUCK YOU DOIN!

Jaquan: If you don't shut the fuck up from the back seat bitch I swear I will pull over and drop your ass off.....Yea, that's what the fuck I thought.

Tabby: Well, I'm gonna let you go.

Jaquan: Yea, you do that, Tabby. But before you do, one more thing. I left my lawn mower in your garage; I need that. It's still in the box, and I need to sell it. I'll be by after I drop Angela off.

Angela: OH, HELL NO

Jaquan: Bitch SHUT UP!

Tabby: Jaquan, don't come over here late, and don't come with an attitude. That's all I ask.

Jaquan: I'll come when I want and how I want, the fuck

Tabby: Jaquan, you need to come another day when you're not dealing with all these issues at once.

Jaquan: Issues? So, I got issues now?

Tabby: Jaquan, everything is a fucking argument with you right now, and I'm not gonna do this; I gotta go.

I hung up the phone before he could say anything else. He called right back, and I sent him to voicemail. Immediately a flurry of text messages came through with him cussing me out, calling me a cougar, and then demanding that I make sure his lawn mower was ready and available to him when he got there. I swear he was acting like a crackhead. If I didn't know Jaquan, I would think that. But Jaquan was just selfish, just like James. What was mine was his, and what was his was also his alone. I thought about what kind of day this was turning out to be when I got a knock at my door. Maria was off, so imagine my surprise when I answered to see a white man in a suit,

White man: Tabitha Monroe?

Tabby: Who are you? Who's asking?

White man: I'm looking for Tabitha Monroe.

Tabby: Must you say my government name like that?

White man: Ms. Monroe, you have just been served.

Tabby: I'm being served? For what?

The man hands me an envelope, and I open it. It read; JAMES TAYLOR VS. TABITHA MONROE. What the fuck was James up to? I read the document. James was hauling me back into court in 3 days to schedule a hearing to renegotiate the terms of our divorce. WHAT? How could he even do that?

I picked up the phone and called James.

Keisha: Hello, Tabby. We were expecting you to call

Tabby: I'm sorry, I must have the wrong number; I was trying to reach James.

Keisha: Are you playing games, sweetheart? James and I are engaged to be married. So, of course, I would answer his phone.

Tabby: Oh, is this Keisha? I'm sorry, being engaged sure isn't good enough to answer that man's phone, and you know how he gets; remember when I was his WIFE, and you felt you had privilege? Does James know you answered his phone? You better give that man his phone before an argument ensues. Better yet, you better hang up and delete my number from his phone log.

Keisha: Are you suggesting that I'm insecure, Tabby?

Tabby: Well, in the country, they say, "hit dogs holler."

Keisha: Is there something we can help you with, Tabby? James is not available right now, but I'll make sure to give him the message.

Tabby: Yea, you do that, Keisha. Tell your man to call me; we have business to discuss.

Keisha: Well, whatever business you have to....

Click. I hung up on that simple bitch. I paced the floor, trying to figure out what to do. The conversation with Shaquita, Jaquan, and Keisha was too much for me. I wanted to get away, but I knew I had no time to run from what was happening. I took a deep breath in and out and called my attorney, Yvette Stevens, who also was expecting my call.

Yvette: Good afternoon, Tabby; I received some information by courier today; I was just about to call you. Tabby, we need to act fast.

Tabby: Yvette, what's happening?

Yvette: According to our county law, either party in the divorce proceedings can contest the divorce with proper justification, and according to Mr. Goldstein James' attorney, on paper, he has a valid reason. Now when that happens, your case has to go back before a judge for renegotiations. As stated in your documents, a few days from now is just the preliminary.

Tabby: So what does all this mean, that James can take everything from me and take me through this all over again?

Yvette: He can try. But like I said, this is preliminary. Let me make a few calls to the judge and Mr. Weinstein to see what their strategy is. In the meantime, Tabby, my advice is to make sure you still have funds outside of account number 8.

Tabby: I have a smaller account with some money in it.

Yvette: Good. And in the meantime, do not move any money into your smaller account. Liquidate some things if you have to. These cases rarely appear in court, so this may take a while.

Tabby: And your fee, Ms. Stevens?

Yvette: Tabby, for now, don't worry about it. My job is to get on top of this immediately. I'll get back to you by tomorrow morning with my findings.

We hung up the phone. My head was spinning a little. This was way too much to take in, and being in this big empty house was way too depressing. I didn't want to stay there, so I booked a hotel room courtesy of account number 3. That was where most of the funds I got from the divorce proceedings went. I know what Yvette told me, but I had to make an exception for myself. So I packed my things and headed out to get away. When I got to my suite, I drew a nice big bubble bath and settled into my thoughts. I wondered at first what I did to deserve all that was happening to me. Did I get smug? Did I get cocky? Was it something I did while I was married to James? Was it all the previous dicks inside me? I had no idea. Whatever it was, I had to get a hold of things, but I didn't know how. One thing I did know is there was nothing I could do until I heard from Yvette. So I decided not to worry about any of it and got out of the tub and relaxed in my robe with a glass of wine.

As the afternoon turned into nighttime, the lingering thoughts of my upcoming court date were a faded memory. I spent the night scrolling through social media, posting, and chatting. Jaquan called, and I sent him to voicemail. He sent a text, and I didn't respond. Immediately I received a Facetime,

Jaquan: Where the fuck are you, Tabby? Are you playing games with me? (laughs) Listen, I know you probably boo'd up somewhere with some nigga, but I told you I was coming by, and all I want is my lawn mower, baby. Tell that nigga I said hello, by the way.

Tabby: (sighs) Let's not do this, Jaquan. As you can see, I'm not home. You can come tomorrow when I am home and get your lawn mower.

Jaquan: No, I'm getting my shit tonight. Let me get my lawn mower Tabby.

Tabby: I know you don't think I'm leaving this hotel room to come open my garage! Like I said, you can get it tomorrow. Hell, I'll even bring it to you.

Jaquan: Nah, FUCK THAT! Why can I get my shit Tabby! It's MINE! You didn't buy that! COME, GIVE ME MY SHIT!

Jaquan takes the camera and walks up towards the driveway of my home. I yelled,

Tabby: JAQUAN! What are you doing? NO! JAQUAN! PUT THE BRICK DOWN!! DON'T DO IT!

CRASH! It's all I heard and saw as Jaquan sent the brick from my beautiful landscape sailing through my window. He then looked at me through the Facetime and said,

Jaquan: I told you to give me my shit. You fucking Cougar!

Jaquan hung up the phone, and there was no sense in calling him back. My alarm company notified me there was a disturbance and that they were sending a police cruiser to my home. Since I wasn't at home, the police agreed to survey the area overnight until I returned. I hoped Jaquan wasn't stupid enough to go back and get his lawn mower. If he was, then that would be on him. I finally laid down and tried to get some sleep. I was restless all night as I thought of this upcoming court case with James, the possibility of losing everything, and then cleaning up the mess that Jaquan made. I woke up the following day achy and a little uneasy.

The madness continued that morning, as true to her word, I was contacted by Yvette bright and early.

Yvette: Good morning, Tabby. How are you?

Tabby: I'd be much better if you had some good news for me; please say so, Yvette.

Yvette: I have some good news, and the rest you probably need to sit down for.

I sat down and braced myself. My heart began to increase its speed in my chest.

Yvette: The good news is that you or James won't have to appear in court in a couple of days. But the unfortunate news for both of you is that certain assets will be frozen.

Tabby: What do you mean frozen? No access to my money?

Yvette: To your money, to the houses, also Tabby. James is fortunate enough to keep the condo he bought for Keisha. But assets accumulated while you were married have been frozen on both ends until we get a hearing which could be months.

Tabby: Are you kidding me? Why is he doing this?

Yvette: Again, everything looks good on paper. Mr. Goldstein definitely did his homework. I have to give it to him. He knew this could drag on for months, and they want to see you suffer. Lucky for me, I love a challenge.

Tabby: Any suggestions for me, Yvette?

Yvette: Here's the not-so-pleasant news.

Tabby: There's MORE!

Yvette: You have 48 hours to remove your belongings from the home. The home will go in escrow until the hearing is set.

Tabby: You've got to be kidding me!

Yvette: I never joke about these matters, Tabby. My advice to you would be to play nice while I handle this. Remove your things, set up temporary housing for a few months, and let's negotiate one hell of a settlement for you. The new judge seems fair and impartial; James has 90% of his assets frozen. Do you think that he is a happy camper?

Tabby: Fuck him. He did that to himself. Thank you for the news, Yvette. Let me figure this out.

I hung up the phone and sprang into action. I knew I had built up a substantial amount in my primary checking, so I wasn't worried about account number 2 being frozen as I had anticipated. I would get my personal belongings, put the rest of my things in storage and get a hotel suite for a few months; perfect, I thought. I also had enough to give Maria four months' worth of salary until we sorted this out. I couldn't leave my girl Maria hanging like that. She was kind of like my ride-or-die! When I left James, so did she, and for that, she deserved more from me than two days' notice. I pulled out my phone to check my bank balance. My jaw dropped. That couldn't be right; the balance was off by about $50,000. Not now, I thought, no alerts, no nothing? This was all too much to deal with. I got in my Mercedes truck and headed to the bank to figure out what was happening.

Several hours later, I had come to the truth and had felt like a fool. And once again, Jaquan was at the center of it all. Over the course of our living together, Jaquan had gained access to a second bank card that had arrived in the mail. And thus, the withdrawal of funds from my account. I reviewed my statements that I had ignored for a whole year; purchases at Louis, Versace, and all the other places we both enjoyed. Hotel room purchases when we went out of town, that son of a bitch! Lucky for me, I was able to deactivate his access. And to be certain, I created a whole new account with new cards that only I could access. I got sick on the inside. I had half of what I anticipated in my account, and I still had 48 hours to hire movers, get my things in storage and find proper housing to figure out a game plan. I still had to pay Maria, which would mean exhausting almost all of my bank accounts. But I still planned to do right by her, so I had to figure out another way for myself.

I drove up to the house and looked at the damage. I got out of the car in numbness from the exhaustion of the last 48 hours. I stepped over the glass fragments to see Maria sweeping up the remaining pieces. She smiled at me like a loving mother and finished. I asked her to come in and gave her the news. She seemed sad, but I assured her it would be temporary. I promised her a three-month severance by the end of the week. Maria seemed a little relieved and asked if I would be ok. I assured Maria I would be okay no matter what life threw at me. Maria also asked me if there was anything she could do. I thought about asking her to put me up for the next three months, but who does that? I told her I would be ok and that I would have her severance by the end of the week. Maria sprang into action by arranging moves on a budget for me while I tried to figure out where I was going to live. I then asked Maria to follow me to the dealership in my Mercedes truck. I sold my baby and got the funds within a few hours to my bank account. And just like that, two problems were solved; my things would be moved into storage, Maria would get her severance, and I could live in a suite for a couple of months. If I was honest with myself, I knew if this battle with James dragged beyond a few months, I would have to figure out other options. Plus, I knew that once Jaquan figured out his access to my money had been cut off, he'd somehow decide to come for me. Why was I still dealing with this fool anyway? We were not even together anymore! I braced for the next few months ahead, knowing I still had two battles before me.

Over the next couple of days, I got everything out of the house. I even called Shaquita to come and get the lawn mower that Jaquan threw such a fit over. Plus, I was curious as to what this chick looked like. I wanted to see his "friend" that he chose over me. A last bit of closure, I guess. Nah, I still had feelings for this man. There was no closure yet. I was exhausted dealing with him, and I wanted to be done. I didn't have the time or energy to deal with Jaquan. I decided to let my best friend karma take care of him instead. After busting my window, and finding out he had access to my money all this time, surely he had a bit of it coming. And I knew my relationship with karma; when somebody does me dirty, my homegirl always allows me to see my justice served. I smiled about my girl karma as a beat-up chevy malibu pulled into my driveway; it was Shaquita.

My meeting with Shaquita was as uneventful as she looked. I was even shocked. Shaquita stepped out of the beat-up malibu in a skinned tight grey sundress that clung to her enormous body. I looked down at the multiple jelly rolls that layered her thighs, legs, calves, and ankles. Her waist was surprisingly small for all the fat distributed elsewhere on her body. Shaquita's dress came to mid-thigh, her hair was pulled back in a crackhead ponytail, and there were multiple visible Keloids on her face and neck. Shaquita also wore a pair of dirty white flip-flops, and there was no appearance of lotion anywhere on her body. Shaquita greeted me and was pleasant enough, friendly even. Shaquita picked up the lawn mower, and that was the end of that. Uneventful, as I stated before. In the back of my mind, I was hoping that Shaquita didn't see me wearing a look of shock when I saw her. However, I couldn't stop Maria from her horrific gasps, and I'm sure Shaquita took notice. After Shaquita departed, Maria looked at me and said, "Aye, Aye, Aye." I told her, "My sentiments exactly." Maria and I said our goodbyes for the next three months as the movers loaded my things to put into storage. I then settled into my hotel suite, the place I called home for the next few months.

The first few weeks went along pretty well. I had gotten into the routine of getting up, hitting the hotel gym, and applying for positions I didn't want. I knew I wasn't meant to work for someone these days, but I didn't know what I could do for a living to bring in money. I thought about it for weeks, and nothing came to mind. I knew I couldn't sit around and do nothing, and I hadn't been in corporate America in what seemed like forever. I was secretly hoping and praying that Yvette could work her magic and get me a decent settlement. In the meantime, I would make things work with the money I had, even if I had to work at McDonald's. I cringed at the thought. Then I thought about going to Arizona to live with Vincent.

Sure, he would take me in; but he was my son who acted like he was my father. And then there was Vanessa, struggling to make a situation work that seemed impossible. I also thought about reaching out to my second-best bestie, but last I heard, she was out of the country with Lady Gaga. She was starring in an upcoming documentary, and Samantha would be gone for at least six months. And to be honest, my pride wouldn't allow me to reach out to Tara for help. She never liked Jaquan and felt the relationship was doomed from the start. So, what were my options but to go through this alone?

My phone rang, and it was an out-of-town number. I noticed it was from Daytonia, and only one person I know lived there, Angela. I answered the phone and proceeded with caution to hear a bitter voice on the other end of my phone,

Angela: Tabby, do you have a minute?

Tabby: Angela, to be honest, if it has to do with Jaquan, I want no part of the conversation.

Angela: I swear to God I have never had anything against you, Tabby. It's just that Jaquan's and my relationship is complicated, and he never told you the truth about everything. But since his ass played me once again, I don't GIVE A FUCK!

Tabby: Angela, what the fuck are you talking about?

Angela: Like I said, I never had anything against you. Jaquan and I have been mostly friends throughout the years, but occasionally we have had times where we been together. I didn't think it was serious when he got with you at first. Then when y'all moved in together, I kind of fell back. Then he started paying bills over there off the money I had been helping him get from me stealing, and I got tired of that shit.

I know this bitch was not complaining about my man doing things for me! She had such audacity! I listened to this bitch go on and on. She said,

Angela: After a while, I told him I refused to do it any longer. We fell out a few times while y'all were together, and then towards the end of y'all's relationship, Jaquan started acting weird. He was being extra nice and flirting. I started complaining about you and what you weren't doing at home. He even started bragging about how he had access to your account and would take money out to buy you things. Did you know that?

I played dumb.

Tabby: What!

Angela: Girl, yes! You need to throw his ass in jail. I heard what he did to your window.

Tabby: Don't worry, I'll handle Jaquan.

Angela: Good. I got some tricks for his ass myself

Tabby: Angela, why are you telling me all this?

Angela: Because I'm sick and tired of Jaquan treating me like shit! He wouldn't have half the shit he does if it weren't for me, and he had the nerve to move back in with Shaquita! I SWEAR TO GOD, I HATE HIS WHOLE LIFE!

Tabby: He and Shaquita are just friends, right? I had a conversation with her.

Angela: Don't believe that shit. Jaquan is over there fucking and sucking on her fat ass every night. That girl is in love with him.

Tabby: And you, Angela? Are you in love with him too?

Angela paused…

Angela: I don't love Jaquan, but I got love FOR him. Jaquan was there for me when I was homeless. We both were homeless together. Jaquan looked out for me even when I had no one. So, I don't love him; I got a whole other nigga I fuck with. But Jaquan acts weird about him.

That was too much information, and Jaquan was too complicated for me. The woman told me another one was in love with him and was lying to me. And then, the way she talked, she appeared to be in denial about her feelings for him. And then there was me; I still loved Jaquan, and I felt like when we were together, he loved me. Was I a fool all this time? I said,

Tabby: Angela, that is way too much information for me.

Angela: You just need to know who you are truly dealing with. Like I said, I got something for him. Jaquan went to the casino and won $20,000 that day. He was arguing with you on the phone. We were supposed to go to dinner and go out that night, but he stayed at the tables. Then he said he would make it up to me the next day after I hit the stores. I stole all this merchandise the next day, and we sold it all, and he made another $6000. Do you know this nigga only gave me $150! I was pissed!

Tabby: Well damn!

Angela: He knows I have kids to take care of! He had the nerve to tell me fuck me, and he already had another booster! THE FUCK! He knows can't nobody steal like me, but he tryna cut me out COMPLETELY! Well, since he tried to be slick, I called all the buyers and told them that he was gonna be out of town for a few weeks and that I was gonna be handling business. Then, I called the stores. I called Lowes, I called Home Depot, and I called Walmart. I told them everything that was going on. He has been laying low the last few days because the main stores have been swarming with cops. (evil laugh) They gonna get his ass!

Tabby: Angela, that's a little extreme, don't you think? You've been dealing with Jaquan for years. Telling on him, not only hurts him but you too.

Angela: Do you think I give a fuck! I told you I was done with him. I mean that, Tabby. (She cries) I just can't take this anymore. I'm ready to change. I'm tired of going through this with Jaquan...I'll get a job before I fuck with him again.

The conversation went on for about an hour. Angela went on and on about how much she hated Jaquan and wanted to ruin his life. No love was lost between her and Shaquita; what was up with that? On the surface, Shaquita seemed nice and genuinely cared about his best interest, which he needed. I knew this wouldn't be the end of things, so I decided to sit back and watch how things would unfold.

A few days later, I received a call from Shaquita. She filled in the missing pieces of the conversation I had with Angela a few days earlier. According to Shaquita, Jaquan had taken her and Mickey into Home Depot to do a return while his new booster when to her designated isles. When they went to make the return, they discovered that Home Depot had established new rules for the number of returns that could be exchanged. Their policy went from $2000 a gift card to $250.

Shaquita: We looked embarrassed as we had to haul thousands of dollars of merchandise back to the car after being questioned. Jaquan got into an argument with the manager, and the manager called him by name. He said he heard about him and not to come back to their location. Jaquan was pissed and confused. Jaquan got angry and knocked over several displays before we left the store. The same thing happened when we went to another Home Depot. They're on to him. Right now, he's sitting around the house listening to old-school music, trying to figure out what to do.

I listened to Shaquita talk. I knew what she was trying to insinuate with the old-school music. He was thinking about me. So I tried to let her words go in one ear and out the other and let her vent.

Shaquita: He been drinking heavy, which is not like Jaquan. I just don't know what to do, Tabby, but to watch him self-destruct.

Tabby: If I know anything about Jaquan Shaquita, I know that he always has a plan B. Give him a few days he'll figure it out

Shaquita: Yeah, you may be right, but I guess we'll see.

Shaquita and I hung up the phone. I knew Jaquan would work out his situation, and I had my own to think about. We were broken up, remember? Months ago? Why was this man still entangled in my everyday affairs? It was like we had broken up, but somehow we were still together. One of us had to let go at some point, but who?

A month into my stay at the suite, as my funds got lower, karma pulled Jaquan and I even closer in the strangest way. I was in my suite minding my business one evening pretending to look for a job while I scrolled through social media. I received a phone call from Shaquita that I sent to voicemail. She called again, and I let it ring. She followed up with a text that said, "Please answer; Jaquan almost died tonight!" I picked up the phone and dialed,

Shaquita: Tabby, I really need your help.

Tabby: What do you mean Jaquan almost died, Shaquita?

Shaquita: His car caught on fire and almost blew up on the freeway!

Tabby: Oh no! Is he ok!

Shaquita: Yes, thank God! Jaquan is about 3 hours away, and my car can't make it that far. He's stranded outside of Springtown.

Tabby: Wait a minute, what was he doing there? That's where the amusement park is. Why would he be headed there tonight?

Shaquita: Apparently, he was taking a female down there. And Angela was with him too.

Tabby: Angela, interesting. The last I heard, she was done with him.

Shaquita: That girl has been texting him for weeks, begging him to talk to her and telling her how she's lost without him and how much she missed him. She's sick. He started bringing her back around, and suddenly, the new booster got caught in the store. The other day, he got mad at her and made her sleep in his truck. Now all of a sudden, it catches on fire! Coincidence, I think not.

Tabby: It could be karma.

Shaquita: I thought about that too. Jaquan has done some bad things to people throughout the years, and little things happen, but he seems to get away with a lot of shit. Well, karma came tonight. Maybe this was a wake-up call for him.

Tabby: Yea, let's hope so. So, what do you need me to do? Honestly, I don't want to see Jaquan's face right now. Or Angela's, for that matter. I don't want to see him stranded, but I'm not picking him up.

Shaquita: I tried to call his cousin Link, but he was busy, as always. Tabby, please, no one I know has a car.

Tabby: I tell you what. Come by the hotel I'm staying at and leave your car here. Then, you can come and get your car when you pick them up and drop them off.

Shaquita: Thank you, Tabby, I know Jaquan may not say thank you, but he really will appreciate it.

We hung up the phone. Several minutes later, I received a "thank you" text from Jaquan. I guess I would be humble, too, if I were stranded. I fell asleep over the next few hours waiting for Shaquita to return. She returned in the wee hours of the morning, exhausted from her driving. The following morning there was a knock at my suite, and it was Jaquan. Why did Shaquita tell him I was here? I opened the door, and he entered.

Jaquan: Tabby, thank you again for letting Shaquita get the car yesterday. I don't know what we would have done. The police had pulled up; we ain't have no license; that shit was wild.

Tabby: So, what are you gonna do now?

Jaquan: I don't know yet. I have to use Shaquita's car for now, but her shit is damn near broke down. Plus, I gotta find some other stores;

shit is slow now. I can't even make half the money I used to, and some of the buyers are acting funny. I don't know what happened or how they even caught on; we been doin' this for years! Do you know they called me by name in Home Depot, Tabby? I can't go back in there.

Tabby: Jaquan, maybe it's a sign you need to slow down

Jaquan: Or that somebody out to get me. So why are you here anyway? You been staying in a hotel? What's going on, Tabby?

I opened up and told him about the situation with James. He came over, drew me in for a hug, and kissed me on the forehead. This was the Jaquan that I remembered. He said,

Jaquan: Baby, I am so sorry you are going through this with that asshole. I know I have done some fucked up shit, but I would never take everything from you that you had.

I looked up at him. He knew that I knew that he had taken almost half the money out of my account. He said,

Jaquan: I'm sorry, Tabby, I know! But I was trying to keep up with your lifestyle and keep you at the same time. I didn't want to lose you.

Tabby: But you didn't think I would eventually find out! What if we were still together and I found out? It would have been worse, Jaquan!

Jaquan: Do we have to talk about this right now? I just came to say thank you, Tabby, that's all.

Tabby: You know you're right; we're not even together anymore. Why are we even talking about things that happened and why we were together?

Jaquan: Because that's you. You bring it up, not me, Tabby.

Tabby: And you always have to have the last word Jaquan.

Jaquan: I do because I'm always right! You know what, Tabby? I still can't get out of the back of my mind the burning feeling that somebody has been trying to set me up. And to be honest, there could only be one real person mad at me, and that's Angela.

Tabby: Well, since you mentioned it, I would say be very careful with her.

Jaquan: I mean, we're cool right now, but I wonder.

Tabby: Well, if you have that feeling in your gut, I say go with it.

Jaquan looked at me deep into my eyes. He was bearing into my soul, and I knew it.

Jaquan: Tabby, you know something that you ain't telling me, are you?

Tabby: Why would you?

Jaquan: Stop playing games, Tabby; we're supposed to be better than that baby.

I told him about my conversation with Angela. Jaquan was furious. He called some of his buyers, who had confirmed that Angela was cutting into the flow of his business. Angela had even contacted some of them and offered to do business with them. Jaquan paced the floor back and forth, consumed in anger. Finally, he demanded I call Angela and put her on speakerphone.

Tabby: Hey Angela, I was checking on you. I heard that you were with Jaquan yesterday when the car caught fire. I thought y'all weren't speaking.

Angela: He started hitting me again, saying he wanted me to train his new booster. Girl, what he fails to realize is that I'm the ONLY bitch! Fuck Shaquita, fuck that new bitch. So yes, I called the store that day, and loss prevention was on high alert, looking for her ass! (laughs) I swear to God, that shit was so funny!

Tabby: So what you gonna do about Jaquan, Angela?

Angela: I don't know, we cool for now, plus I need the money.

Jaquan yelled, "hang up on that bitch."

Angela: Oh, hell no, Jaquan is there with you! You bitch!

Jaquan grabs the phone from me and says,

Jaquan: How 'bout this, Angela; don't call me, don't text my phone begging me to talk to you, nothing. Leave me the fuck alone! Go take care of them ugly-ass kids of yours. As a matter of fact, go kill yourself, girl!

Jaquan hung up the phone and sat down on my sofa. He looked up at me and said,

Jaquan: That's real fucked up what she did, Tabby. You can't trust nobody these days. Outside of you and Shaquita, I really ain't got no one.

Tabby: Right now, I feel you. I have a few people, but...

Jaquan: You got me, Tabby. You always got me. I promise.

We looked at each other, and the room went silent for several minutes. He said,

Jaquan: It looks to me that we both have to figure something out with our lives. Our lives are fucked up, Tabby.

He laughed, and so did I. There were no lies detected there. We both seemed to be walking through living hell; perhaps the trauma forever kept us bound.

Jaquan: So how long you gonna be going through this shit with your ex?

Tabby: Who knows; it could be a few months, or it could go on for almost a year.

Jaquan: That's really fucked up. I know you can't afford to stay in this suite forever, either. How much longer you got there?

I didn't want to be vulnerable and tell this man my business. But Jaquan knew me too well for me to lie to him.

Tabby: A few more weeks. I have a few more weeks to figure something out before my money dwindles, and I need to downgrade seriously.

Jaquan: That ain't your style; you the shit, and you know it. Won't you pick up a corporate contract gig or something? You're smart enough.

Tabby: I thought about it, but I need something quick.

Jaquan: You'll figure it out, ain't that what you always tell me!

Tabby: Yea, you're right. Things always seem to have a way of working themselves out.

Jaquan: Most definitely. As a matter of fact, I may have a solution that could benefit both of us, hell, all of us.

Tabby: All of us.

Jaquan: Just hear me out, Tabby. You just told me this court shit could go on for a while, right? Well, I was thinking, since you gotta downgrade your living, why don't you come and stay with me and Shaquita?

Tabby: Nigga what! Oh, hell no.

Jaquan: Tabby! For real, think about it. That way, you can save money cause she lives in section 8, so she don't have to pay rent. Her ugly ass sister just moved out of the extra bedroom down the hall. It's completely empty. You can bring your bed and whatever else to make you feel comfortable.

Tabby: You cannot be serious, Jaquan. Move in with you and your "friend." Yea, that's another thing Angela told me about; how friendly the two of you are.

Jaquan: Yea, we're fucking, so what? You not jealous, are you? She's just somebody I fuck. You should know that.

Tabby: Jaquan, I don't give a fuck who you're giving it to. (I lied) but don't you think that the whole situation would be awkward? How will Shaquita feel about this?

Jaquan: Shaquita is a good person; that's why I like her. Plus, she'll do anything I ask her to. This is about you, Tabby. I can't see you falling off if there is something in my power to do to help.

Tabby: I know, but this is doing a lot, Jaquan.

Jaquan: Yea, it ain't the best situation, but as long as we all respect each other, it should be ok. Hell, we can even have a threesome! She can play with her toy while she watches me hit it from behind. (He laughs) I'm just joking

Tabby: Oh, that shit would never go down.

Jaquan: I told you I was playin', girl. Chill out! But I was serious about the offer, Tabby. Think about it and let me know.

Tabby: Ok, Jaquan, give me a few days to think it over

Jaquan left my suite, and I began springing into action, trying to find alternatives to his offer. Vincent had announced that Hope was expecting, and they were already planning to decorate their extra bedroom. Antonio's parents, sister, and her four kids had moved in with Vanessa. Samantha was still out of town, and my pride STILL wouldn't let me reach out to Tara. I followed up with Yvette on the court proceedings, who informed me we would be looking at at least six more months to get a court date. I felt helpless and alone. I had no one but the one person I didn't want to rely on. I had no other options. Finally, I called Jaquan and told him I would take him up on his offer.

Jaquan had talked to Shaquita, who seemed to be ok with it. He filled me with promises of a short-term ceasefire between us. We all even sat down to figure out how to map out a strategy for Jaquan to get another car quickly, and they promised when I moved in, it would be like I wasn't even there. So, like a sheep headed for the slaughter, I moved in with Jaquan and Shaquita and began what turned out to be a complicated situation. One that was more than Poly; it was toxic and destructive. Love's Journey had started to meet up with Karma, and the lessons I learned from that decision changed the course of my life forever. From love's journey to love's lesson to a situation that was just flat-out complicated, no one would really understand it unless you were there. One so complicated that there would be too many books to tell their tales.

6

ALMOST POLY

Poly.... What is it? It's an old term becoming new in western culture. But poly has many meanings. The term itself means many; an indefinite number other than one. In relationships, polyamorous people are described as being in loving, intentional, and intimate relationships with multiple people at the same time. And then there is polygamy, which is the same dynamic but involves married folks. I'm taking you on a journey, and I need you to follow me with this; in the dynamic of love's lesson, Jaquan had an indefinite number of ladies other than one. Although his actions were always intentional with us, the love and intimacy were never there, just manipulation. So, Me and Shaquita lived there, and then there was Angela and the one-offs. It still blows my mind how I ended up living with my ex and his new-old situation. Our dynamic for those who knew us wondered, "what were they anyway." Were we poly? No, almost, I guess.

Jaquan walked in and looked at Shaquita, and scoffed. Shaquita looked up at Jaquan, evil-eyed. Angela walked in behind him, smiling as she helped him bring in all his latest toys. He said,

Jaquan: Tabby! Come, see what I bought! We 'bout to go out tonight; I'm about to be FRESH! Look at you looking all sexy in them leggings, girl.

Angela and Shaquita looked at him, and I could feel the hate for me coming from them. I smiled and laughed to myself, and Jaquan took his time showing me his outfits, shoes, hats, and watches. He intentionally joked and flirted with me in front of them, and I could feel their jealousy rising. I entertained him for a few minutes and decided to go to my room. I wanted no part of the shit that was taking place. Jaquan left his bags in the living room, and before he left the house again, he said to Shaquita,

Jaquan: Bitch, what are you crying for NOW! Always crying, I swear! That's why I call you Big Baby. I'm about to make some money right now. So why are you stressing about MY MONEY? I'll make that overnight cause I'm THAT NIGGA! Man, I'm outta here.

Jaquan left the house with Shaquita in shambles. Shaquita stomped up the stairs and down the hall to her room. I opened the door to see a crying Shaquita tearing her room apart. I ran down the hall and asked,

Tabby: Girl, what are you doing? Stop it!

Shaquita: (sobs) I swear I'm tired of this, Tabby...what did I do to deserve this? I don't understand. I want him out of this room, fuck that! I'm putting all his shit in the basement.

Shaquita continues to tear her room apart. She takes down all the pictures and takes his clothes and belongings out of the closet. She cries as she disconnects his gaming system and the television. I watched Shaquita, true to her word, remove all of his things out of her room. Some things went into the basement, and others in the living room. I looked around her bare bedroom. Outside of the bed and the TV stand, there was nothing left. She truly had nothing of her own. What a sad state of life to be in. Shaquita, however, seemed to be content. She sat on her bed, got on her phone, and began to play online games. Shaquita lit a cigarette, and tears rolled down her face as she played the game. She said,

Shaquita: Jaquan ruins everything. Thanksgiving is next week, and we have no car....no furniture...we were supposed to have some people over...(sobs)

Tabby: Don't worry about it, Shaquita. It will work itself out, I promise. Furniture is a small thing. As a matter of fact, I have some furniture in storage you can have. It's very nice and matches that big area rug Jaquan bought for the living room. So, girl, don't worry; the universe always has your back.

Shaquita gave a half smile. She thanked me for the offer and asked if I had any weed. I went to my room and grabbed my stash, and we rolled up and smoked while Shaquita released the stresses of her life known as Jaquan. That man was once my love's journey. Now he served as my love's lesson. I sat and listened as she talked about all she had put up with over the years of him being in and out of her life. Jaquan had been around since Mickey was a baby. Mickey, now 6, had grown attached to him being around and looked at him as a father. Mickey's father left town as soon as he found out Shaquita was pregnant. In his new town, he found a new job, a new boo, and became a father to a new child. That left Shaquita to do only what she knew and was raised to do, be a section 8 Momma. But, according to Shaquita, there was a time when she had a good job.

Shaquita: I was making 14 dollars an hour when I met Jaquan. We met on Tinder and hooked up that night. I was living with my mom then, so he talked me into getting an apartment and promised to help with the bills. He never did, and he cheated on me in MY APARTMENT!

Tabby: Bitch, what! Wait, hold on...

Shaquita: Yea, Tabby. And he got me fired.

Tabby: Hold up.

Shaquita: Yea... Jaquan is selfish, and he don't care about nobody but himself. Like I said, I had a good job. I was answering emails for customers, and I was really happy. My auntie went out of town and asked me to watch her dogs, Bo and Joey. Well, Joey really liked Jaquan, but Bo didn't. So, I kept them in the cage while I was at work. A few days in, Jaquan called me to tell me Bo got out and ran away. I panicked, but he told me not to worry. He would find him. I agreed to stay at work, but I was still worried. So about 30 minutes later, I decided to leave. When I got to the house and opened the door, I saw Jaquan jump up from on top of some white girl pulling his pants up, saying, "we ain't do nothing." I was devastated.

Tabby: Oh, HELL NO! he fucked her in your HOUSE!

Shaquita: He said he didn't. But I was so distraught at the time that I started looking for Bo. I couldn't find him. I started crying, and after about an hr. I headed back to the house. Jaquan was still there with the white girl and had changed his clothes. He and the girl left, and he didn't come back for hours. He acted like nothing had happened, played the game, and went to sleep.

Tabby: Damn, girl. And you didn't mention it again? So, did you get fired for leaving work?

Shaquita: No. I got fired two weeks later when he and the white girl showed up at my job. That white girl has a name, by the way. It's Shanna.

Tabby: Showed up at your job? Girl, what?

Shaquita: Yea, they both showed up at my job unannounced. I had already been to work for a couple of hours. I had my headphones on, and I was answering emails. I had just gotten paid the day before and had my hair and nails done because I also had the day off. I was in a really good mood. I was working alone until I noticed people looking out the window. I wondered what was going on, so I got up and went to the window with the rest of my teammates. I looked out the window and saw Jaquan and Shanna out there arguing. He was all in her face saying, "fuck you, bitch" and she started hitting him. Jaquan pushed her away from him, and she fell to the ground. I walked away from the window and tried to leave the office area secretly while they watched on. I sure didn't want them to know that I KNEW THEM! But some of the girls knew already. They had seen Jaquan drop me off a few times, and I saw one of my coworkers look over at me. Then, out of the blue, I heard Shanna and Jaquan from the window!

Shanna: HELLLLPPPP. SOMEBODY HELP ME! JAQUAN, GET AWAY FROM ME!

Jaquan: BITCH, GET OFF THE GROUND! AIN'T NOBODY DO NOTHING TO YOU, DUMB BITCH!

Shanna: HELLLLLPPPP! SHAQUITA! SHAQQQUUUUIIITTTTAAAAA TURRRNNNNEEERRR! SHAQUITA TURNER HELP ME PLEASE!!!

Shaquita: Everybody turned and looked at me. I grabbed my purse and walked out of the office and into the parking lot. Jaquan was still standing in the same spot telling her to get up, and she was still screaming my name on the ground with one hand over her face like he was gonna attack her. She looked over at me and started screaming about how much of a piece of shit Jaquan was. I got closer to her. Close enough to help her up off the ground. I was in tears. I asked her to please leave my job. She refused to go with Jaquan. She yelled,

Shanna: He's gonna beat me up if I leave with him.

Jaquan: Bitch, SHUT UP! You know I ain't never put my hands on you! C'mon get in the truck.

Shanna: No! fuck you!

Jaquan: Girl, we need to go before the police get here; if you don't get your ass in this truck.

Shanna: NO! Shaquita, please.... Can you take me home? I can't go with him, PLEASE!

Shaquita: I thought about it for a second. Tears streamed down my eyes. I knew the police were well on their way, and I didn't want to add anything to the situation; Jaquan had a warrant. Jaquan jumped in his truck, told her she could stay if she wanted, and pulled off, leaving us in the parking lot. What choice did I have? I dropped Shanna off and went home. Jaquan was there already apologizing and promising never to come to my job again. I cried for the rest of the night. The next day as I was getting ready for work, my manager called me. She told me that I no longer had a job and that they would be mailing my last check and my belongings to my apartment. And since then, I haven't been able to find a job.

I took in the story Shaquita told me—thinking about how crazy it was. This was not the man that I knew and loved at all. Maybe I really didn't know him at all.

That evening Jaquan returned home from his return operation and set up the living room as his new resting place. He turned on the music and yelled at Shaquita to be ready to take the rental back in the morning. He then came upstairs and asked if they could use my car to return the rental. He told me he planned to get the money he needed for his car, and I was genuinely happy for him AND me. They could finally have their own transportation and stop using my c300. My poor baby had taken a beating she wasn't used to the last several months. Shaquita came out of her room, and Jaquan openly flirted with me. He then got in the shower, dressed, and headed out for the night. When he returned in the wee hours of the morning, I could hear him downstairs playing his gaming system with the volume up really loud. I also heard Shaquita sobbing lightly in her bedroom. I looked around my room at the vision boards on my wall. I knew that somehow, I had to get out of there, and that pleasant thought drifted me off into a deep sleep.

The next morning, true to fashion, Jaquan and Shaquita took back the rental and returned to the house, still not speaking to one another. Shaquita retreated to her room, and Jaquan took my car to make his daily runs. I went back to my room to make plans to get my furniture here. I called a discount mover who was available in two days. "Just in time for Thanksgiving," I thought. Maybe there would be a weird bright side to the holiday. I knew from time's past that this little spat between Jaquan and Shaquita would be temporary. He'd eventually weasel his way back into her bedroom, and all would be well again. I recalled a time when we first broke up after I had the pleasure of meeting Shaquita. They had gotten into a fight, and she started crying. He said,

Jaquan: Big Baby, why are you crying? There's food in the fridge; you just got some dick. What is it?

She looked at me like she wanted to say something, and he ushered me out of the house. He took her on a long car ride where they smoked and talked, and everything was well again. That was the cycle of their relationship.

Later that night, Jaquan returned and began his routine of turning on his gaming system to wind down for the day. I was a little thirsty, so I went to the kitchen to get something to drink. On my way back upstairs, Jaquan called to me softly. He sounded like the man at the beginning of love's journey. The one who loved me, who handled me with care. He asked me to join him on the couch. He said,

Jaquan: Thanksgiving is coming up, and I want peace. I remember when things were peaceful when you were my peace.

Tabby: Jaquan, so much has happened...

Jaquan: I know; I was thinking back.

Tabby: Yea, to be honest, I don't want to have you two fighting during the holidays.

Jaquan: I tried to text her, but she ignored me. It's all good, though; I can't worry about that, Tabby. I'm gonna look at some furniture tomorrow. I swear I ain't sleeping on this shit down here one more night fuck that.

Tabby: Well, you don't have to worry about that, Jaquan. I'm gonna go ahead and give Shaquita the furniture that's in storage. So don't worry, we'll have furniture for the holidays.

Jaquan: See, you shouldn't have to do that, Tabby. That bitch needs to get off her ass and contribute to this household. Do you know she ain't even buy this trash-ass furniture in here? She got it from the thrift store. I swear everything she has is borrowed or given to her. She's so low budget, Tabby, not like you. You the shit, and you know it.

That was one of the things he loved to say to me when we were together. I had to admit feelings were stirring up a bit, and I had to remember where I was and who I was. I couldn't let him get to me. Jaquan said,

Jaquan: I also found a way to get a new car, Tabby.

Tabby: Jaquan, I'm so proud of you! I know you always have a backup plan!

Jaquan: Yea, that's me. But anyway, one of my buyers got tired of me not being able to fulfill all their orders because of my transportation issues, and you know shit has been slow for a few months too. So, they agreed to front me most of the money for a truck I saw. I just need a couple more thousand dollars, and I got it. Tabby, I don't wanna have to keep waiting to get a truck, and you know how business has been since I started fucking with Angela again. Slow as fuck.

Tabby: Well, you know SHE'S the reason your business is slow, Jaquan.

Jaquan: Do we have to talk about that now, Tabby please, be my peace, ok?

Tabby: You're right. I shouldn't have brought it up.

Jaquan: Tabby, I need you. Can you give me $3000 for this truck? I know you don't want me to keep riding around in your Mercedes, girl. This will benefit both of us.

I thought about it for a Moment. It would be beneficial. Shaquita could stop using my car for errands which would give her a rest. Jaquan could do his thing in his own car, and it would free me up to formulate my exit. I agreed.

Jaquan: Tabby, you are the bomb! You always come through for me when I need you. Nobody has ever been there for me like that. All you need to do is come with me to the dealership, and we can put the truck in your name.

Tabby: Wait, what?

Jaquan: Yea, you know my license is suspended, girl.

Tabby: I know, but why don't you ask Shaquita? She has a clean license.

Jaquan: To be honest, although my last truck was in her name, I don't want her to have access to it like that. Her behavior has been on and off, and it's no telling what she would do with the car in her name. Shaquita's changed. A lot. It's like she's tryna be somebody she's not. She thinks she is on the same level as you and feels I should give her the same respect I gave you. You were my girlfriend; Shaquita was always a jump off. Did I tell you I met her on Tinder?

I was a little surprised because, in Shaquita's mind, she had been his girlfriend at one time. That was always her way of distinguishing herself from Angela. According to her, she and I were ex-girlfriends, while Angela was just his pet. I said,

Tabby: Yea, she shared a little of how y'all met. But I'm not touching that, Sir.

We laughed. I also agreed to put the truck in my name to keep the peace. Once again, I became his peace, and in a sick twisted way, I felt good on the inside. We smiled and smoked a little, and I watched him play the game for a little while. We had a conversation and even watched a movie. Once I got tired, I headed up the stairs to bed. At the end of the hallway, I could hear Shaquita talking on the phone to what appeared to be... ANGELA!! I couldn't believe it. I knew it was Angela because I heard Shaquita say her name! I tiptoed down the hall and put my ear to the door. Shaquita had the phone on low speaker volume.

Shaquita: Angela, it's just not fair. What did I do to deserve this?

Angela: Girl, fuck him AND her! That bitch is giving y'all furniture and buying his TRUCK! Oh, you can't trust her! I SWEAR TO GOD! Next thing you know, that bitch will be fucking that man down the hall in the bedroom you let her sleep in. I hate that bitch!

Shaquita: Oh, that bitch would NEVER! We ALL would be fightin' in here!

Why was I not surprised? Shaquita had been watching the cameras from her room and listening to our conversation. This was ridiculous; was she that insecure? I shook my head, tiptoed back into my room, closed the door, and fell asleep. Several hours later, I could hear Jaquan coming up the steps and heading to Shaquita's room down the hall. Apparently, they had made peace with the situation already. Perhaps Shaquita thought it would benefit her to allow Jaquan back in her bedroom to fuck him. Maybe, she was that insecure. It also made me wonder if Jaquan was playing me yet again.

The day before Thanksgiving, the movers delivered the living room furniture to Shaquita's house early morning. I got up and got ready to head to the dealership with Jaquan. Everyone was in good spirits. Shaquita was buzzing around the house, prepping the food for the dinner she was cooking. She was all smiles in her mini dress that clung to her body. Shaquita was not thick; she was obese. But she seemed to act as if it didn't bother her that she was unattractive and overweight. She walked around her section 8 palace like she was the queen of it. Apparently, Jaquan's dick did her some good. Speaking of dick, I figured Shaquita shouldn't be the only one getting some. I made a mental note to hit up an oldie but goodie and get some real soon. I texted Ahmed to wish him a happy holiday. He responded,

> Ahmed: T Baby! How are you? Happy Thanksgiving! You cooking, T?

> Tabby: Nah, you know my situation here, go figure, but she is.

> Ahmed: Well, won't you come over tomorrow… I'm cooking.

> Tabby: I could stop by for a plate. But because she's cooking, it's only right to hang out here for a bit.

> Ahmed: T Baby! I'm tryna see you. Can you come over tonight? I'm gonna be getting the food started tonight, and the boys will be doing what boys do, lol. I'm making a lobster casserole that's gonna be FIRE!

> Tabby: Oh, you FEEDING ME!

> Ahmed: Oh, ima feed you, then fuck you real good! (eggplant emoji, devil emoji)

I smiled and texted back.

> Tabby: I think I can swing that. I got some running around to do, and I'll hit you up when I'm done. (heart face emoji)

Ahmed: Coo! Bring some shells with you! I got some tequila and some fireweed. It's called RUNTS! (strong arm emoji, 100 emoji)

I looked up to see Jaquan staring at me with an impatient look. He said,

Jaquan: Can we get going? Damn, I'm tryna get this car, Tabby. I know you are all on your phone with that nigga, but I got stuff to do too. Big Baby! We'll be back, girl!

I rolled my eyes at Jaquan. Shaquita gave a half smile and went back to the kitchen to do whatever she was doing. Then, Jaquan and I headed to the dealership to pick up his new baby, the chocolate-colored Cadillac Escalade.

Jaquan got behind the wheel of his new vehicle. He put on his sunglasses and smiled. He talked to me about everything he was going to do to the car, all the plans he made for his new ride. I listened and nodded. Jaquan sounded like a prisoner with promises of being a better man. This Escalade was his freedom, and now I'm sure he would act accordingly. We both departed ways, and I headed to Bath and Body Works and a few other places in preparation for my evening ahead. I got home and greeted Shaquita, still buzzing around, to let her know I wouldn't be home that night. She smiled and encouraged me to "get my freak on." She said that Jaquan had planned on coming back early this evening, and they were gonna catch up on a few episodes of "A love like Ours."

Shaquita: The results of the pregnancy test will be back

Tabby: Pregnancy test? Who's taking a test? One of Pastor Doug's daughters? I know they've been showcasing his family on that show. Which one? The third child? I could see that heffa getting knocked up.

Shaquita: (laughs) no, silly! Keisha is taking a pregnancy test. Although I do agree, daughter number 3 is off the hook!

Tabby: You have GOT to be kidding me! There is no WAY Keisha is pregnant. That's strictly for the cameras.

Shaquita: You think so? Umm... I don't know, Tabby.

Tabby: I don't know why y'all like that show anyway; it's a bunch of bullshit.

Shaquita: Actually, Keisha is pretty cool. I understand her.

Shaquita gave me a cool look. I looked right back at her. The unspoken had come to the surface without her even coming clean about it. This bitch genuinely DID have an issue with me. Between the conversation she had last night with Angela and her so-called love for Keisha, this bitch seemed to be getting bolder and bolder. I said,

Tabby: Yea, apparently, the two of you have a lot in common: my exes.

I smiled and retired to my room to get ready for the evening. I wanted to drown out the sound of Shaquita, but she did that for me by turning on her favorite artist, "Jaquees," in the living room. I thought about that reality show. I had only gotten four episodes in. I turned on the television and began episode five. I watched as Keisha took in every word of wisdom Pastor Doug put out there like it was the gospel. "You are such a saint and a blessing, Pastor Doug," "Pastor, you're so full of wisdom," it was sickening. Maybe because I couldn't stand the sound of her voice. And then there was James, who seemed annoyed most of the time about Keisha's wild antics. I know this whole reality show idea was Keisha's, not his. James was always a very private man in his dealings.

Having his whole life displayed on National TV must have been exhausting. But I did not pity him. This was the life and the bitch that he chose. I got in the shower and dressed while I watched episode seven. Yep, that bitch was claiming she thought she was pregnant. Poor James. "No fuck him," I thought. I couldn't believe I was getting sucked into this. I thought about it for a minute. I knew my new followers would want my opinion on the outcome. So, why not watch it? I looked down at my phone. It was about that time. I packed my overnight back, grabbed the shells from my drawer, and headed out to have fun with Ahmed. "A love like Ours" could wait until I got back.

I got to Ahmed's, and the smell of the food was amazing! He greeted me at the door with a light snack he had put together. He fed me and asked,

Ahmed: You likey?

Tabby: Oooh, it's delicious! Give me more, daddy!

Ahmed: And ya know there's more where that came from.

Ahmed kissed me and gave me the biggest smile. I always liked that about him. He was young, playful, and energetic—the things I missed about my relationship with Jaquan. But Ahmed was more grounded and responsible at the same time. I liked being around him, but I knew what we had was simply a fling. Ahmed and I knew what it was, and he understood his assignment. Being a young single dad, he didn't seem to mind.

Ahmed: I got it all worked out tonight, T baby! The boys got the whole basement to themselves with everything they needed down there! So I'm gonna feed you a little lobster dip I made from the casserole, pour you a shot of tequila, and roll up! Oh yea, we gotta catch the next episode of "A Love Like Ours," that shit's DOPE, YO!

Not him too! Was everybody hooked on their celebrity status? Ahmed handed me a blunt and told me to light up. I inhaled and exhaled. He was right; this was some good shit. I could feel the effects of the weed from the first hit. I felt mellow and relaxed already. I rolled with the night and told him to pour me a shot. I sat down and got comfortable, and Ahmed laid out the spread, and we relaxed into the show. Between the effects of the weed and the tequila, I got through it. It was not that bad, if I was honest. And Keisha surprised everyone with a positive pregnancy test.

Keisha: Oh, James! We're gonna be parents again, can you believe it? I'm too old for all this. (cries)

James: C'mon, babe. I love you, and this is a blessing from God. Ain't that right, Pastor Doug?

Pastor Doug: A blessing of the Lord, it is James.

Pastor Doug looks at Keisha with endearment and draws her in for a hug. He locks her in an extra-long embrace that's common for Pastor Doug. He places both hands on the side of her face and says,

Pastor Doug: My beautiful daughter. Why are you so worried about how old you are? You're only forty-one, and God's favored. Do you not remember that Sarah was ninety when she first conceived? Oh, glory! The word I gave James years ago is coming back to me! James truly has the spirit of Abraham!

James: Hallelujah! Pastor, you are truly a prophet of God. I forgot about that word.

Pastor Doug: You've been through a lot, son. But never forget, You had to get rid of that wicked Hagar and her children to TRULY have the promises of God. C'mon SOMEBODY!

He draws her in for another embrace, and Keisha cries a little, then wipes her eyes.

Keisha: Oh, Pastor! You always know exactly what to say. James, everything we've been through is gonna be so worth it. This baby is truly a gift from God. I mean this from the bottom of my heart when I say this baby...

The camera zooms in on Keisha as she embraces her belly and strokes it like she's about seven months pregnant. The camera then zooms in on Keisha's face as she says...

Keisha: There will truly never be "A Love Like Ours."

I rolled my eyes. She was so dramatic, I swear. And the shade of it all! The whole Abraham and Hagar dig was a low blow! I couldn't believe they put that out there! Any of Pastor Doug's congregants would know that he used to be married to me. Especially since our breakup and my getting "put out" of the church was announced on national television years ago. The funny thing is I didn't even know I wasn't allowed back until I saw the broadcast; go figure. This trio was trying to destroy everything I had, and I was getting tired of that shit. But there was nothing I could do until the new court date. Until then, I would wait this out and endure. "When am I gonna finally be happy?" I thought to myself. Frozen bank accounts and living with my ex was not a good look. The show ended with a prayer from Pastor Doug, and I took another shot in celebration. Ahmed rubbed my shoulders, and I relaxed and forgot what I blamed for my unhappiness. Ahmed said,

Ahmed: T Baby, you so tense, let me give you a massage and rub your booty.

Tabby: (laughs) boy, you crazy!

And just like that, Ahmed took my mind off "a love like ours," and we retired to the bedroom for my massage.

I lay on my stomach across Ahmed's bed. Ahmed smacked my ass playfully, and I giggled. He was such a fun lover. Ahmed turned on his trap music and grabbed the baby oil. It was time, and between the weed and the tequila, I was ready to forget about all my life's troubles. Ahmed straddled me and massaged my shoulders and neck. It felt so good. He gave my shoulders deep intentional rubs, and I moaned a little. I needed this. Ahmed's hands moved to my back, and I wiggled and giggled as he reached the edges. I was ticklish there. He laughed with me and gave my back more tickles. I wiggled some more and begged him to stop. He did, and Ahmed took the bottle of baby oil and poured a little on my back. He rubbed the baby oil on my skin in slow, methodical strokes. Boo Boo Kitty's juices started to peek from her opening. She was so nasty. Ahmed edged back and dripped baby oil onto my booty. "My favorite part right here," he said. Ahmed rubbed the baby oil into my behind and started smacking my cheeks lightly. He rubbed my bottom, took his hands, and made them clap. He rubbed and massaged me for a little while and then pulled my body to the edge of the bed. Ahmed commanded that I get on all fours from behind. If he wanted to get right to it, I was game. Then, Ahmed did something that surprised me. Ahmed spread my cheeks and began to lick.

At first, I felt squeamish. I couldn't get past the fact that he was eating my ass. Then I decided to focus as he licked. Ahmed had my cheeks spread wide. His tongue danced in and out of my ass, and my clit began to flicker. Ahmed gave her the attention she needed with his fingers as he licked my ass in tandem. He could feel kitty's wetness. Ahmed lifted my ass and let his tongue taste my clit. I moaned loudly. He flipped me over on the edge of the bed, and his hands spread my lips wide. Ahmed started licking me slowly, and my juices began to mount. I moved my hips in tandem with his tongue. He was fucking my pussy so good. I told him so. As he held my lips widely and licked, I played with my nipples. I stroked my twins as he licked and sucked, and my juices began to sprout from Boo Boo Kitty. I moved my hips faster. Ahmed took one finger and circled my wet anus as he licked my pussy. My body went crazy. Ahmed placed his finger in my ass as he licked. I took my hands and held my lips open. I moved my hips, and he licked and fucked my ass. I screamed, "oh god, yes," and I came.

Ahmed got up from his knees and pulled me closer to the edge of the bed. He entered me, and I gasped. Ahmed stroked me long and deep. He grabbed my hips and stroked. My juices made a music symphony as he pounded in Boo Boo Kitty. He said,

Ahmed: Your pussy is so wet, T. Damn, this feels so good.

Tabby: Ooh baby, don't stop fucking me yes

Ahmed: This some good ass pussy, baby; let's fuck all night.

Tabby: Ooh, yes, baby, give it to me, don't stop.

Ahmed continued to stroke my pussy with his shaft. My hips matched his energy. I moved in circles, and my wetness poured all over his dick. Ahmed stroked faster. I moaned. He went deeper inside me, and I said, "CUM FOR ME, BABY"! Deeper and faster, harder and harder, until finally, I let him cum inside me.

Ahmed collapsed on top of me for a few minutes. We laid there and talked and laughed. We finally settled in, smoked another blunt, and cuddled ourselves to sleep watching Netflix. That was the perfect way to start the holiday. Maybe going back to that temporary place I called home wouldn't be so bad after all. But I decided to take my time getting there. Being with Ahmed at that moment made me happy, and I wasn't in any rush to go back to unhappiness. I closed my eyes, dozed off to sleep, and thought about happy thoughts.

The following day, I woke up to breakfast in bed. This man loved cooking, and I was the beneficiary of it. I looked over to a chicken omelet with broccoli and cheese, fresh fruit, coffee, and his award-winning smile. If I wasn't in such a fucked up position, he might make a good man for me. But another boyfriend was not on my radar, especially since I hadn't found a way to escape the entanglement with my ex. Plus, Ahmed didn't seem like the settling-down type. He liked to hit me up every now and again to play, and I was okay with that. So I enjoyed the rest of the morning at his house, gathered my things, and headed home.

When I returned to Shaquita's late that morning, the house was quiet. Mickey was in her room watching YouTube and Shaquita was in the kitchen basting the turkey and prepping the side dishes. I said good morning, and she gave me a half smile. Jaquan entered the kitchen fully dressed and ready to head out. He said,

Jaquan: Tabby! Where you been, girl? We were supposed to watch our show last night.

Tabby: Our show? Oh, you got jokes, I see.

Jaquan: (laughs) you know I'm fucking with you. I'll be back, y'all. I gotta see my son today. Tabby, are you making the potatoes? You know how I loved those last year.

Jaquan winks at me and heads out of the house. I looked confused and asked Shaquita what time the company was coming over. I was going to try to make other plans and get out of there. Shaquita tells me between her sobs that she doesn't know, and she doesn't know what she did to Jaquan to make him act like this. Some holiday this was turning out to be, I thought. I retired to my room and sent out my holiday texts while waiting for the food to be done. When Shaquita was finished, there was still no sight of Jaquan. Shaquita fixed herself a big plate, went to her room, and closed the door. I made Mickey a plate and sent her to her room as well. Since I wasn't hungry, I decided I would eat later.

There was nothing to be thankful for in this house. Around 9 pm, Jaquan returned to the house with two of his buddies. He called me downstairs and asked me to fix plates for him and his boys. As I fixed the plates, he flirted with me. He talked about our last holidays together and how different everything was. I looked at him, and he looked into my eyes. I could see a little bit of something in there; I always knew how he was feeling. And right now, I believe it was a little regret. Jaquan looked away and then started talking to his boys. I fixed their plates and made sure they were comfortable. Jaquan asked me to stay downstairs for a while with him, so I did. Whatever was going on with him and Shaquita, it was apparent that they didn't want to be around each other today. After a few hours, Jaquan got himself together, changed his clothes, and packed up his boys to go out for the holiday. Before he left, he said to me,

Jaquan: You know she's jealous of you, right?

Tabby: Huh?

Jaquan: Shaquita...she's so jealous of who you were to me, it drives her crazy.

Tabby: And you know what, Jaquan, you don't make it any better, do you?

Jaquan: I know (laughs). That girl is in love with me and will do anything for me. She has never been anything more than a jump-off.

Tabby: That's so disrespectful, Jaquan. She may not be your woman now, but I'm sure when she was, things were different.

Jaquan: Who told you that she was my woman EVER? Look at her; I can't take her nowhere in public. Look at you, Tabby. Even at your worst, you outshine that bitch without even trying. And for that, she's jealous cause she knows it.

Jaquan looks at the camera and says,

Jaquan: Now eavesdrop on that (laughs)

Jaquan kissed my forehead and walked out of the house. I stood in shock for a Moment for a couple of reasons:

1. I was trying to digest the fact that everything was coming out in the open; the woman who asked me to move in was jealous of me.

2. Jaquan's forehead kiss.

3. I knew Shaquita was watching through the cameras.

I knew from experience that this would not turn out well, and she and Jaquan would be into it again. I didn't want to be here to experience it, but I also couldn't keep running to a hotel every time shit got hot here in the hood. I kept my big girl panties on, went to my room, and retired for the night. The next few days were awkward. Shaquita and Jaquan were hardly speaking, Jaquan was flirting with me, and Shaquita was in her room crying. Maybe Jaquan was right; she was a big baby. After about a week, they went for a ride in the truck, and all seemed to be well again. I swear I couldn't wait to get the hell out of here. I texted my attorney,

> Tabby: Hey, Yvonne, I'm going INSANE over here. Any updates?

> Yvonne: Good morning, Tabby. No updates yet. We should know before January about a new court date. Hang in there, Tabby, and stay positive.

> Tabby: January??

That was way too long just to get info on a court date! How was I supposed to stay positive in this emotional circus that surrounded me? These two together were worse than when they were apart. A giggling Shaquita and Jaquan interrupted my thoughts.

Jaquan: Tabby, I got an announcement to make. Thanksgiving was shitty here, and we were not about to do that again with another holiday. I decided that I was gonna make up for that at Christmas. I want all of us to be together as a family for Christmas, Angela included. I'm buying all my girls Christmas gifts.

Shaquita giggled, and I looked at both of them like they were insane. Jaquan was making up for Christmas by having us all together in one place. What the fuck? When I say all, I mean everyone; me, Shaquita, Angela, and all our children. Hell, he even encouraged me to invite Vincent and Vanessa. There was no way in hell I was doing that. In my mind, I started making other plans for Christmas because this situation that Jaquan was trying to create was doomed to fail.

As the weeks went by, Jaquan became serious about the situation. He had Angela in the stores hot and heavy, and in the evenings, he was bringing items into the house for Christmas. He bought a tree, decorations, and plenty of gifts. I hadn't seen him like this since we were together. All through December, the house was filled with Christmas spirit. And when Christmas Eve came, Jaquan got his wish; we were all there. The living room was alive with the sound of children playing and running around. Angela had three kids, and Mickey was excited to have someone to play with for a change. Shaquita was in her room wrapping gifts. She indicated she would be wrapping all night, so I offered to help. Shaquita declined because some of my gifts were mixed in with the others, and Jaquan didn't want me to see them. I had no choice but to join everyone downstairs not to seem like I wasn't in the spirit. Angela's ugly ass was plopped on the floor by the sofa in front of Jaquan. MY SOFA, I thought. Jaquan popped in a movie, and about halfway through, I was done pretending. I said goodnight to everyone and retired to my room.

I woke up on Christmas Day with gratitude in my heart. Vincent called me from Arizona to wish me well.

Vincent: Merry Christmas, Mom! I have a gift for you, but to be honest, I didn't want to send it to that address. I hate that you think you have to live like that, Mom.

Tabby: Son, I'm ok. This will be over soon, and all my assets will be unfrozen.

Vincent: Mom, come to Arizona; you'd love it here. You can leave all that mess behind, and I'll make sure you're ok.

Tabby: Son, I appreciate you. I know you love me, but I'll be ok. I have to deal with this situation head-on. I can't run from it anymore.

Vincent: And what about Jaquan? Mom, that man is toxic, and you need to get away from him. He's a scammer, a thief. And you know the saying, there is no honor among thieves. A thief is one of the worst criminals because they have no moral code. Remember I told you that.

Tabby: Son Jaquan and I are not even together

Vincent: You're not, but you are. I swear I hate seeing you in this. But it's Christmas, and I didn't call for that. I love you, Mom, and I am just a flight away; remember that.

We hung up, and the tears in my eyes began to develop. He was right, and I knew it. I could not break away from Jaquan and this sickness as long as I lived with him and Shaquita. Perhaps I should take him up on his offer. And just as I was about to look up one-way flights, there was a knock on my bedroom door. It was Shaquita.

Shaquita entered my bedroom with tears in her eyes. I could hear the children downstairs playing and was excited to open their presents. Shaquita closed my door.

Tabby: Shaquita, what's the matter? Why are you crying? It's Christmas!

Shaquita: Jaquan fucked Angela last night downstairs!

Tabby: What! Impossible. The kids have been downstairs all night with them. Are you sure?

Shaquita: (sobs) yes, I'm sure.

Tabby: Holy shit, I forgot about the cameras; did you see them? That's pretty bold.

Shaquita: No, but I heard them.

Tabby: Ok, Shaquita, slow down. You actually didn't SEE them, so you really don't know for sure.

Shaquita: Tabby, I know what the fuck I heard. He fucked Angela in my dirty ass basement.

Tabby: Ewe. That's trifling if she allowed that

Shaquita: Well, that's the kind of bitch she is.

Tabby: Shaquita, start from the beginning, please.

Shaquita: Ok, so after you went to bed, I was still wrapping presents. After about an hour, Jaquan checked in on me to see how I was doing. He asked me how much longer, and I told him I had another hour. He said OK, and by then, when I looked through the cameras, the kids were on the couches sleeping, and the two of them were on the floor watching movies. About 15 minutes later, I heard noises. I thought maybe it was the TV, so I looked at the cameras. They were not in the living room or the kitchen. The noises went on for about 10 minutes, and then they stopped. I opened my bedroom door and headed down the hall. Jaquan darted into the bathroom, and I heard the sink running. Jaquan came out of the bathroom and headed to our bedroom without looking my way. He then wrapped himself in the purple and black blanket that he loves so much, the one that reminded him of Angela.

I was in complete shock. Did he REALLY fuck this girl in Shaquita's house? That was hella disrespectful. Not only that, the mystery about the purple and black blanket he loved so much had been solved.

Tabby: Shaquita, what are you gonna do?

Shaquita: (sobs) nothing...what can I do?

Tabby: Bitch if you don't put your big girl panties on and MAN UP! but not today, sweetie, it's Christmas.

Shaquita: Please don't say anything, Tabby. I'm just gonna finish the cooking, and then I'm going to my room for the rest of the day.

Shaquita exited my room and went downstairs to join everyone else. A few minutes later, there was another knock on my door. It was Jaquan. I opened the door in the holiday spirit and said,

Tabby: Merry Christmas, Jaquan.

Jaquan: Tabby, what's wrong with Shaquita?

Tabby: Is something wrong with her?

Jaquan: Yea, she down there crying like a big baby.

Tabby: Nothing's wrong that I know of, Jaquan.

Jaquan: Tabby, quit playing with me. I know that you know something is wrong. Please don't lie to me.

Tabby: Jaquan.

Jaquan: Tabby, what is it for real?

Tabby: I think she feels bad. She wasn't able to get Mickey presents herself, and it is weighing on her; that's all.

Jaquan: I don't know why that bitch would be mad about that...she never has money to buy that girl anything. I swear she better not ruin my holiday.

Jaquan walked out of the room and back downstairs. Shaquita was still crying, and he didn't know why. Jaquan decided to ignore her and let the kids open their gifts. There were plenty of mini trampolines, basketballs, dolls, coloring books, and such. The kids loved it! Jaquan gave Angela and me our gifts. Angela had a pair of Nike tennis shoes and a bottle of perfume. He gave me a new tablet and a Bath and Body Works in my favorite fragrance. Shaquita ended up with a small body wash sample from Walmart. She looked so disappointed, and Jaquan saw it. Immediately his mood changed. Jaquan showered and announced he was going to see his son. Angela went with him and left her kids at the house. That bitch used any opportunity to dump her kids off. Since they weren't my responsibility, and I didn't like that bitch, I went to my room and closed the door. Shaquita was stuck with not only Mickey but Angela's kids. That had to sting, considering Jaquan had just fucked Angela in her house earlier, according to her. Shaquita finished the food through tears and went to her room, leaving the kids downstairs alone.

A few hours later, Jaquan and Angela returned with Tiquan, his son, in tow. Tiquan saw me and ran and gave me the biggest hug in remembrance. Angela rolled her eyes in jealousy. Jaquan told Angela to get her kids together and have her sister pick her up. She was fuming. Jaquan set up the game in the living room, and he and Tiquan played the game and enjoyed the food that Shaquita had made. After spending time with Tiquan, Jaquan packed up his son and thanked ME for being the only person who made the holiday worthwhile. The sad thing is he said it in front of Shaquita. I felt terrible for her. Jaquan said to her, "Bitch, don't wait up" she laughed and left the house. Tears rolled down her face, and I embraced her in comfort. She said,

Shaquita: Why is he doing this to me? What did I do to deserve this?

Tabby: Shaquita, why are you basing your life on Jaquan? You have a beautiful daughter that needs your attention. You have your own place and could have a good life if you want. The new year is coming. You can change your circumstances if you want.

Shaquita: Tabby, we are not all like you. We all can't BE you. Tabby, I just realized something right before Christmas. And this is why this is affecting me this way. I am in love with Jaquan. I know it's ridiculous to think he will ever feel the same, but I have to be honest with myself. And that's why it hurts so much that he did this to me!

Poor Shaquita. I understood all too well what it was like to be in love with Jaquan. He was amazing when he was on point, but if he ever felt like you crossed him, he could be the most vindictive person hell-bent on proving a point. And whatever was going on between him and Shaquita; he was getting his point across. I didn't know what to say to Shaquita, so I said nothing. I got my stash from upstairs, and we sat and smoked while I let her talk about all her problems that stemmed around Jaquan. I even offered to watch that stupid show, "A Love Like Ours," with her, and she declined. She and Jaquan did that together, and she wanted to wait for him to come back to his senses. This girl was truly living in a fantasy world. Shaquita had dealt with Jaquan for almost six years, and he still never made an honest woman out of her. Shaquita said,

Shaquita: Before Jaquan came back, I was actually in a good relationship. His name was Todd, and he was older. He worked every day, came home, cooked for me, and rubbed my feet every night. Damn, I miss how he treated me.

Tabby: Well, what happened with that?

Shaquita: Towards the end of your relationship, I ran into Jaquan at the corner store, and I was with Todd. We had a pleasant conversation, and I thought nothing of it. When we got back to the house, Todd began questioning me about Jaquan. We had a fight, and Todd went to work and never came back. He told me he could see I was in love with Jaquan. I denied it and asked him to come back. He refused.

Tabby: Well damn. That man could see from one conversation that you had feelings for Jaquan.

Shaquita: Yea. And I begged him for weeks. We talked a lot and were getting to a better place, then BOOM, the two of you break up, and Jaquan hits my doorstep, needing a place to stay. When Jaquan first moved in, he was still sad about y'alls relationship. Then after a few weeks, he started making moves to be in my bedroom. I got weak and gave in. Well, the night I gave in was the same night Todd decided to come back to me. I forgot he still had a key, and when he entered the house and saw me and Jaquan in the bed together, he was done. That's why I say Jaquan ruins everything. I had a chance with a good man to have a good life. Tabby, if you don't get away now, you'll never leave. Jaquan has that kind of hold on people. Look at me; look at Angela. Jaquan ruins things.

I thought about everything Shaquita had exposed. I took it all in. The more I learned about Jaquan, the more I wanted to escape this situation. Finally, I could see this man's true colors. Jaquan was all about Jaquan.

Over the next few days, things remained the same in the household. New Year's Eve was approaching, and I had to make some solid plans. I was determined I would not bring in my New Year around Jaquan, Shaquita, or Angela. He may have had a hold on these broads, but I was my own woman. I looked on social media to see what events were taking place. As I began figuring out my plans, I didn't realize another storm was brewing. Shaquita burst through my bedroom door in anger with Angela on the phone. I sighed.

Shaquita: This nigga done lost his mind. Are you serious?

Angela: Yes, girl, he just called me.

Tabby: What's going on?

Shaquita: Jaquan's truck is in the impound.

Tabby: The impound? That truck is in my name.

Angela: You better not help him either, that son of a bitch!

Tabby: Ok, Angela, slow down; what's happening here?

Angela: Yesterday, Jaquan came by and told me he needed some money and didn't have time to sell any gift cards or anything. He took the 70-inch flat-screen that he gave me and pawned it. Come to find out that he got a hotel room with one of these bitches here in Daytonia. He pawned MY TV to get a hotel with another bitch that I KNOW! I SWEAR TA GOD IMA LOSE IT!

Tabby: And how does this concern me outside of the fact that I have to get the car out of the impound?

Angela: Do NOT get that truck out of the impound! He's gonna give you all a lie and an excuse, and I'm tired of his shit!

Shaquita: Me too. Who is this other woman?

Angela gave Shaquita a name. Immediately Shaquita went to social media and looked her up. The two women went on and on about the new chick. Oh, this was definitely a poly situation. And I was exhausted by it. My phone dinged, and it was Jaquan.

Jaquan: I need your help.

Tabby: What is it?

Jaquan: My truck is in the impound, and I need you to get it out.

Tabby: The impound? What happened?

Jaquan: Why the fuck are you asking me what happened? What difference does it make?

I showed the ladies our conversation. I was irritated at the fact that he had an attitude toward me. The ladies then began to champion me to snap back at Jaquan. I did.

Tabby: The difference is you are asking me for MY HELP for a vehicle in MY NAME, so again I ask what happened.

Jaquan: Are you getting the truck out of the impound or not?

Tabby: With that attitude, definitely not.

I turned off my phone and got in the shower. I decided to spend the day away until the impound lot was closed. That would show him not to fuck with me. Jaquan could disrespect those other ladies, but I refused to allow him to address me that way. I got dressed and headed to the nail shop for a mani and pedi. That would kill a couple of hours, I thought. I then would stop at a couple of shops and take a long drive. I needed to think anyway.

At about six in the evening, I returned to the house to see a pissed-off Jaquan and his friend waiting on me.

Jaquan: Where the fuck you been? I been calling you!

Tabby: Jaquan, I had things of my own to do. And considering the sun doesn't rise and set around you like you think you do, I decided to put myself first.

Jaquan: I can tell by the way you look; new wig, new nails must be nice to be out having fun when my truck is in the impound.

Tabby: Jaquan, we'll get it tomorrow. I'm sorry I had things to do.

Jaquan: No, we getting my shit tonight. C'mon, let's go.

Tabby: Isn't the impound closed by now?

Jaquan: That's wishful thinking on your part. Let me get my truck Tabby, and I promise we ain't even gotta have words no more.

I conceded, and we got in my car and headed to the impound. I let Jaquan drive, and his boy sat in the back seat. Jaquan was pissed at me and began talking shit to me. And knowing the person I am, things took a turn for the worse quickly.

Jaquan: Bitch, you thought you was really slick, tryna stay away all day. Ima get my truck regardless. You know not to play with me, Tabby.

Tabby: You know what, Jaquan; I don't have to be slick, considering that truck is in my name.

Jaquan: So, you think you own me because that truck is in your name?

Tabby: Jaquan, I never cared to own you; I give no fucks about you.

Jaquan: You sure gave a fuck when you were questioning my whereabouts. Do you wanna know what I was doing? I was with a bitch. YES! And that's how the truck got impounded. DAMN!

Tabby: Again, you talking to the wrong female, Jaquan. I give no fucks about what you do and who you're with unless it affects MY livelihood!

Jaquan: (laughs) yea, right. You're a joke. Look at you. You are living with me and my trick. You ain't got shit goin' on for you, Tabby.

Tabby: Your whole life is a series of shit NOT going on. Look at you. You're pathetic. You need ME for YOUR livelihood.

Jaquan: Bitch, you need me; always have.

Tabby: Oh really? When I met you, I didn't need you.

Jaquan: Yea, you needed your ex-husband, who took very good care of you. And look at you now. Who's taking care of you now, Tabby? (laughs)

Tabby: Do you REALLY want the truth Jaquan? Cause I sure don't think you can handle it... The truth is that dating you was a serious downgrade for me. I was used to the finer things in life, and I settled with your young ass. I've been to Paris, Italy, Spain, hell, all over the world. Where the fuck have you been except the casino? Grow your young ass up, little boy!

My last remarks heated Jaquan. He sped up in the car and looked at me as he drove. I looked right back at him like, "I dare you to wreck my shit." Jaquan put on the brakes of my Mercedes and snatched my wig off of me, and threw it out of the car!

Tabby: Really, Jaquan?! That shows how much of a piece of shit you really are.

Jaquan: Fuck you, Tabby!

Tabby: The problem is you wish you still could

Jaquan: That's laughable. Don't nobody care about your tight wet pussy.

Tabby: And there it is. Yes, my tight wet pussy is a compliment.

Jaquan: You fucking old-ass cougar.

Tabby: Again, a compliment. Funny thing is you could never keep up with this old-ass cougar BITCH.

Jaquan: (laughs) Your mouth is real slick, right now.

Tabby: Just like you ain't to be fucked with, baby, I can give just as good as I get. Let's get this shit over with, shall we? We can argue this whole way to the impound, or you can shut the fuck up.

Jaquan: Yea, I got your bitch...you know what, ima shut the fuck up. Cause you the shit. (laughs). But Ima go back and get your wig cause bitch you look like a chia pet right now.

Tabby: That may be so, but I'm STILL the baddest bitch you ever fucked with, and I'm still THAT BITCH.

Jaquan busted a u-turn and headed back in the direction where he snatched my wig off. Luckily, it was still there. He got out and picked it up, shook it out, and handed it to me. I propped it back on my head as if it was never removed. Jaquan and I got to the impound, he got his keys, and we parted ways. I dialed Shaquita to tell her what happened. The phone didn't pick up. I knew Jaquan was already in her ear.

About 30 minutes later, as I headed back to the house, I received a phone call from Shaquita crying. She asked me to meet her up the street from her house. Jaquan had gotten pulled over on his way to the house. Since he had no license and a bench warrant, they were getting ready to take him to jail. Talk about karma. I agreed to meet her up the street so she could retrieve Jaquan's truck. When we arrived on the scene, the police were still there. I explained that the truck was in my name, and they handed me the keys. Jaquan was put in handcuffs and taken to the county jail.

Shaquita drove the truck to the house in tears, and I was a bit confused. Earlier, she and Angela were furious because he was with another woman; now, she was bawling her eyes out. Did she forget so quickly? All this was a bit much for me. Jaquan had done way too much in 24 hours. When I got back to the house, I went straight to my room. I would let Shaquita deal with all of this; I wanted no part of it. But another 30 minutes later, MY PHONE rang, and the number to the county jail appeared. No matter how much I didn't want to be involved, Jaquan was making sure I would be. I answered the phone, and Jaquan sounded so humble.

Jaquan: Hey, Tabby.

Tabby: Jaquan, are you ok?

Jaquan: Yea, I will be. I need to speak to Shaquita; I don't know her number by heart. I need her to get in touch with my cousin to post this bail for me.

I handed the phone to a crying Shaquita. She looked at me, puzzled.

Shaquita: Hello? Jaquan, oh my goodness, are you ok?

Jaquan: Yea, quit crying, girl. I need you to focus. I need you to call my cousin Link to post my bail.

Shaquita: Ok, I will. I miss you already. Why didn't you call my phone?

Jaquan: I couldn't remember your number; give it to me before I hang up.

Shaquita: I will. You need to be in contact with me only until you get out. I promise I will handle it for you. And baby, I'll make you cheeseburgers when you get out.

Shaquita gave Jaquan her number before she hung up. She handed me the phone, rolled her eyes, and went to her room to make phone calls. I heard her talking to Angela and then his cousin Link, who was supposed to get in touch with a bail bondsman. They seemed to have it handled, so I left Shaquita to her affairs. I knew that Jaquan would be spending the night in jail even if his bail was posted this evening. Shaquita spent the rest of the evening ignoring me, and I knew she blamed me for what happened. Well, my suspicions were confirmed when her phone rang several hours later.

Jaquan: Did you call Link?

Shaquita: Yea, he's getting the bail-bondsman

Jaquan: Ok. Cool. Yea, I want those cheeseburgers, girl.

Shaquita: Anything for you, Jaquan. Now I'm gonna be honest and tell you something.

Jaquan: What is it?

Shaquita: Don't you find it suspicious that you and Tabby get into it, and then you're arrested? I think she called the police on you. Jaquan, I want her to pack her shit and get out of my house.

Jaquan: That's a big hell no! You really think Tabby had something to do with that or would do that to me? You don't know her, Shaquita. That woman has never done anything to cause me harm.

Shaquita: Well, I don't believe it. I want her out. I can feel it in my gut. I don't wanna look at her here another day.

Jaquan: Well, if you put her out, then WE gonna have problems. She had nothing to do with it. I was already pulled over doing some shit, and you know this neighborhood.

Shaquita: Jaquan...

Jaquan: Shaquita drop it. The only thing you should be focused on is handling my business. Quit focusing on dumb shit. Can you do that, or not? Fuck it; I'll call Angela.

Jaquan hung up the phone. Ain't this some shit! This bitch thinks I called the police on him. And she wanted me out. What a sneaky snake. It made me wonder if this was their first conversation about my living arrangements. The writing on the wall was obvious; my time here was coming to an end. And with New Year's Eve right around the corner, my "new year, new me" was starting to kick in. I laid down to sleep to formulate a plan to make my exit shortly after the new year.

A few hours later, Shaquita awakened me. She opened my bedroom door and woke me out of my sleep.

Shaquita: Tabby, can I ask you a question?

Here we go, I thought. I was ready, though. It was overdue for her and I to have a heart-to-heart if she needed to. But in light of everything that had already gone down, I knew if she confronted me, things would not go well. It was, like I said, a new year new me. I looked at Shaquita as if to say, "tread lightly."

Tabby: Absolutely, Shaquita. Is there something on your mind that you want to share?

Shaquita: No, not at all. I just have a question about getting a bail bondsman. I called Link several times this evening, but he hasn't responded. I don't know what to do.

Tabby: Simply find another one.

Shaquita: How do I do that? Jaquan is gonna call, and I know he's gonna be pissed. He called Angela to handle things, and she was asleep! She just called me crying because he cussed her out.

At that moment, my phone rang. It was Jaquan from the county jail. I put the phone on speaker and answered.

Tabby: Hey, Jaquan,

Jaquan: Hey, Tabby.

Tabby: How you holding up?

Jaquan: I'm ok; it's jail, you know. Is Shaquita up?

Tabby: Yea, she's right here. I have you on speaker.

Shaquita tries to grab my phone; I look at her like, "bitch, back up." The phoenix in me was beginning to rise; I could feel it. She did as my eyes had instructed and stood down. Jaquan said,

Jaquan: Shaquita, have you talked to Link?

Shaquita: Umm, no not yet.

Jaquan: Why not?

Shaquita: Because he texted earlier and said he couldn't get free to get a bail bondsman. He was babysitting.

Jaquan: Well, did you go pick up the money?

Shaquita: Well, I called for that, but he's not answering.

Jaquan: So why didn't you just go over there? Did you try to find another bondsman?

Shaquita: No

Jaquan: Man, DAMN! Shaquita, what is you good for? I swear! Man, Tabby, are you still there?

Tabby: Jaquan, I'm here.

Jaquan: Can you please help me find a bondsman, PLEASE!

Tabby: I can do that, Jaquan.

Jaquan: Shaquita, are you still there?

Shaquita: Yes.

Jaquan: Well, you and Angela got work to do to get this bail money. As a matter of fact, y'all thought y'all was slick earlier. You took Angela's sister's car to Daytonia, picked up Angela, and took her to the stores on some revenge shit. Who y'all think y'all are, Bonnie and Clyde? (laughs evil) So, get some sleep. Get her sister's car again, and you and Angela get them returns popping! Fuck Link!

The prison intercom message broke in and said, " YOU HAVE ONE MINUTE LEFT."

Jaquan: Shaquita, I'll call you in the morning.

Tabby: I'll get the bondsman info and give it the Shaquita.

Jaquan: Nah, give it to my boy. He'll help them handle it.

Then the phone went dead. Shaquita left my room in silence and a little defeated. I laid back down and slept peacefully.

The next day we all completed our assignments. I located a bail bondsman; the girls and his friend completed the return operation, found the buyers, and got his bond before the clerk of courts closed. I even picked him up, which they all seemed to have an attitude about, except him because he called me. I dropped him off at his vehicle, and we all went our merry ways for the rest of the day. Tomorrow was New Year's Eve, and I overheard them talking about having a set at the house. You know, weed, liquor, ghetto music. Real trappish. Oh, don't get me wrong, there was a time for all of that, but New Year's was a time of creating a vision for my life and being around people I wanted to spend the rest of the year with. So that was a solid hell-no for me. I silently made plans for tomorrow. Even if I had to bring it in with strangers, I was ok with that. I went to the house, did a quick meditation, packed a suitcase, and looked for a room in the city. I knew it was the last minute, and I prayed there would be something that would accommodate me that was up to my standards. DAMN! All booked up. I thought about it; wait a minute; Tabby, have you forgotten who you are? You have connections, dear. Oh yes, I started talking to myself again. I thought about my second best-bestie. I gave her a text.

> Tabby: Hey, Foxy, I need your help. I need a hotel, and it's all booked up in the city. I know we haven't talked in a while; long story. Anything you can do?

> Samantha: SEXY MAMI!!!!! Where you been, Mami? Yea, we need to talk. I got you. Give me 10 minutes, Chica. (kissy face emojis)

> Tabby: Just know I'M BACK, FOXY! (2 high-heel emojis)

And just like that, ten minutes later, I didn't have a hotel room; I had an upgrade! I had a penthouse high rise downtown with an amazing view of the city. I finished packing my suitcase, jumped into my Mercedes, and headed downtown. I pulled the sunroof back a little. Although it was chilly, I didn't care. I wanted to feel the wind on my back from the night air. It felt refreshing for the first time in a long time. This was how my life would be, I decided. I drove towards downtown, not knowing exactly where life was taking me next and how and when I'd get there, but I knew it would be sooner than later. I took in the beautiful scenery as I got to my destination.

I opened the door to the penthouse and looked around. It was beautiful. The kitchen had stainless steel appliances and a huge marble island with chandelier-style lighting that hung above it. The cabinets were a stunning dark wood that matched the specks in the marble flooring. I smiled as I walked into the living room to see a huge window with a view of the city. I opened the patio doors and took in the night, and smiled. This would be my home for the next few days. I texted Sam to say thank you.

> Tabby: Foxy! This is amazing! Any chance I can have an extended stay?

> Samantha: Aye, Sexy Mami! I wish you could! It's booked for the rest of January. Now, if you can make it through the first of the year, I got you for February!

I picked up the phone and called her.

Samantha: Hey, Sexy Mami!

Tabby: You have no idea what I have been through, girl!

Samantha: And you know what? I don't care! I love you; you're my second best-bestie! I know it's more than James and Keisha, and we'll talk about it when you're ready to talk. But I got you!

Tabby: Foxy, I love you so much, Mami!

We hung up, and I felt another glimmer of hope. Things would work out for me. I just had to endure just one more month. My phone dinged, and it was Shaquita. She asked if I had a moment to talk. I answered when she called.

Shaquita: Hey girl, where did you go? We came back, and you were gone.

Tabby: Oh, I already had plans for New Year's, so I packed a bag and headed out.

Shaquita: Oh, ok. Perhaps that's a good thing. I want Jaquan to have some peace around here, and to be honest, the last time the two of you were in each other's space, y'all had a big fight.

Tabby: Well, you don't have to worry about that. I won't be back for a few days. So here's a happy new year early if you don't hear from me. And Also, you don't have to worry about me being in your space much longer; I've arranged to be out by the beginning of February.

Shaquita: (pauses) well ok, then, all's well that ends well

I hung up the phone. I wasn't giving her passive-aggressive ass any more of my energy. I unpacked my suitcase, hopped in the shower, and settled into my room. I was feeling myself. I wore a black lace Cami and my favorite red see-through robe. My hair was brushed back in a ponytail, and I could feel my natural beauty. I looked in the mirror at myself and smiled. I decided to win. All the hell I had been through was worth it. I got on my phone and began to look up the local events near me. It turns out there was a party right here in the building for the guests. I would be bold again and go. That would be my New Year's Eve, bringing it in with strangers. I also texted my hair stylist. She was able to squeeze me in for tomorrow. I guess it was the added bonus I was giving her to come to me. I had to look my best if I was bringing in the new year at my best. I went to the closet and picked out the lucky outfit for the evening. It was sleek and elegant. Classy even. A drastic change from how I had been living as of late. As I started to reflect on my journey, my phone rang again, and this time it was Yvette. Well, look at the universe!

Yvette: Good evening, Tabby. I hope it's not too late. How are you?

Tabby: Actually, I'm fantastic! And I'd be a lot better if you had some good news for me! You still working at this hour?

Yvette: You know high-powered attorneys never stop working, even if it's temporarily pro-bono. As a matter of fact, I've been working on your behalf.

Tabby: Well, if you're in overtime, I know it's good news! You're good at what you do!

Yvette: Absolutely, I am. I wanted to circle back with you and let you know I managed to get before the judge. It just so happens that we both are members of the same country club. The judge has agreed to hear your case before the court on Tuesday, March 5th.

Tabby: Are you serious? Well, hell yea, I'll take it!

Yvette: Now, Tabby, I will let you know that this judge will want us to renegotiate some of the settlement, so we will need some time to prepare.

I took a deep breath in and out. I thought about the next fight ahead. James would want everything. Hell, they had a new mouth to feed. I didn't care, though; I knew my worth. I said,

Tabby: Well, let's renegotiate. I'm prepared for whatever. If I have to lose it all and start over, I'm prepared to do that too.

Yvette: (laughs) Tabby, that's a bit dramatic. Did you forget who I am? We'll negotiate a settlement that will be very comfortable for you. James and Keisha are celebrities now. Do you think they want any nasty publicity? I'll negotiate a considerable settlement to make this go away as quietly as possible; trust me, I got you.

We hung up, and I screamed out loud! Things were starting to turn for me. I opened the double doors to the balcony, stepped out into the night air, and took in the night lights. It was beautiful. I sat on the landing of the balcony and thought about the last two years. Love's journey turned into love's lesson when Jaquan and I parted ways before I felt stripped of everything. Lonely, hurt, confused. Now here I was, alone again but sitting in my power. I looked over the balcony at the lights and the midnight sky. I thought about what was next for my life. I thought I had gotten back to happy when I met Jaquan; hell, if he acted right, we would have been. We were almost there. I took another deep breath in and out and released the heartache and pain into the year that was passing. I decided this time I would finally be there, happy. I thought about what my new life would look like after I left that toxic place those people called home. I sat and imagined in the midnight air as I looked up at the stars. This time I would create my happy, create a new life for just me. I had no idea where I was headed next, but I decided to be in the Moment like a little girl who wasn't afraid to dream her biggest dreams.

7

ALMOST HAPPY

The word almost is an adverb meaning not quite or very nearly. For instance, I almost won the race, or we were almost to the finish line. The word could almost be positive or negative, depending on how you put a spin on it. When I was younger, my Momma always implied that almost was not good enough. I often recall her saying, "Almost only counted in horseshoes and hand grenades," and I was often confused by the saying as a little girl. As I got older, although I understood the phrase, I found it had a ring of truth. After the divorce, I was almost happy. I met love's journey, and we were almost there. But as I bought in the new year on my terms and with peace of and clarity, I knew I would finally get there...Happy.

As I entered Shaquita's house after the turn of the new year, I had a new sense of confidence. The solidified court date and knowing my time at Shaquita's was coming to an end very soon was enough to give me peace of mind. I had one more month to endure these people's shenanigans, and then I could be done with Jaquan, Shaquita, and Angela for good. Just the thought made me jump up and down on the inside. I had an extra pep in my step and a smile on my face! When I walked in, I saw Jaquan and Shaquita sitting on the couch under the blankets, watching television. Jaquan looked up and said,

Jaquan: What's up, girl! Happy New Year!

Tabby: Thank you, Jaquan, happy new year to both of you!

Shaquita: Thank you. Well, you look refreshed, a glow even. I take it you had a good new year.

Tabby: I did! Very relaxing even.

Jaquan: Y'all funny (laughs). So, you movin' out, Tabby? Why? You ready to go, girl?

Tabby: Now you know this was temporary. You two have a vehicle now, and the goal was for me to find another place to stay, right?

Jaquan: Don't you mean I have a vehicle? And Shaquita might need you to take Mickey to school sometimes; I got stuff to do.

Shaquita looks at Jaquan in surprise.

Jaquan: What? Y'all know I gotta get this bread.

Tabby: And I have a life I need to live, too, Jaquan.

Jaquan: We always gone be connected, girl, even when you leave here.

Tabby: Yea, ok.

I looked over at Shaquita, who had an irritated look on her face. I walked into the kitchen to get something to drink, and I could hear Keisha, James, and Pastor Doug on the television in the living room.

Pastor Doug: My beautiful daughter. Why are you so worried about how old you are? You're only 41, and God's favored. Do you not remember that Sarah was 90 when she first conceived? Oh, glory!

Wait? Was this déjà vu? They were just getting around to watching "A Love Like Ours." I couldn't believe it. Jaquan said,

Jaquan: That bitch is too old to be having kids. How old is she 40-something (laughs)? Nah, that's Tabby (laughs).

Shaquita: I can't believe she's pregnant! Now that was a season-ending banger right there!

Jaquan: For SURE! Hit this blunt girl.

A few seconds later, I heard Shaquita coughing. Soft at first, then more intense. Several seconds later, she is coughing and gagging hard, and I become concerned. I walk into the living room to check on Shaquita. Shaquita gags, gets up from the couch, and runs upstairs and into the bathroom. She closes the door, and I can hear her gagging some more. Eventually, she begins throwing up. Jaquan laughs again.

Jaquan: That girl is weak with these blunts; I told her to slow down. This shit I got here is fire. Here, hit this.

Tabby: Nah, I'm ok.

Jaquan: Ahh, you on that new year, new me shit already, Tabby. Just don't get brand new on a nigga, for real.

I change the subject by saying,

Tabby: Is she gonna be ok? She's still in there.

Jaquan: She'll be alright. She be down here smoking again after she comes out. Why don't you go check on her "Mom"?

I looked at him and shook my head. Jaquan always tried to push my buttons. An advertisement came across the 70-inch flat-screen TV; it was James, Pastor Doug, and Keisha sitting down interview-style with the producers of the show. Keisha had a very visible baby bump, but she still looked star-studded. There also sat other cast members of the show who had supporting roles, such as Keisha's best friend, James, and his business dealings, and a few messy Sisters that I remember from the church who had weaseled their way in to give the upcoming season a few twists and turns. They were showing snippets, and messy sister number 1 said,

Messy Sister 1: Well, you know what I think about that whole pregnancy. It's a shame! God showed me the whole thing!

Messy Sister 2: God showed you that about our man of God, but he couldn't tell you where your husband spent the weekend?

Jaquan said, "oh shit, Shaquita, get down here. This gone be good! When is this coming on?"

I rolled my eyes and headed up the stairs. I could still hear Shaquita throwing up lightly, and something struck me like a lightning bolt; if I put my money on it, I would say Shaquita's ass was pregnant.

I thought about the past couple of months, from Thanksgiving to now. This house had been an emotional roller coaster, and Jaquan and Shaquita had several breakups to make up. And in those make-ups were sexual encounters. Shaquita loved sleeping with Jaquan. There were even nights she cried when she couldn't "get any dick." Living with Jaquan showed me he had many options; Shaquita, Angela, the mystery woman in Daytonia, and then there was Marissa, a woman who frequented one of his favorite clubs, "Club Domerique." I found that tidbit of information from Shaquita when Jaquan went to jail. Shaquita accessed Jaquan's tablet and went through his social media messenger. Jaquan was out here living his best life, and I know he didn't use condoms. So, there was a very big chance that my intuition was correct. I got sick on the inside for two reasons:

1. I felt dirty thinking about the number of partners Jaquan had in such a short time. It made me wonder how many people he had sex with when we were together.

2. The possibility of Shaquita being pregnant bothered me if I was honest with myself.

Jaquan and I had been in a relationship. We dated, fell in love, broke up, and went through hell and back. Of course, I would feel some type of way. The truth was that there was still a connection between us and her pregnancy, meaning the nail was in the coffin, the writing on the wall. Perhaps it was the perfect gift from God to me, the ending of a painful lesson, a cycle. As I walked up the steps to the room, I reminded myself to check on the planetary alignments for the next few months, but for now, I had to see if I was right about Shaquita. The bathroom door opened as I hit the top of the stairs. I said,

Tabby: You, ok?

Shaquita: Yea, girl, I hit the blunt way too hard down there. And I been smoking cigarettes all day too. The acid reflux just got the best of me, that's all.

Tabby: Umm hmm...

Shaquita: What? (giggles)

I summon her into my room and say,

Tabby: So, I noticed, over the past month or so, you have been sleeping more, and now you are throwing up. Are you sure you're not pregnant, girl?

Shaquita: Are you serious (laughs)? Of course not! I had my period last month, and as a matter of fact, I'm supposed to get it in a few days. Which reminds me, I need to get some tampons.

Tabby: Well, ok then! I'll leave it alone! You know your body better than me, Sister.

She laughs and assures me everything is ok. Shaquita goes back downstairs, and she and Jaquan spend the rest of the day watching movies in the living room. They then took a midnight ride and returned from Walmart with a bunch of household items from the gift cards Jaquan had from his latest returns. So all was well in the Universe. Perhaps the new year would bring a new Jaquan and Shaquita. Who knew? All I knew was that I was biding my time. "Thirty days," I thought. "Girl, you got this."

I closed the door to my bedroom and plopped on the bed. I sent a text to Ahmed to see what he was up to. He was in Atlanta for the new year as he was invited to some A-list reality show gala there. He was moving up in the world. I pulled up my phone and pulled up the internet. I looked at the moon cycle and found something interesting. The full moon was in Pisces, which represents releasing past karma. Karma was here to assist with releasing old patterns of behaviors, people, and things that no longer served you. Interesting. Karma was also here to serve her dish hot or cold depending on what you had given to her and others; in essence, it was time to pay the piper. It was also a time of truly getting on with your life's purpose. Time to move on. I pondered those words. Moving on.... This time I was truly ready to. But as I said, the full moon was in Pisces, so Karma was shaking things up in our household, and this karmatic cycle was not set to end until Scorpio season. Those fucking water signs will pull every emotion out of you, with Cancer season midway through. I was delusional in thinking that my departure from Shaquita's would be smooth sailing.

A couple of weeks passed, and I received a text from my second-best bestie. Samantha explained that she had to push my stay at the suite back a couple of weeks until two days after Valentine's Day. Son of a bitch! I wanted to get the hell out of here. Apparently, a very important client had something prepared for his wife. They wanted to make sure the suite was immaculate up until his stay. I understood, but I was literally on a countdown. Things were getting tense again around here. In only a short week after watching movies together, they barely spoke. I thought it was odd. I also noticed Mickey wasn't talking to Jaquan either. It made me wonder if something had happened that I didn't notice. But I had no time to think about that. I had to tell Shaquita I needed to stay at least two more weeks, which was daunting to me. I decided to get it over with and opened the door to my room. Jaquan was in the hallway getting something out of the closet. I saw him pick up the box of tampons and shake his head. He looked at me and said,

Jaquan: Can't trust no one, swear.

He walked away and headed down the stairs and out the door. I approached Shaquita's partially opened door and knocked. She signaled me to come in. Shaquita was sitting on her mattress and box spring, smoking a cigarette. Tears began to roll down her face, and I asked her what was the matter.

Shaquita: The worse thing ever... Oh, I'm just having a baby with a man I'm in love with, and he told me he didn't wanna have a baby with me.

Tabby: I knew it! When did you find out?

Shaquita: Well, I'm not 100% sure. I took a home pregnancy test about four days ago. It came back positive. I was shocked because I didn't think I could have more kids. And to be pregnant by his ass.

Tabby: Well, the reality is you're pregnant.

Shaquita: I told you I don't know for sure.

Tabby: Bitch, did you not just have a positive pregnancy test?

Shaquita: (laughs) I know, but I want to know for sure. I told Jaquan immediately, and then his whole attitude changed. He stopped talking to me and barely touched me. He even wraps himself up in that damn blanket that reminds him of Angela. That's so disrespectful.

Tabby: Damn. Shaquita.

Shaquita: Yea, it's not like he said he didn't want any more kids. He doesn't want ME to have his baby... he makes me feel like he's embarrassed by me. That hurts so bad.

Shaquita begins to sob, and I reach in and comfort her. What else could I do? I ask,

Tabby: So, what are you gonna do if you are pregnant?

Shaquita: Like I said, I have to find out for sure. I made an appointment at the clinic for tomorrow. I asked Jaquan to take me, and he said he was busy. I was stupid to think he would be a little bit happy about having a kid. Why would he want to take me to the doctor?

Tabby: If that man can stick his dick in you, he can take you to the doctor.

Shaquita: Fuck Jaquan. Tabby, will you go to the doctor's with me tomorrow, please? I don't wanna do this by myself.

Tabby: Of course, I can. Nobody should ever have to go through this by themselves.

Shaquita: Thank you, Tabby; I really appreciate it. Oh, shit, you came in here to talk to me, and here I am putting all this on you; I'm so sorry.

Tabby: Girl, it's not a bother taking you to the doctor. But I did come in to let you know that I have to stay a little longer, only a couple of weeks.

Shaquita: That's perfectly fine. You can stay as long as you need to.

I thanked her, and we ended the conversation. I went back to my room and processed all that just discovered. Jaquan and Shaquita would be having a baby. Love's fucking lesson indeed.

The following day, I got up early, and Shaquita, Mickey, and I headed to the clinic. Jaquan slept in on the living room couch. Mickey and I sat in the waiting room until Shaquita was done. When she exited the office with a small bag in her hands, I already knew what my suspicions had confirmed. Shaquita looked at me and nodded. We both understood. Shaquita stuffed the bag in her purse so Mickey could not see the contents. She pulled me to the side to tell me what we both knew. Shaquita had a blood test and a GYN exam. The doctor sent her home with a bottle of prenatal vitamins, a bag of information, and goodies and said they would be in touch if there were an issue with the blood test or exam. Shaquita scheduled an appointment for the following month for her next visit. We got in the car, and Shaquita gave Mickey her phone to distract her. Mickey immediately turned on YouTube. Shaquita said,

Shaquita: I can't believe this is happening to me right now

Tabby: So, how do you feel now that you know?

Shaquita: Mixed feelings, to be honest. I've always wanted a boy, and because of my weight and health issues, I never thought I would get a chance again. But on the other hand, it's Jaquan, another baby daddy that doesn't want to be a father.

Tabby: Well, you can't make your decision based on him. The two of you were grown enough to create this situation. Also, what are your options anyway?

Shaquita: I could not have it.

Tabby: And who's paying for that?

Shaquita: Well, it just so happens I have a little money aside.

Tabby: Excuse me? Where did this money come from? And when?

Shaquita: Well, I got a new Netspend card in the mail the other day. I hadn't had a Netspend card in about three years when I got fired. I activated the card, and out of curiosity, I checked the balance. Apparently, the IRS had released my tax return from 2 years ago on that card, and I didn't even know it! I had been walking around for a year with money and didn't even know it! $3000! Oh, things are about to change around that household. I may or may not have a new baby to take care of.

I looked at Shaquita and nodded in approval. This chick wasn't dumb. Maybe this pregnancy would be a good thing. She could finally get her shit together too. The sad reality, however, was that having a baby with Jaquan meant she was forever tied to him. I truly felt sorry for her.

We left the clinic and returned to the house to see that Jaquan had gotten up, dressed, and ready to go. Shaquita stormed past the living room upstairs to her bedroom and slammed the door. Mickey looked at Jaquan, rolled her eyes, and went to her bedroom. He looked at me and laughed and said,

Jaquan: Funny how everybody in the house is mad at me when all the shit in here I put in here!

Tabby: Jaquan, please don't start.

Jaquan: NAH, FUCK THAT! That girl or her daughter wouldn't have SHIT without me, even this section 8 apartment. Who do you think got her this apartment? Did I tell you that, Tabby?

Shaquita yells down the stairs,

Shaquita: OH, YOU REALLY THINK SO! WHO THE FUCK HAD TO GO FILL OUT THE APPLICATION?

Jaquan: YOU WOULDN'T EVEN KNOW ABOUT THE APPLICATION IF IT WASN'T FOR ME!

Shaquita: AND! SO, I OWE YOU SOMETHING?

Jaquan: BITCH, YOU OWE ME YOUR WHOLE LIFE!

And it was on and popping! Shaquita's bedroom door flew open from upstairs, and she came downstairs. The two of them were in each other's faces unloading all of their frustrations from what appeared to have been bottled up for years!

Shaquita: NIGGA, YOU GOT MY SISTER'S CAR REPOSSESSED! WHAT ABOUT THAT?

Jaquan: WHAT ABOUT WHEN YOU AND YOUR UGLY ASS SISTER GOT IN A FIGHT! YOUR FAMILY STOLE MY CLOTHES BECAUSE THEY WAS MAD AT YOU!

Shaquita: JAQUAN, NOT ONLY DID YOU FUCK THAT WHITE BITCH, SHANNA, IN MY HOUSE BUT WHEN WE BROKE UP, YOU DESTROYED THAT APARTMENT AND RUINED MY CREDIT!!!

Jaquan: BROKE UP? (LAUGHS) YOU WASN'T EVER MY GIRLFRIEND! GIRL, LOOK AT YOU, A WHOLE MESS (LAUGHS)!

Shaquita charges toward Jaquan, and he matches her energy. I step in between them before an actual fight breaks out between them. Shaquita tells Jaquan to get the fuck out, and he assures her since everything in this bitch was his that, he would return. Shaquita went back to her room and lit a cigarette. Jaquan grabbed his keys to the truck, and just like that, he was gone, and the living room, which had become the new warzone, had a temporary ceasefire. That argument was just a glimpse of the hostility that would become my last 40 days in that household. Forty days and forty nights of hell that, if I didn't break free, would have aged me 40 years.

I gave Shaquita her space and time to process what was happening because sometimes I know it's better to think that way, so I went to my room and closed the door. My phone dinged, and it was Jaquan. Oh, hell no! This was way too much for me. He texted, "where you at" "I know you see my text, girl, don't be funny" then he called,

Tabby: Jaquan, what is it?

Jaquan: Tabby, I need to talk to you, but I can't come back now because I need to calm down. Can you come outside?

I sighed deeply, agreed to talk to Jaquan, and put on my shoes and coat. I began feeling more like a parent or mediator in this toxic situation. I got in Jaquan's truck, and he put it in drive, and we left the section 8 townhouse that was supposed to be our home. We drove without saying a word as Jaquan let the lyrics to the music describe how he was feeling. The lyrics from mo3 belted from the speakers as the bass shook and pounded, driving the point loud and clear, "everybody ain't yo' friend, everybody ain't yo' partna." Jaquan was feeling deceived. Interesting. After several minutes of driving, Jaquan pulled into a mini-park's parking lot. He put the gear in Park and said,

Jaquan: I know you know what's happening, Tabby; this shit is sick.

Tabby: First of all, you need to apologize for getting in that girl's face like that, Jaquan.

Jaquan: I know, but she pissed me off, Tabby. You think you know everything; that's your problem, Tabby.

Tabby: I know you ain't trying to take this shit out on me, Jaquan. Trick no good, Sir.

Jaquan: Oh, so you REALLY brand new (laughs). You know what, all y'all brand new, you, Shaquita.

Tabby: Jaquan, why am I here?

Jaquan: Shaquita has changed. She used to be sweet and nice and didn't argue. Then, when she contacted you, and you came around, she started changing, switching shit up.

Tabby: So, you're blaming me for a grown-ass woman's attitude, ok Jaquan? Did you forget you put this whole thing in play?

Jaquan: See, it's that sassy ass shit. That slick mouth. Do you know Shaquita and I have never argued in years?

Tabby: What is your point? So, are you gonna hold me responsible for you getting her pregnant too?

Jaquan: Nah, I blame that shit solely on her sneaky ass.

Tabby: And you had nothing to do with it, ok.

Jaquan: Nah, for real! That bitch is slick. You don't think I watch that bitch's cycles? I know when to fuck and nut in her and when not to. I'm the one who gotta pay for her tampons with my gift cards. I told her I didn't want no kids by her, and I meant that shit.

Tabby: So, she wasn't lying about that. Wow!

Jaquan: Yea, I told her I would never have a baby by her, so I was also watching for her cycles. When I start arguments, it's to get away so I can fuck somebody else why she's ovulating. A couple of months ago, when she put me on the couch, her fat ass made her way downstairs and on my lap. I thought I was dreaming until I came and opened my eyes.

Tabby: Well, damn, she just took it? Big girls can do that?

Jaquan: Apparently, they can.

Tabby: At 300 pounds?

Jaquan: Now, who's tryna be funny? But anyway, I noticed the throwing up a while ago. I noticed her period ain't come on the day it was supposed to, so I let a few days go by to see if she would bring it up. Then she was like, "oh yea, it's about to drop; I can feel it." So we got tampons, and she pretended to use them. There were empty, non-bloody tampon remains in the trash.

Tabby: Well, damn, weren't you an investigator!

Jaquan: Hell yea! That bitch ain't slick! So, when I say she on some new shit tryna trap a nigga and that shit ain't gonna work, Tabby. The worst part is I know she got that tax money. She don't THINK I know. And the fucked up part is she ain't offer me nothin' after all I did for her.

I looked at Jaquan in shock. Just like he saw through Shaquita's bullshit, I could see right through his. I had seen this before, but just not this volatile. Jaquan was a gas lighter. Probably one in denial. What made him think he had any right to a woman's hard-earned tax money from a job that he got her fired from? As his mouth was moving with tales of all he had done for Shaquita, I wondered what the next 40 days would be like. "Hang in there, Tabby," I thought to myself.

Jaquan: So, do you see my point of view? After everything I've done for her, I should always be good. She should at least consider helping a nigga out, but every time she has a come-up, it's all about her. So, I thought you should know all that, Tabby, before you go judging the situation.

I agreed to see his side of things. I disagreed, but I decided to understand. Jaquan dropped me off back at the house, and I went up to my room, plopped on the bed, and fell into a deep sleep. I must have been exhausted from the day before because I slept well into the next morning. I was awakened out of my sleep by a tap from Shaquita,

Shaquita: Tabby, can I talk to you?

Tabby: (sleepily) Umm, yeah, Shaquita, what's going on?

Shaquita: The doctor's office called me to reschedule my appointment for my first prenatal treatment, and they did an over-the-phone assessment.

Tabby: Shaquita, what's the matter?

Shaquita: Well, they say because I have fibroids, I have a risk of them growing as the baby grows. They can't do nothing until I have the baby, but I'm high risk because of my weight. They were also surprised I got pregnant due to the number of fibroids.

Tabby: Awe, Shaquita, that's so sad... I'm sorry.

Shaquita: I swear, I need my Momma more than ever right now. When me and my sister, Jaleese, got in that fight, she accused me of loving Jaquan more than them. They all turned against me. I really miss my Mom.

Tabby: Mothers and daughters have a special bond, you know that. It has been about six months, right? Think of it this way. The new baby could be a way to bring you and your family back together. No grandparent wants to miss out on that, trust me.

Shaquita smiled. I encouraged her to reach out to her mom soon at some point when she was ready. She agreed to think about it and said she had more news.

Shaquita: So, on top of all I told you, there's something else. Can I use your car to pick up my prenatal vitamins and prescriptions?

Tabby: Of course, Shaquita.

Shaquita: Not only will I be picking up prenatal vitamins, but a prescription for a fucking STD! Jaquan's ass gave me chlamydia.

Karma. That bitch was wreaking havoc in our household already. I opened my mouth in shock, but nothing came out. Shaquita calmly grabbed the keys to my Benz and quietly exited my room. Wow, she was taking this well, I thought. Almost too well. Holy shit, it was about to get REAL. Shaquita's mental was only calm before the next big storm brewed.

Shaquita returned home from the pharmacy and began dismantling her room again. This time she didn't throw or break anything but removed Jaquan's items and took them into the living room. The calm before the storm...Shaquita sent then Jaquan a text telling him that she no longer wanted him in her room and that she had moved all of his things into the living room. She also told him that she didn't think they should live together anymore. She also told him she wasn't putting him out but advised him to set up in the basement until he could find another place to stay. She also told him not to worry about the baby. Shaquita decided to have an abortion. That was a power-packed text that Shaquita sent; honestly, I had no clue how Jaquan would respond. When she showed me the laughing emojis in response to her text, I knew things were about to get wild.

Several hours later, Shaquita was in her Zen. She had an empty room with just her bed and her speaker, and she was listening to music and rotated between smoking weed and her cigarettes. Shaquita kept Mickey occupied by ordering her favorite meal from Doordash, McDonald's. The small wave of peace slowly dissolved as Jaquan walked through the door with Angela and his new hanging buddy as of late, Little Damien. Let me take a pause here for a Moment and make mention of little Damien. Damien lived true to his name and was a spawn of all evil and hood-like. If there was madness and mayhem, Little Damien was front and center. Damien was eight years younger than Jaquan, so most of his behavior was chalked up to his immaturity. Drama and Damien went well together, and he loved to be in the middle of it all. Jaquan looked around the room that was in disarray. He said to Damien,

Jaquan: Can you believe this bitch tried to put me out? Yea, it's all good; I ain't goin' NOWHERE!

Damien: (laughs) you wild boy! What you gone do? You need to handle this, yo!

Jaquan: Fuck that hoe. Get the mattress out of the car.

Jaquan turned on the speaker downstairs and blasted his favorite music. He then instructed Angela and Damien to get to work. Jaquan and Damien bought a new mattress and box spring and began setting up Jaquan's things in the basement. The three worked diligently like worker bees until Jaquan had a laid-out mini apartment in the basement after a few short hours. Jaquan had taken his 70-inch flat screen from the living room along with the TV stand. He then went upstairs to the linen closet and removed all the extra toilet paper, toothpaste, and paper towels. He even took Shaquita's tampons. I heard him say, "They ain't gone be using my shit!" and I chuckled. I had seen this level of petty before, as a matter of fact, not so long ago.

I understood and knew he could go there, but Shaquita was a bit surprised, which was weird considering she had known him much longer than me. Jaquan continued his celebration in his new apartment downstairs. He came up, took a shower, and even gave Angela the go-ahead to freshen up. Then, he yelled, "She's my guest, so y'all bitches better not say nothing." Bitch? Who was he calling a bitch? I chose to ignore Jaquan because I knew he was in a volatile state of mind. He was angry but also afraid. The sad truth is that Jaquan needed Shaquita right now and had a little fear of not having control of the situation. Jaquan was looking for anyone to place the blame on.

Jaquan's housewarming party went well into the late evening until they decided to go out for the night. On his way out the door, he yelled upstairs,

Jaquan: YEA, I AIN'T GOT TO GO NOWHERE!

Damien: WHAT'S THAT YOU SAY, MY NIGGA? YOU AIN'T GOTTA GO NOWHERE?

Jaquan: YEA, YOU HEARD ME. I GOT KEYS, AND I GOT MAIL HERE. SO I AIN'T GOTTA GO NOWHERE TILL I'M READY!

Damien: I know I'm ready to hit this club, my nigga, and throw these stacks at some bitches.

The two of them laugh and head to the club, leaving Angela in the basement to enjoy all the pleasures of Jaquan's new apartment. Meanwhile, Shaquita sat in her room like a hostage listening to music streaming from her phone. I decided to go in and check on her.

Tabby: Everything ok?

Shaquita: Yea, I'll be fine, I think. I can't believe all this is happening to me.

Tabby: Shaquita, you know how Jaquan is. Do you really think that sending that text was the best thing? And you didn't even mention that he gave you chlamydia. So what's up with that?

Shaquita: To be honest, I didn't think he would handle things like he did. I was a little pissed too. This man burnt me, and I bet he has no clue where it came from. And then he got that bitch in my basement ready to fuck and suck on her AGAIN in my house; that shit's so disrespectful! So, I decided I'm gonna take my medicine and have this abortion, and when he moves out, I'll let him and that bitch know they been burning. And if it takes months, it fucking takes months!

She smiled wickedly at me. I said,

Tabby: Do you really want to do that man dirty like that? And second, do you really want to have an abortion? Your heart is not built like that.

Shaquita: I don't want to, Tabby, but I don't want to be tied to a man like that for the rest of my life. I made up my mind. I have an appointment tomorrow for a consultation. I finally broke down and told one of my sisters what was going on. She agreed to take me tomorrow, and I'm paying for the abortion.

Tabby: You doing everything tomorrow? What the fuck?

Shaquita: (laughs) No, silly! I go to the consultation tomorrow, and they will explain everything. Then I pay for the meds to start the abortion. I don't get the prescription for the meds until one day before the procedure. So I take the medication the night before and then go for the abortion.

Tabby: So, when are you having the abortion?

Shaquita: Early next week. I already told Jaquan.

I was in shock. And Shaquita seemed to be at peace with it. I knew deep down, though, that decision should not and could not be made overnight and lightly. So I waited to see how this would play out and went back to my bedroom and marked the day off my new calendar. Thirty-nine days to go, I thought and laid my head down to rest.

The next day, Shaquita went to her appointment, and Jaquan and Angela went about their days like Bonnie and Clyde. Shaquita told me she paid for the abortion and showed me her pamphlets. She also showed me some material from the protesters, and I could tell she was not sold on giving her baby up. I talked to her about it and told her to make the right decision for her. She lied and said she was 100% sure that getting rid of the baby was the right thing to do. I let her live in her truth and decided to live in my own; I had an epiphany; my Momma was right, almost was not good enough. Even in Shaquita's lie, she was 100% sure of her decision, or so it seemed. I knew that to move forward with this situation and even deal with James and Keisha; I had to be 100% sure of what I wanted. I had to have time away from all of this to figure it out. Sure, I knew I wanted to get the hell out of this townhouse and into that beautiful suite, but what next? When Jaquan presented the idea of moving in here, I wasn't completely sold on it, but I did it anyway. When James and Pastor Doug talked me into a whirlwind marriage, I settled and stayed there way too long. In both situations, I was almost happy. To me, that was no longer good enough. I could hear my Momma's voice ringing loud and clear, "Almost ain't good enough, Tabby. Almost only counts in horseshoes and hand grenades. Nothin' good comes from almost." Deep down, I deserved better than this, much better than almost happy.

Over the next week, there seemed to be a ceasefire in the household. Jaquan hung out in the basement, and Shaquita kept residence in her room. Shaquita had taken Mickey to her sister's house in preparation for her procedure, and everyone seemed to stay out of each other's way. Jaquan and Angela would spend their days doing what scammers do and their nights doing what Jaquan and I used to do, hell, even what he and Shaquita used to do. Shaquita spent her days discussing the upcoming procedure and how to get out of her situation. She then spent her nights sobbing as she listened to Jaqua and Angela into the midnight hours. The whole thing was depressing.

And to make matters worse for me, there was not a dick in sight. I was used to using sex as a sweet escape from reality, but right now, too much of it was smacking me dead in the face. I had to deal with all of this reality before I could indulge in my fantasies. I had less than 30 days, and all this would end. When I walked away from this situation, I promised myself I would never look back. It no longer served me, and I knew my worth.

Shaquita decided to keep the baby. There was no big surprise there. The pressure of the protestors outside of the building was just too much for her. She told me she couldn't even go in. When she got home and called the clinic, they told her that her money was non-refundable. Shaquita had wasted $700 on an almost decision. Yea, my Momma was definitely right. But the plot twist to the story is that she didn't want to tell Jaquan. I didn't think that was a good idea. I told her,

Tabby: If you keep this baby, that man has a right to know Shaquita.

Shaquita: Oh, you think so? That man has been downstairs fucking Angela every night. And he's doing that to taunt me. He started texting me, apologizing at first, then when I wouldn't respond, he started texting mean shit like I'll be glad when you go get that abortion and how he can't stand to look at me. The last message he sent was telling me not to worry. He was moving to Daytonia with Angela.

Tabby: You can't be serious.

Shaquita: Yea, he said he was moving out when you moved out.

I shook my head. At first, feeling stressed, but then I realized none of this was my concern anymore. I was done and like completely done. These grown-ass adults would need to handle their own business, all three of them. If Shaquita wanted to let Jaquan walk all over her with another woman in her basement, have at it. If she also wanted to be treacherous and keep the fact that Jaquan had a baby on the way AND an STD, she would reap her own karma for that. And if Jaquan and Angela wanted to play house for however long hell, they could do that too. I was gonna be happy the last few weeks here, and nothing these crazies did was gonna destroy that for me. So I decided to have fun, be lighthearted and focus on my upcoming exit. And if the three of them had drama, I was gonna sit back and enjoy the show.

The next few days in the house were filled with my pleasantries and their hostilities. Jaquan had shifted from acting like he didn't give a fuck to pure anger towards Shaquita. He would walk around the house talking shit about her looks and saying she was a man. Shaquita ignored him at first. But then begin to reply. I came out of my room, and Angela came up from the basement. Call us Ms. Cleo, but we knew another storm was brewing, and we were both front and center. Jaquan said:

Jaquan: Can somebody please help Mr. Turner over there? He needs help screwing that guardrail back on (laughs)

Shaquita: Yea, I may look like a man, which makes you my little bitch now, don't it.

Jaquan: Your ugly ass got a fly ass mouth this morning. Watch yourself, girl.

Shaquita: I bet I don't watch shit! I'm sick of your smart-ass comments nigga! This is MY HOUSE!

Jaquan: And you wouldn't have this shit if it wasn't for me, SO SHUT THE FUCK UP!

Shaquita: How bout you shut me up!

Jaquan: (laughs) look at you, bitter ass bitch! You mad cause I moved on WHAT!

Shaquita: Moved on? I don't give a fuck about you moving on! What do you have to offer besides that limp-ass COMMUNITY DICK?!

Jaquan charged at Shaquita and got in her face. The yelling ensued. Jaquan did something that shocked me. He grabbed Shaquita by the neck and began to choke her. Shaquita sprang into action and started swinging, trying to get Jaquan off her. The two tussled around the room for a few seconds, and Jaquan pushed Shaquita's body into the wall. A big hole was created instantly, and Shaquita got visibly angrier. She was beginning to overtake him. Angela ran over and tore the two apart, and I jumped in front of Shaquita, and Angela jumped in front of Jaquan.

Jaquan: You scratched me. You FAT BITCH!

Shaquita: Jaquan, get the fuck out my house!

Jaquan: Don't worry, Angela and I will be gone in a couple of weeks; till then, I ain't goin' NOWHERE BITCH!

Jaquan punched the wall, which created another hole. Angela was in his corner, trying to convince him to calm down. I was in Shaquita's corner, not only doing the same but trying to be the voice of reason in the whole situation. After all, I was the only adult in the house, so it seemed. In a matter of minutes, the two retreated to their respective places in the household, and I convinced them to stop communicating with each other over the next few weeks. They both agreed. Jaquan and Angela went about their normal days, making plans for their move, and Shaquita was looking forward to her freedom.

One afternoon while Jaquan and Angela were out being Bonnie and Clyde, I was sitting in Shaquita's room, keeping her company. Her phone rang, and she answered and put it on speaker. Mr. Brown, her landlord, owned the strip of townhouses on her row. He said,

Mr. Brown: Good Afternoon, Ms. Turner. How are you?

Shaquita: I'm good, Mr. Brown. Is everything ok

Mr. Brown: Well, that's why I'm calling Ms. Turner. I received an anonymous call from someone indicating that you have unauthorized tenants living there and suspected domestic violence. As the owner and landlord in good standing with section 8, I had to file a formal complaint.

Shaquita: WHAT! MR. BROWN, PLEASE DON'T DO THIS! I can't lose my section 8. I have a baby on the way!

Mr. Brown paused for a second. He said,

Mr. Brown: Ms. Turner, what is really going on over there? And I need you to be honest. I'm getting all kinds of complaints, and if I ignore them, this woman threatened to go directly to housing development!

I could see Shaquita looking a little scared and shocked but then a look I had never seen before and couldn't place the emotion. Shaquita begins to tell Mr. Brown the honest truth, all of it. But the thing is, she lied. Yes, she lied. Shaquita told a lie so unbelievable that it made me wonder who this woman was. She said,

Shaquita: Mr. Brown, the truth is, I ended up letting my boyfriend move in. He had nowhere to go, and since we had been dating, I knew it wouldn't be long until he got on his feet. Well, when he moved in, he stopped working. He began drinking more and then would start saying mean things to me. Those mean things turned into physical abuse. I wanted him to leave, but he refused. And then, when I found out I was pregnant, he started throwing things around the house and destroying them. I begged him to leave, but he refused. I'm like a hostage in my own home, and to be honest, I'm really scared. I can't change the locks because I'm afraid he'll bust a window. Mr. Brown, I need help, please!

There was another long pause on the phone. Mr. Brown told her he felt bad that she was in her situation, and he didn't want to see her out in the streets in her condition. He also told her she had 24 hours until he would come over for an inspection to assess the damage.

That would determine how he moved forward with section 8. Shaquita got off the phone, and she texted Jaquan to let him know, who didn't seem to care, and Shaquita and I cleaned up the best we could.

Early the next morning, Mr. Brown showed up at the door. He walked in and looked around the living room at the gaping holes in his wall that Jaquan and Shaquita had created. He shook his head in disbelief. He then walked around the rest of the property at the half-cleaned rooms and minor wear and tear on the home. He went into the basement where Jaquan and Angela slept, and he turned and headed back up the stairs. He looked at Shaquita and said,

Mr. Brown: I'm gonna be honest with you. When I decided to rent to you, you seemed like a very sweet woman; how could you get yourself into this? And to allow my property to be damaged like this is very disappointing. I don't want to see anyone out on the streets, but you can no longer live here. If you agree to leave in thirty days, I will rescind the complaint sent to section 8, and you can still find another place to rent. I just want you out of here.

Shaquita began to cry, but he thanked him. Mr. Brown wished her well, and he left. It looked like we were all getting a fresh new start, whatever that meant. All I knew was that the Universe was confirming it was time for me to break free. The cycle here was complete, and I was more than ready. I smiled on the inside and prepared for my move.

The next few weeks went by quickly for all of us. Shaquita had made amends with her family and had found another apartment. It was a smaller place, with only two bedrooms on the opposite side of town. It wouldn't be ready in time for her soft eviction date, so she and Mickey would stay with her mom until her apartment was ready. She also broke down and told Jaquan she was still pregnant, but she still didn't tell him that he needed to get tested. Jaquan seemed to take the news without exploding as if he already knew. He seemed a bit nicer to her, even cordial. Jaquan and Angela had also put a lot of his stuff in storage. Angela's two-bedroom apartment was too small for all his things and her kids, making me wonder where they were while she was playing house here. The two of them were arguing more these days. Jaquan's reality of living with Angela full-time was starting to sink in. He didn't want to be almost an hour away from his business operations, and being with Angela could put a damper on things. But just like Shaquita, I no longer gave a fuck. Jaquan was reaping what he had sown over the past year or so.

Moving day arrived, and we were all ready to go. Shaquita's family showed up to help her move, and I hired movers to store my things. The landlord also arrived to make sure we were all left by the agreed-upon date and to retrieve the keys to the townhouse. Jaquan and Angela moved their things quickly for two reasons:

1. Most of his items were already in storage except his clothes.

2. Shaquita's family still hated him and wanted to hurt him. And now that she was having his baby, they hated him even more.

Shaquita's family was project worthy. They were hood-like people that appeared not to have anything and thus didn't see the value in what others had. Her sisters looked me up and down as I directed the movers. I saw them whispering and making snide comments, which told me that Shaquita also had some things to say about me in this situation. I heard one of them say, "yea, that bitch better than me to have the bitch he in love with livin' in her house, Shaquita, we might as well call you Ms. Celie," and they all laughed. I shook my head. What the fuck did I do to that bitch but show her kindness? Her fat ass used my car to ride around and do her errands, AND she was keeping the furniture that I put in this place! The furniture cost more than everything she owned, probably more than her family owned collectively. I stopped caring, knowing I was done with this cycle of my life. I would let all their karma be THEIR karma. And this time, I didn't need to be around to see it.

As Shaquita and I finished moving, she handed Mr. Brown the keys. He said,

Mr. Brown: Ms. Turner, again, I am sorry it has come to this.

Shaquita: Me too, Mr. Brown. I am really a good person. I didn't mean to allow all of this to happen.

Mr. Brown: As I look around, I see a lot of damage. I'm just very disappointed. I just couldn't continue to ignore the complaints from the neighbors.

Shaquita: That's what I don't understand. I have talked to a few of the neighbors; I mean not about this situation but overall. They seem very nice and understanding.

Mr. Brown: Well, since you're moving, I'll be honest with you. It wasn't so much the neighbors but their guests. Apparently, some of the things observed were when your neighbors had guests, and one began to call a lot. What was her name.... Rose...Angela Rose...

Shaquita's jaw dropped open, and I was a little surprised too. It was Angela. Wow. Angela had been calling Mr. Brown, making complaints about Shaquita, and eventually getting her a soft eviction from her place. Now that was fucked up. I thought about all the late-night conversations between her and Angela about not trusting me. Now here Angela was, trying to take away her whole livelihood. These were some treacherous bitches. Shaquita said,

Shaquita: Angela Rose, oh really (laughs evil) whoever she is, I'm sure what goes around definitely comes around.

Tabby: (laughs) it sure does. And on that note, I have to get to my next destination, which I call home. Mr. Brown, it was nice meeting you. Shaquita. Thank you for your hospitality, beloved.

Shaquita: So, what will you do next?

Tabby: What's next? Who knows? But whatever it is, it DEFINITELY is not this.

As I walk out the door, I hear one of her sisters say, "everybody say goodbye to Shug Avery." I kept my head up, knowing that these people would never reach the heights I had already soared.

I reached my hotel suite and looked around again. I smiled. I put my things on the sofa and headed to the bedroom. I plopped on the bed and rolled around. I had done it! I was free! I walked away from Jaquan and that toxic situation and was determined not to look back. I pulled out my phone and sent Samantha a big thank-you text. She responded, "You know I always got you, Chica," and I knew I had my power back. I then initiated the block feature on Jaquan and Shaquita's numbers. I never had Angela's number stored because I didn't think that bitch was worthy. I went to social media and blocked Jaquan. I went to block Shaquita but couldn't find her on my friend's list. That bitch had already blocked me first. I swear she was a fucking weirdo. I was learning that Shaquita was a lot like Jaquan. Shaquita played both sides of the fence in every situation to make it beneficial for her. Shaquita tolerated my presence in her household to benefit not only Jaquan's needs but my furniture, babysitting her daughter, and using my vehicle. Once she got what she needed, she was done. Jaquan was the same way, but he tried to keep his doors open. Hell, he did it for years with these two women. I wondered what in my energy attracted these kinds of people to me; what was the great lesson I was supposed to learn? I did know there was no honor among thieves, and these three didn't know any other way but dishonor.

After blocking my adversaries, I thought about my present future. It was a couple of days after Valentine's Day, and the holiday had just floated by like another day. With all the trauma that was happening, who thought or even cared? Last year's memories came flooding back to me with the help of my social media memory timeline. Videos of Jaquan surprised me, and the apparent joy of us being "couple goals." An apparent happy, almost happy. Butterflies tried to appear in my stomach of the memories that once were until my conscious mind reminded me of the money he took from my account. I got off Facebook and decided to switch gears.

I had less than two weeks to face off with James and Keisha, and I had no clue what I was going to do or even what I wanted. Over the last month, I had not reached out to Yvette, given the circumstances, but I was sure she was handling things on her end. I knew she and I needed to meet, but I also had to get myself together. I had once again gone through hell and back and needed time to relax, assess, and regroup. I also needed to figure out what I wanted to do about this situation and everything else in life. I had to ask myself again and quickly what I really wanted. I began to talk to myself.

Tabby: I want to be happy...finally there. Like, for real, there. But what is that gonna look like, Tabby? You can't just say you wanna be happy. You have to DEFINE happy and what it means to you. What THINGS, what PEOPLE, what will you DO to be happy? How will you create that? You gotta be more specific about what that will mean to you. And by the way, this rest you have been giving Boo Boo Kitty is well deserved. She's worth so much more than you've been giving her.

I smiled. Yea, I was gonna be happy no matter what. And I decided whatever I wanted to do was my responsibility to create my happiness.

I spent the next few days relaxing, meditating, and enjoying my peace. I also spent a lot of time thinking about what was next for me. I didn't know for sure, to be honest, but I knew that I was ready to leave this city, hell, this state. I had spent my whole life here and believed the universe was telling me I had worn out my welcome. I had been born as a result of a secret relationship to which my father denied me; I had a childhood in the hood where family compliments were scarce. I then hooked up with a baby daddy out of convenience, who never committed, and gave me two kids out of wedlock. In trying to secure an amazing future for them, I married James, who turned out to be a fanatic controlling narcissist. From there, I left Jaquan and a string of lovers behind. It was time to go and start over. Create a new life; have new stories and adventures to tell. I contacted Yvette to set up a meeting, as it was about a week before our court date. We agreed on a sit-down at Callahan's, one of my favorite rooftop spots. I ordered a light salad and mimosa, and Yvette and I dived into the conversation.

Yvette: So, tell me, Tabby, how have you been? You look a lot better since I saw you last. I hope you have been taking care of yourself.

Tabby: As a matter of fact, I've been taking very good care of myself the last few days; thank you for asking. So, Yvette, tell me, what is the state of affairs with James?

Yvette: Well, Tabby, to be honest, James really wants a fight. He feels like you shouldn't be entitled to anything, and he's willing to bring your most recent character into question.

Tabby: You know, this is typical James. He can't stand to lose in any situation. But you know, Yvette, over the last few days, I have had a lot of time to think. The house he's fighting for that he built for us he can have. It was a prison that he built for me anyway. And in the end, it became empty, and I realized I didn't want to be there anyway. But, hell, you know what? He can even have the beach house in Atlanta. Yvette, I'm so over him, Keisha, and Pastor Doug. It's time for me to truly break ties and cut free.

Yvette: Tabby, I understand how you feel, and as your attorney, I will honor your wishes. But we have to be strategic with James and his attorney Mr. Goldstein. If you are willing to give back both homes in this settlement, then it must be worth your while as well. We have to have a starting point, so I advise you to aim higher.

Tabby: Ok, what would you advise?

Yvette: You giving the homes back is a very strong opening offer. But you know James is most upset about the distribution of the funds in account #8. So if you want to walk away from James completely, I would advise you to give back a percentage of that judgment.

I thought about it for a moment. I had been awarded 3 million dollars from that account that had just been sitting there growing interest. Things with Jaquan happened so fast that I didn't have time to tap into that money. I had been living off the alimony and a mortgage-free house, thanks to James. Giving James a portion of the money back would not be a bad idea if I could be totally done with him. I raised my hands in surrender and said,

Tabby: You know what, I'm willing to do whatever I need to at this point, Yvette. Let's say one million dollars?

Yvette: Excellent. Tabby, this is a solid offer that we will not bend on. If Mr. Weinstein is a smart man, which I know he is, then he will advise James to take it. Once James accepts the offer, the business will be settled, and there will be no need to go to court.

Tabby: Now that sounds even better. The last thing I need is to see those too. Hell, I've seen enough of them on television.

Yvette smiled and said,

Yvette: Yes, they seem to have a fan base and another season. So Tabby, don't be surprised if this settlement makes social media headlines or their future storylines. Brace yourself

Tabby: After the hell I just walked through, Yvette, I can handle anything. Even though I'm settling, I still feel like I have won. As a matter of fact, I did win. I won me. Control of me again.

Yvette: That is excellent news Tabby. So, I'll have the paperwork drafted up to send to James' attorney. I will give them 24 hours to respond, and once they accept our offer, which I am confident they will, I'll let you know. I'll then deliver the settlement to the judge, and your funds will be released within 48 hours.

Tabby: So, you mean my money will be released in 48 hours?

Yvette: More like 3 to 4 days. Depending on James and how long it takes for him to mull over the decision. But more or less, yes, Tabby.

Tabby: YES! I'll be rich again! Of course, a million dollars less rich and your fee, but I still have enough to start all over. And you know, Yvette, that's precisely what I'm going to do.

Yvette: Good for you, Tabby; starting over is good. And from the looks of it, it already suits you. Well, let's have a pre-celebratory toast before I draft this proposal.

Tabby: Oh, I'm all for that! What are we toasting to?

Yvette: To new beginnings and a fresh new start.

We clinked glasses. I took in the toast, and Yvette and I finished our conversation, and I released her to handle her business. I drove back to my suite excitedly, knowing that things were falling into place.

Things from then on begin to move quickly. The next evening, I received a call from Yvette telling me that James had accepted my offer! Yvette knew how to do her job. She assured me that since he accepted so quickly, my funds would be released at noon the next day. I then had 48 hours to transfer the funds I agreed upon back to account number #8 for James. Yvette was suspicious that perhaps he needed access to his money too. For them, both houses and another million dollars was a win-win. I called my girl Samantha and told her the good news.

Sam: I told you it would work out, Sexy Mami! Sometimes you win when you walk away. So, what's next? What you gonna do, Mami?

Tabby: To be honest, it's time to leave this place.

Sam: Aye!!! I'm so proud of you! You have only been talking about it forever! Come to LA! We'd have so much fun! I got connections. You know that!

Tabby: Girl, LA is way too fast for me! Although I would be close to Vincent, you know they have a baby on the way real soon.

Sam: All the more reason! You coming?

Tabby: Nah, I got my heart set on somewhere else. Somewhere I can settle in. Somewhere with a southern draw, but still has that Midwest feel? Being with James allowed me to travel around the world, and I still wanna do that. But I see myself in a high rise, right by the river.

I told Samantha where I was headed. She championed me for venturing into territory I had never been to. There were no friends, family, or lovers where I was going. It was time to start over. Time to make new memories. As usual, my second-best-bestie had connections there as well. She said,

Sam: I see what you're trying to do on social media. Let me connect you with my girl Tierra. She is a stylist, videographer, and director extraordinaire. She will turn Tabby into a whole brand if you let her. Now her services don't come cheap, but I promise you that everything about you will be recognizable if you connect with her. Why let James and Keisha get all the limelight? It's time for YOU to shine!

We laughed and ended the conversation. I was grateful for having a good friend like her in my corner.

Before my departure, I had decided to tie up my last few loose ends. I called Vincent and told him about my plans, and he approved them for the first time in a long time. I smiled. I then went to say goodbye to Maria. I then wired her another nine months' worth of salary, and she assured me she would be ok.

Tabby: You could always go back and work for James and Keisha.

Maria: And deal with that Diva of a woman, no thank you.

We laughed, and I headed to the car wash to clean up my Mercedes. Got her spic and span for the ride to the dealership. I picked up my daughter, and all she knew was we were taking a ride. When we got to the dealership, they had my new baby ready. She was a sturdy silver Mercedes G550 with a black interior. She was an SUV with the look of a Jeep but had the quality and excellence of the Mercedes brand. I was in love at just the sight of her. When I saw her, I already had a name picked out for her, Meagan. She was big and luxurious, like Meagan Thee Stallion. She was also new to the industry but still top-notch and a champion. Me and Meagan were DEFINITELY gonna have some great adventures together! Vanessa said,

Vanessa: Oh my Gosh, Mom, is that for ME!

I looked at her like she was crazy, and she laughed. I signed all the papers and handed Vanessa the keys to my baby. I said,

All the maintenance has also been done and paid up for the next year. So here's your new baby. This is your reward for moving out of that slum of a neighborhood and getting that new position as manager at that tax office. I also paid your rent for the next year. So now the rest is up to you, baby. Now when I come back to town from time to time, I expect to have a place to stay, baby girl.

Vanessa hugged me and cried. It was a little for what I had done for her and more because I knew she would miss me. But I knew I had put things in order for her and that she would be ok. Vanessa and I said our goodbyes, and I headed back to my suite to pack my belongings. I had one more night in the suite and gathered my things quickly. To be honest, there was not much to grab. To took my clothing mostly, and my high-rise suite by the river was fully furnished. It would be my home for the next 12 months. I showered and poured myself a glass of wine. I took a few sips and dozed off, dreaming of my better life ahead of me.

The following day, I showered and put on my yellow long flowy sundress. The day had a beautiful spring-like feel, although it was still winter. It was the Midwest; sometimes, you could experience all four seasons in one day. And today, it felt like spring. I looked at myself in the hotel mirror one last time and smiled. I was saying goodbye, and I was on my way to happy. I put on my shades, left the suite, and headed to my baby, Meagan. I turned on the smooth engine of my Mercedes Jeep, which purred like a kitten. I said to myself and Meagan, "Y'all ready to go"? I put my destination in the GPS and made sure my Bluetooth was connected. It was about a three-hour drive, and I wanted to take in the sunny view of something classical yet purposeful. I pulled my sunroof back, turned on "Royalty" by Kimberly and Alberto Rivera, put Meagan in drive, and smiled. I took in the sunny breeze and knew I was no longer striving to get back to happy, nor was I even almost happy. After all the hell I walked through, I rose like the Scorpio, the phoenix that rose from the ashes, and I was finally there....

Epilogue: Finally, There: 6 Months Later

When my GPS said, "Welcome to Louisville," it seemed like my life had hit the ground running. Samantha had connected me with Tierra, who knew everyone there was to know in the city. Tierra showed me that there was a whole other side of Louisville that was not tapped into. The Black elite in that city was the best-kept secret. I remember our first conversation. I said,

Tabby: What is there to do in Kentucky anyway outside of the derby?

Tierra: Do your research, Suga. Stick with me, and you'll quickly discover how things move around here. Trust me; you're gonna love it!

She smiled and gave me that southern charm, and just like that, we connected! Tierra became my stylist and the creative director for my "All Things Tabby" brand. Tierra helped me with my look, image, and social media presence in a few short months. She even presented bomb ass ideas for ways to bring in several side streams of income. Tierra was turning me into a social media influencer right before my eyes. I was in my stride, and to be honest, for the first time, I was focused on the focus. It felt good.

One night while preparing for my photo shoot the next morning, I called Tara before I tuned into "A Love Like Ours." Yes, I was still watching that shit. It was starting to be my guilty pleasure. There was just enough church foolishness to keep me entertained, especially since they added the messy sisters to the show. Two of them didn't like Keisha, so I tuned in for that. Plus, the season finale was going to show the baby's delivery, and I definitely couldn't miss that. I still couldn't believe James' old ass had another child on the way. Then I was secretly grateful that I never gave that man a seed; I'd probably still be stuck till this day. I switched gears and called Tara, who picked up on the first ring.

Tara: GIRL! I am so glad you called! Have I got some tea for YOU? Let me send you this article. Ain't this your people (laughs)?

I pulled up the article, BOOSTER INVOLVED IN LOCAL RETURN RING ARRESTED. I looked at the photo. It was Angela! I said,

Tabby: Holy Shit! What the fuck!

Tara: Well, you can read the article if you like, but I have the inside to the inside. Jaquan showed up at the bar a couple of days after she got arrested.

Tabby: Bitch, WHAT!

Tara: Hell, yea, girl! I was in the office when I saw him. I told the bartender on duty to continue to serve him and get all the tea. Shortly after he got there, another man arrived. He looked too young to be there, but I let him stay since it was a slow night during the week. My bartender listened to the whole conversation and got it ALL.

Tabby: That's little Damien. I see some things haven't changed. Talk about our town being small. Give me the tea, girl.

Tara: Well, it turns out that he and Angela had hit up one of the Lowe's that they usually go to. After they left there in their usual fashion, they hit store number two. Angela goes in, and after about twenty minutes, Jaquan notices she is still in there. He gets out of the car and heads toward the building, but his senses tell him to leave, and he does. Angela had gotten arrested, and they figured out it was her from the anonymous tip they had received. The police knew the exact time and location she would be at.

Tabby: Shaquita! That bitch got her revenge. I KNEW IT!

Tara: Well, I'm glad you said that name because, apparently, that's where he's laying low.

Tabby: I am not surprised. Those two bitches are so dependent on that man they would do anything to each other to have him. She should be having that baby soon.

Tara: I assume so, he went on and on about how miserable he was there, and he was just there for the baby. He even had the audacity to try to holler at the bartender.

We laughed and talked a little more. I got her up to speed on everything that was happening. She celebrated my successes, and we ended the conversation, and I turned on my new guilty pleasure.

The season finale did not disappoint, but it may have sparked controversy. Keisha delivered her baby on television, and to everyone's surprise, the baby looked nothing like James. This little girl was fair-skinned, and James was as dark as the midnight sky. Keisha was a lighter brown woman who could chalk it up to her genes. However, a lightbulb came on in my head when Pastor Doug entered the room. And I knew if it sent a signal to me, there was a possibility that others were thinking what I was; Pastor Doug was the father of that baby! I thought back to the birth of his third daughter when we were in the ministry. When the cameras did a close-up, I saw a striking resemblance. I thought back to season 1 and how Keisha always doted on Pastor Doug. Yea, this was going to be a three-ring circus. I chuckled to myself at what karma had administered to those two. Instead of fighting, I walked away, and that girl called justice did what she wanted to do. Things had come full circle, and I vowed to continue to put good things out in the universe with the expectation of getting them back to me. I walked to my French balcony and opened the doors to the late summer sky. I took in the air and breathed. I dreamed a dream, and I was happy; finally, there.

I woke up the next day running late for my photoshoot as usual. Tierra instructed me to pick up some last-minute things, so I headed to Walmart looking a mess. I scurried around the store in a hurry to get my stuff; my full focus was on me these days. I came to an end of an aisle. I saw a tall black gentleman at the other end of the aisle, and I didn't want to even engage in the pleasantries of passing him to say "hello." I was in a hurry, so I turned my cart around and dashed in the other direction. Thirty seconds later, I heard a deep voice say, "excuse me, ma'am, how are you?"

I didn't want to turn around and wished he would leave me alone. I had shit to do. I played nice and turned around and said shortly,

Tabby: I'm fine, and you?

Shawn: I'm good. My name is Shawn. Do you have a man?

Tabby: Well, damn, that was quick.

Shawn: I'm a man that gets to things quickly, and besides, I don't want to be disrespectful if you already have a man.

Tabby: No, I don't have a man

Shawn: Well, can I have your number?

Tabby: For what? What do you want? Do you have a woman?

Shawn: No, I wouldn't be approaching you asking if you had a man if I had a woman.

Tabby: Ok, so you haven't answered the second question. What is it that you want?

Shawn: Can we be friends and see what happens? (laughs) I think you're beautiful and would love to get to know you better. What are you doing right now?

Tabby: I'm on my way to a photoshoot, and I'm running late too.

Shawn: Oh, so you model?

Tabby: A little bit.

Shawn: Well, let's meet somewhere later. I got a little spot I go to a lot; you shoot pool?

Tabby: No, but I sure like having fun trying.

Shawn: (laughs) ok, cool, give me your number. Text me or call me when you're free.

We exchanged numbers, and when I walked away, I called and said, "your name is Shawn, right?" He laughed, and I locked his number in and went to my photo shoot.

After I handled my business, I met Shawn at a pool hall about 20 minutes from where I lived. We had a couple of drinks and got to know each other as we engaged at the table. He was good, and I told him that. It turns out he had a pool table in his house. He said it was a recent purchase because he wanted to practice. His best friend and his wife were pool champions. Like literally. I found out that Shawn owned multiple cleaning franchises here locally and in three other cities. I was impressed. He also had investments and other streams of income. And over the next couple of weeks, Shawn gave me great conversation and vibes. He was 6'4, brown-skinned, and had a swag that was out of this world. He also smelled good and was a Cancer. Being a water sign like me, we were very compatible. He also had a west African background, although he was born and raised in Chicago. A Midwest man, I loved it. After spending time with him, I also realized that our spiritual beliefs aligned. He even turned me on to some things that elevated me. He even invited me to his gated home and was a perfect gentleman, well, almost. We had made out just a little bit in those two weeks of getting to know each other, and we both subconsciously decided to take our relationship to the next level. The sexual tension had been building up, and to be honest, I wanted to see "what that dick do."

I invited Shawn to my place one evening for a late-night chill after I completed my live show. Shawn bought the weed, and I poured the drinks. When he arrived, I opened the door, and he showed up in his distressed jeans. Timberlands and designer tee. He hugged me, and he smelled so good. This man had his gun on his hip and sat it on the bookshelf. He was so sexy, and I wanted him. He drew me in for a long deep hug, smelling me, taking me all in like he wanted me to. We sat down and had a great conversation while I melted into him. Shawn nibbled my ear, and my body tingled. He lifted my face for a kiss that was gentle at first and then a little more intense. I matched his energy. Shawn's hands searched my body, and it felt so good. He removed my twins from her restraint and sucked them lightly, like he knew what I wanted and how I liked it. I moaned, and my juices began to stir. I reached in the direction of his manhood, scared and praying at the same time - praying that a man with his height was truly working with something and also scared at the same time that it would be too much to handle. I reached in for his manhood and felt. I kept reaching and reaching until I reached the end and realized that my prayers had been answered and my fears realized at the same time. This man was hung like a horse. I felt his manhood, and he said, "I'm not even hard all the way." I gasped as he took my breasts in and out.

Shawn switched gears and positioned himself between my legs. He hiked up my dress to reveal that I wasn't wearing panties. He pushed me back on the sofa and began to have his way. Shawn was an authoritative but gentle man. He licked my lips in controlled soft measures. My pussy begged for more of him, and he knew it. Shawn took his time licking and sucking, and Boo Boo Kitty didn't mind. He opened my lips wide and licked every inch of her. Boo Boo Kitty's wetness oozed out of her, and the waterfalls couldn't stop themselves. Shawn gently placed a finger inside me. He licked and sucked as his fingers moved in and out of me. I could hear the juicy swirl that he continually took in his mouth as he sucked. My body lost control from the intensity of it all. With my legs spread open, I let him have his way with me until he knew I couldn't take anymore.

Shawn stood before me, and I knew it was my turn to return the favor. Show him what my mouth could do. I know I mentioned in my previous book that I could suck the soul out of a man's body, and I meant that. Although this mountain was a big one to climb, it was beautiful, and I was about to snatch his soul. I looked up at him and smiled. I winked as I took his manhood in my mouth. I teased him first and licked the tip of his shaft lightly. I stroked his Johnson while I licked the tip and played with his balls in tandem. He moaned as he looked down at me, and I took more of him inside me. My mouth was hot and moist, and my lips took him in and out of me. I took it out, licked him from top to bottom, and took him in my mouth again. I took him out and did the same, adding his shaft deeper into my mouth, and he gasped. I licked him again, took him deeper inside me until I couldn't take anymore, and gagged. I let his dick pound my face as I gagged some more, and the spit covered his dick. I took it out my mouth and licked some more, took it in again, and let him fuck my face. When he almost came, Shawn released himself and looked down at me like I was the champion. I won round two.

Shawn dropped his sweats and sat down on the sofa. I took my dress off and released my breasts from my bra. Shawn drew me in and sat me slowly on top of him. It had been a while, and the walls to Boo Boo Kitty had been closed for some time. Shawn felt that and knew it was apparent. He took his time with me and grinded slowly until Boo Book Kitty had let him into her walls. As our bodies melted into one another, it felt like pure heaven. I bounced up and down on his shaft, and he gave my girls the gentle attention they needed. It felt so good his long penis was hitting spots that I didn't know were there. Shawn picked up the pace; my body matched him as he grabbed me by my waist. Shawn thrusted deep inside me, and the pleasure it gave had me wanting to feel every inch of him. I moved my hips deeper around him, and I looked at him looking at me. He said, "Damn, you're so fucking pretty," and I moaned louder. I bounced higher in the air taking Boo Boo Kitty in and out of him. I felt his hardness get harder with every thrust. He said, "Damn, this pussy's wet as fuck" and I moaned. Shawn took control and thrusted inside me. I moaned. Shawn moved faster and faster. I yelled, "oh God! I'm cumming." Shawn and I exploded, and he looked at me in amazement. I said,

Tabby: What?

Shawn: Nothing, babe. Nothing at all.

Shawn smiled, and we lay together for a few minutes more. I knew his business was taking him out of town for a few days, and he had an early flight. He said,

Shawn: When I get back, I want you to have a bag packed. This event will bring in a lot of money, and I thought we could take a little trip. You don't have anything to do next week, do you?

Tabby: Well, I do have my live show. That's it, though; maybe I can cancel.

Shawn: Nah, don't do that. Just go live from an exotic location; that'll be pretty dope. Plus, I wanna see how you do things anyway.

Tabby: An exotic location? Well, I'm flattered. And yes, that would be a dope idea.

Shawn: Well, don't make any plans because now we have them. I know a lot of people, Tabby, and you have a true market for your brand. Stick with me, baby, and I can show you a world you have never seen.

Shawn stands up and pulls me into him. He picks my naked body up and kisses me. We had one more quickie up against the wall, and then I walked Shawn to the door and sent him on his way to his weekend event with a kiss. He promised to stay in touch, and I knew he would; if anything else, he had been these last few weeks, he was consistent. He seemed solid and true already and was big on honesty and loyalty. This was a man that I could fall in love with, and things were happening fast. I shut the door and leaned up against it, and smiled. I walked to the bookshelf and realized he had left his EarPods and cologne. I knew he would be back, and I was excited about this exotic trip he invited me on. This man had me open already. Once again, I didn't know where this ride was taking me, but I was open and ready to go with Shawn. I wasn't almost happy anymore; I was finally there, and whoever Shawn Mackland appeared to be, this man had me open and intrigued.

THE END!

ABOUT THE AUTHOR

Jaylonna Stevette is an author, speaker, podcaster, mentor, entertainer, and entrepreneur who went from a six-figure salary in corporate America to helping others do their life's work. Jaylonna has a bachelor's degree in Psychology and currently working on her MBA. As a spiritualist, Jaylonna believes we have the greater power inside of us to change our circumstances dramatically. Jaylonna has been described by many as smart, fierce, sexy, and in control. She is known as an executor, one who gets things done.

Born to a single mother of four, Jaylonna understands not only the plight of the single mother but also the many facets of life that being raised in that element brings. Jaylonna had a childhood filled with many memories that left a mark on her life, and writing and entertainment were her way of creating a safe outlet to express her feelings. As a result, Jaylonna's stories are centralized in real-life themes to which the reader can relate.

Jaylonna also has had a life-long passion for those with Autism Spectrum Disorder, as there is a personal connection between her and the diagnosis. Her oldest son Aaron was diagnosed when the disorder was not very common. Jaylonna looks to give back in the form of charities and organizations that are passionate about autism and other developmental delays.

Jaylonna's writing style is unique; she likes to expand her writing, and her works vary from fiction genres to Self-help and personal testimonials. As a writer, Jaylonna has the ability to tap into diverse streams of her artistic talent to perfect her gift. Jaylonna is often looked at as a risk taker and a lot of Jaylonna's writing tends to tie in a central message at the end for her readers. Her writing has great stories that will take you to the depth of your emotions. Jaylonna can add a special touch to her writing, which comes down to the level of her readers, and they appreciate that.

As a writer, speaker, entrepreneur, entertainer, and mentor, Jaylonna shares a host of diverse experiences with her audience in complete transparency. As a result, her following feels safe with her, and Jaylonna's life experience and education combined have been used to greatly help others on their journey to achieve greatness. Today, Jaylonna has a podcast on all major platforms called "Naughty Tales," with listeners in over 25 countries and a lingerie line in the works. Everything Erotica is her brand, and her goal is to let her followers know that sex is healthy but can also be tasteful.

ALSO BY JAYLONNA STEVETTE

Getting Back 2 Happy: The Chronicles of Tabby

CPSIA information can be obtained
at www.ICGtesting.com
Printed in the USA
LVHW021312120523
745408LV00014B/98